My Favorite Bride

Any self-respecting wolf would refuse to eat her. She'd been traveling for four solid days. Her eyes were gritty from lack of sleep, and her feet— She stopped and leaned against a tree. "My feet hurt."

Which didn't matter at all when she heard a crashing in the underbrush. A beast galloped onto the road right in front of her. A man's hand reached down and snagged her by her collar, and his deep voice thundered, "Halt! What are you doing here?"

Grabbing his wrist, she twisted around to look up at him. "Who are you to question me so rudely?"

A big, tall, good-looking man. A healthy head of dark hair cut neatly around his face and ears. Stark cheekbones with shadowy hollows beneath them. A square jaw, thrust forward and tight with determination. And better still, a lovely set of broad shoulders with a narrow waist and obviously strong arms. Beneath her hand, his wrist was taut and corded, and so wide her fingers didn't span it. "I'm Miss Samantha Prendregast and I'm the new governess at Silvermere."

"Where are you from, Miss Prendregast?" His rich voice taunted her.

"She fingered the straps of her reticule. "London."

"You've never been outside of London, have you?" He laughed, a laugh that mocked her ignorance. "You'd better be a first-rate governess." He rode into the woods.

She stared after him, relieved, amazed— alone. "Wait!" she shouted. "You're supposed to rescue me!"

Also by Christina Dodd

CHRISTINA DODD

My Favorite Bride

AVON BOOKS
An Imprint of HarperCollinsPublishers

This is a work of fiction. Names, characters, places, and incidents are products of the author's imagination or are used fictitiously and are not to be construed as real. Any resemblance to actual events, locales, organizations, or person, living or dead, is entirely coincidental.

AVON BOOKS
An Imprint of HarperCollins*Publishers*
10 East 53rd Street
New York, New York 10022-5299

First Avon Books paperback printing: September 2002

Avon Trademark Reg. U.S. Pat. Off. and in Other Countries, Marca Registrada, Hecho en U.S.A.
HarperCollins® is a registered trademark of HarperCollins Publishers Inc.

Printed in the U.S.A.

10 9 8 7 6 5 4 3 2 1

❧ Chapter One ❧

"It's not that you were a pickpocket, Samantha. It's that you persist in exposing your employers' foibles to your employers themselves, and they don't care for it." Adorna, Lady Bucknell, spoke in her soft and husky voice, and anyone listening would think she placidly accepted Samantha's most recent dismissal.

Samantha Prendregast didn't make that mistake. She stood before the desk with her chin up, shoulders back, just as Adorna had taught her. "No, ma'am."

The study of the Distinguished Academy of Governesses had been decorated in shades of pale blue, and Adorna's lush blonde beauty shone like a diamond in a satin setting. "I warned you about Mr. Wordlaw. I told you he was a martinet who believes women should be seen and not heard, and you assured me you would be able to handle him."

Samantha resisted the desire to shift back and forth. "Yes, ma'am."

"Yet in two short months you are back at the Distinguished Academy of Governesses without a job, without a reference, and with a guarantee that Mr. Wordlaw's vengefulness will spread your larcenous reputation among the few of the ton who don't yet know it." Adorna folded her hands beneath her chin and fixed her large blue eyes on Samantha. "So what is your defense this time?"

Samantha thought of what she should say, how she could pacify Adorna, but she had given up lying at the same time she had given up stealing. "He bullies his son. The lad doesn't want to study the law. Little Norman stammers already, and when his father dragged him up in front of the entire family and mocked him, my heart ached for him, and I wanted to"—she grew warm as she thought about that day, or perhaps the heat of a summer day in the City affected her—"teach that man a lesson."

"So you told his wife about his mistress and convinced his mistress to abandon him. How will that benefit young Norman?"

"Mrs. Wordlaw's father controls the money. She has taken her son and left Wordlaw, which she should have done years ago, but she was too proud to admit she'd made a mistake. Norman's grandfather will make sure Norman gets to follow his dream." Samantha remembered how science fascinated the boy. "I think the lad is going to invent something wonderful."

"And the mistress?"

Samantha grinned. "She's a friend of mine from my street days. She relished giving the old whoreson the heave-ho for a chance at young Lord Penwyn."

"How did she get that chance?"

"I arranged it."

Adorna's delicate sigh conveyed resignation. "I'll wager you did."

"My lady, I'm sorry I lost the position and brought disgrace upon the Distinguished Academy of Governesses." Samantha really was sorry, sorrier than she could say. "But I'm not sorry I helped Norman."

"No, I'm not sorry, either. But there are always more discreet ways of maneuvering."

Samantha hated that she had disappointed Adorna—again. "I know. I really, really do. I try to remember what you tell me, but sometimes I lose my temper, and I don't get it back for a long time. By then it's too late."

"Sit down." Adorna indicated the blue velvet chair beside Samantha.

Samantha slid into it gratefully. Adorna had rescued her from the streets six years before, and for the first three of those years Samantha had studied Adorna's every word and move in hopes of emulating her charm and beauty. Now, at the age of twenty-two, Samantha faced the fact that a tall blonde Viking with outspoken tendencies could never squeeze herself into Adorna's dainty, circumspect mold. But the time spent contemplating Adorna had given Samantha insight into the shrewd mind her patron hid beneath her breathy voice and curvaceous body. The worst of the censure was over. Now she must face the consequences.

And she knew how to face consequences. She'd learned that, not from Adorna, but from a father who, from the time she could toddle, taught her to pick a pocket and smile charmingly all the while.

"Mr. Wordlaw had quite the black eye when he came here to complain," Adorna said.

Samantha bunched up her skinny fist.

Adorna nodded. "That's what I thought. Did he attack you?"

"He tried. After his wife had moved out." Their tussle had been brief and sharp, and Samantha's arm ached where he had wrenched it. She didn't allow herself to show the terror that struggle had engendered, nor would she admit how often she came awake, heart pounding, in the grips of a nightmare. "He really is a despicable little man."

"He's over six foot. Most people would not call him little."

"Not in stature. In character."

"Hm. Yes. Be that as it may, he is a respected judge—"

"Respected?"

"For the moment. Until I can spread gossip to the contrary."

"You are good, my lady." Samantha folded her hands in her lap and tried to appear demure.

She obviously didn't succeed, for Adorna's voice sharpened. "Even then, my dear young crusader for justice, there are those who believe a woman should honor her vows regardless of how corrupt her husband is."

"Men, mostly."

"Mostly." Adorna tapped her nails on the open letter before her and stared beyond Samantha. "Part of the problem with placing you is that you're an attractive young woman."

"Thank you, my lady." Adorna had taught Samantha many things, among them how to make the most of her best features. Samantha braided her platinum blonde hair and wrapped it over her ears, and into a loose knot at the back of her neck. She used her large brown eyes to flirt and admire, and never did she allow them to reveal her intelligence. Her lips were generous—too generous, in her opinion, but Adorna had told her men would want to kiss them. That turned out to be true, although she hadn't cared for the experience.

She was too thin. She knew it. Adorna agreed. But something about her smooth, strong shoulders, her slender body, and the way she walked, brought her attention. More attention than she wanted, usually, for her early life had given her an unvarnished knowledge of men and women and how their bodies worked, and Samantha wanted none of it.

Nothing Adorna said to the contrary had changed Samantha's mind.

"The problem with placing you is your former profession. If you hadn't been such a famous—or shall I say infamous—pickpocket, things would be easier now."

Samantha dropped into the street language of her youth. "Oi just gave them what they wanted, Miss. A little adventure, a little excitement. Oi can't 'elp it if they bragged about 'aving their purses nabbed by the likes o' me."

Adorna did not smile. "That's the problem. You were well dressed. You were glamorous. You lured them into dark alleys and robbed them, and they liked it."

Samantha abandoned the Cockney and returned to the pure upper class English accent Adorna had taught her. "The men did, anyway. The women were not so tolerant."

"I thought myself quite tolerant. I didn't have you hanged."

"I've never understood why not." Nor had Samantha understood how Adorna realized her purse had been cut, but in the years since she'd learned that Adorna had a sixth sense about people and a frightening awareness of everything around her.

"I saw something in you that I liked." Relenting, Adorna laughed. "You reminded me of me."

"My lady, you've never had to steal in your life."

"No, but I had a father who wished me to marry for his profit." Adorna looked down at the letter open before her. "I have a solution to your problem. You must leave London."

Samantha found herself on her feet. "Leave London?" she shouted.

"A lady always modulates her voice."

Samantha tried to speak normally, but discovered her modulator wasn't working. "Leave London?" she whispered.

"I have here a letter from Colonel William Gregory of Cumbria."

"Cumbria?"

"In the Lake District."

"The Lake District? But that's . . . in the country."

"Fresh air," Adorna agreed.

Samantha waved a feeble hand. "North . . . far north. And west. Mountains. Tall, menacing mountains."

"Snow. Brisk, clean, white snow. Clear streams. Beautiful blue lakes. I envy you. Every day will be a holiday."

Distraught, Samantha looked at Adorna, seeking any indication that the lady was jesting.

She was not. "Colonel Gregory is in desperate need of a governess for his children. You are a governess, and a very good one."

"I know, but . . . the *country*." A painting she had once viewed in the Royal Museum rose in Samantha's mind. A winding, country road. Lush, green trees. A deer half hidden in the forest. And off in the distance, an azure lake and rugged mountains shrouded in clouds. The most horribly bucolic scene Samantha had ever viewed.

Adorna did not relent.

"To work for a . . . colonel?" In Her Majesty's army?

"A younger son, sent into the military and serving in India with honors. He married an Englishwoman while abroad—Mrs. Gregory had a reputation for beauty and kindness—and they were quite happy. Three years ago, his elder brother died, and Colonel Gregory inherited the family estate.

"Before Colonel Gregory could return home, his wife was killed in mysterious circumstances. It is said that he must have been deeply in love with her, for he hasn't looked at another woman since."

Adorna waited, and finally Samantha realized she expected a suitable comment. "Tragic."

"Indeed. When Colonel Gregory returned with his family, the story was the talk of London." With a slight smile, Adorna played with her pen. "Because, of course, the matrons hoped he would reside in London, where he would find a new bride. Instead he went at once to his country home of Silvermere, near Devil's Fell, and there he has stayed."

"Devil's Fell?" At once a picture formed in Samantha's head of a decrepit castle, perched on top of a stony crag, jagged and black against a stormy sky.

"It's reputed to be a lovely place."

If you like bats. Samantha asked, "Have you met Colonel Gregory?"

"No, but he is an officer and a gentleman, well thought of by his subordinates, and with a strict and sterling reputation." Adorna viewed Samantha. "I feel sure he'll offer you no reason for another scandal."

"I hope not, my lady."

Adorna cleared her throat.

Samantha hastily amended, "I'm sure not, my lady."

Adorna donned her glasses and read from Colonel Gregory's letter. " 'While my home is isolated—' "

Samantha whimpered softly.

" '—the governess need not worry about her safety. The roads are patrolled by the local militia, which I organize and which is enforced by my men.' "

Impervious to Samantha's revulsion, Adorna said, "And a few paragraphs down, Colonel Gregory says, 'I offer a salary of four pounds a month, an allowance for tea and sugar and, with that, a half day off every week. I will also allow the governess a week off a year to visit her family.' " She looked over her glasses. "Very generous. Much more generous than anything you can make here in London."

"But my lady, the locomotive doesn't even go there." If Samantha had to leave the City, she wanted to be assured she could return in a hurry.

"The train will get you close," Adorna assured her. "Colonel Gregory writes, 'She should take the train to York, and from there transfer to the coach, which will carry her on to Hawksmouth. At the inn she will tell the innkeeper who she is, and he will send her in a conveyance on to Silvermere, where her charges and I will be awaiting her.' "

"That's why he's paying four pounds a week." Samantha could well imagine the rugged country to which Adorna wished to condemn her. "No one would ever want to live out in the wilderness."

"Actually, that's not why." Adorna examined the letter. "It's the children."

"The children?" This got worse and worse. Samantha tried to read the letter upside-down. "What's wrong with the children?"

"Colonel Gregory says there's nothing wrong with them."

"If he says there's nothing wrong with them, then there most certainly is something wrong with them."

"True. I thought that myself. There are certainly an abundance of the little dears."

"An abundance?" Alarmed, Samantha asked, "What constitutes an abundance of children?"

Adorna consulted the letter. "Six, ranging in ages from four to twelve."

"Colonel Gregory's been a busy lad!" And he was just what Samantha didn't need. A curmudgeonly chap who wanted a governess to care for his abundance of children so he could go chasing around the countryside after vicious bandits. "My lady . . ." Samantha spread her hands, palm up, in appeal.

Adorna took off her glasses, folded them, and placed them on the table with a precision that boded ill for Samantha. "I am resolute that you shall take this position."

Oh, no. Adorna seldom spoke with such determination. She almost always got what she wanted, true, but normally she did so with tact and guile. When she spoke so directly, the intended victim had no chance of appeal. "My lady?"

"You struck at Mr. Wordlaw's income, his status, and his masculine pride—and that pride will find no satisfaction with anything but the complete annihilation of your reputation. I cannot find you another position here in London."

"But . . . but I've never left London."

"You've made your bed. Now you must lie in it." Adorna stared at Samantha. "You *are* going to the Lake District."

Heart sinking, Samantha stared back at her.

Briskly, Adorna said, "I've already sent a letter to Colonel Gregory telling him to look for you within the fortnight. And Samantha?"

Adorna's serious tone made Samantha pay particular attention. "Aye, my lady?"

"Do not, under any circumstances, tell Colonel Gregory about your past." Adorna folded her hands before her on the desk. "I have investigated him, and I'm told he is a good man, a fair man, but intolerant."

"A thief is a thief until the day she dies?" Samantha could scarcely swallow around the lump of resentment in her throat. "There's nothing new in that. I could make of myself a saint and still the bastards would judge me."

"Don't be vulgar," Adorna rebuked. "And promise me you'll be discreet."

Samantha smiled bitterly. "I promise, my lady. I will tell this righteous curmudgeon nothing."

❧ *Chapter Two* ❧

Slack-jawed, Samantha stood in the grass next to her trunk and stared as, in a cloud of dust, the cart raced back down the dirt road toward the village of Hawksmouth. "What did I say?" she yelled after the youthful driver, who ignored her with steadfast disregard.

All she'd done was inquire if wolves still ate the villagers. Whether she would have to rescue the children from bears. And if Colonel Gregory kept his livestock in the house. They were all questions that needed to be raised, but the groom from the Hawksmouth Inn had taken offense and dumped her here.

The scenery proved as terrifying as she had feared. Trees lined the road and extended back into a dark forest where, she was sure, bears lurked with long claws and blood-flecked teeth. Bears which now stalked her while slobbering with hunger, waiting only till dark to leap on her and rend her to pieces. And just ahead, she could see an open area. One of those meadows, she supposed, like so many the coach had passed on its trip up here. A meadow, vast and green, rising and falling, etched by lines of white drystone fences that extended as far as the eye could see. Sheep strolled the meadows, large-eyed, chewing grass, watching constantly for . . . wolves.

Yes, wolves. She would wager there were wolves here. She could imagine wolves slinking along, their red eyes fixed on a meal of fresh mutton, when suddenly they veered away, for they spotted a larger, more tender meal. *Her.*

She shuddered and slowly lowered herself onto the trunk. Adorna must have felt sorry for her protégé, for she had taken care that Samantha should be well dressed for her exile, gifting her with an extravagance of gowns, shawls, petticoats, hats, and boots. Unfortunate that they would be left to rot on the side of this lane; for night would descend, Samantha would still be sitting out here, every fanged creature would take its chance to eat her, and no one would hear her screams.

She came to her feet and started toward Silvermere. Her skirts swished in the dirt. She glanced behind her, and all around. The shadows were deepening in the trees. The sun dropped toward the horizon, toward the maw of the mountains, where it would be devoured. If she were wise, she would go back to the trunk and spend her last precious moments with her garments, but the will to survive was too strong. Even though she knew it was useless, she had to try to get to Silvermere.

She adjusted her reticule on her arm. She only hoped the decaying castle waited at the end of the road.

She passed beside a lake, a still, blue, frightening depth, cold and deep. *Things* inhabited it. She knew they did, because occasionally something plopped on the surface. It might be a fish. On the other hand, it could be a monster, lurking in the depths. She'd heard about lake monsters. She'd just read a novel about one in Scotland.

As she began to trot, she remembered the gothic novels she had so lovingly packed in that trunk. If she lived through this, she was going to toss them . . . well, not in the lake. That might disturb the monster. But away.

She looked ahead, hoping to see a building. Any building. There was nothing. Nothing but the road, twisting and turning, rising and falling. The trees, a relentless green. And above everything towered those mountains, austere, rocky, uncaring. The young driver had pointed them out and had told her they called them "fells" here in Cumbria. She had asked whether they were called that because people fell down them, or because they fell down on people. It seemed a logical question, but he'd begun to get surly right then.

The sun sank too rapidly, touching the peaks with red. Mist boiled out from the trees in puffs, then slid away as if sucked in by the breath of a hidden giant. Dusk gathered in the pockets of the forest and the dips in the road.

A stitch grew in her side, and she slowed down and pressed her hand to her corset.

Actually, any self-respecting wolf would refuse to eat her. She'd been traveling for four solid days—two days on the train, a brief night in an inn in York, then two days on the coach. Her eyes were gritty from lack of sleep, her gown of sturdy brown worsted looked much the worse for wear, and her feet . . . she stopped and leaned against a tree. "My feet hurt."

Which didn't matter at all when she heard a crashing in the underbrush. She didn't even try to see what or where it was. She took off in a sprint.

A beast galloped onto the road right in front of her, forcing her to a stop.

"Ruddy 'ell!" Before she could turn and dash the other direction, a man's hand reached down and snagged her by her collar, and his deep voice thundered, "Halt! What are you doing here?"

A horse. A horse and rider.

She could scarcely speak for relief. "I'm trying to get to Silvermere."

"Silvermere? What for?"

Which was when she realized he had her by the collar. This man clutched her by the collar as if she were a puppy. Grabbing his wrist, she twisted around to look up at him. "Who are you to question me so rudely?"

She filled in her own answer. *A big, tall, good-looking man.* She couldn't make out the details, the dusk had grown too thick, but what she could see looked quite marvelous. A healthy head of dark hair, cut neatly around his face and ears. Stark cheekbones with shadowy hollows beneath them. A square jaw, thrust forward and tight with determination. A thin nose. A long nose. Some might say a big nose, but one that sat well on that face of crags and valleys.

And better still, a lovely set of broad shoulders with a narrow waist and obviously strong arms. Beneath her hand, his wrist was taut and corded, and so wide her fingers didn't span it.

She couldn't see his eyes, though, and without them she couldn't read his mind. Well, except for his hostility.

She would have thought, when he saw her, a slender young woman, he would release her, but instead he tightened his grip. "Answer me. Who are you, and why are you going to Silvermere?"

Her initial relief at seeing a man, not a wolf or a monster, faded. He held her so close she could feel his horse's warmth and smell its sweat. The proximity of its crushing hooves, so close to her own feet, made her try to back away, and when he simply moved the creature closer, she gave a shriek. "Would you stop? That beast is going to step on me."

"Stand still and all will be well."

She precisely remembered the tone of a constable's voice when he collared a thief, and this fellow had that tone. Gritty. Disdainful. Implacable.

"I'm Miss Samantha Prendregast and I'm the new governess." She did *not* ask him if they kept livestock in the houses hereabout. No one could say she didn't learn from her mistakes.

The fellow let go of her collar.

She gave a sigh of relief and straightened her gown. "That's better. Now—who are *you* and what are you doing riding the roads and grabbing young women by the—"

Leaning over, he removed her reticule from her arm.

She grabbed for it.

He held it away from her.

"What are you doing?" she shouted. She *knew* what he was doing; she just couldn't believe it. What an irony, for her to have her purse nicked as soon as she left the City.

He felt the outside of the soft black velvet, then brought forth the contents. A handkerchief. The key to her trunk. The stub of her train ticket. And a modest, very modest, sum of money.

She never made the mistake of carrying any but the least of her funds in her reticule. She kept most of her money strapped beneath her garter. Tonight, if her bad luck held, he would realize that and be under her skirts at once.

But he put the contents of her reticule back in and handed it to her.

She snatched the purse and wondered if madmen and bullies always roamed the countryside.

"Why are you afoot? Was there an accident?" For all that he had let her go, that commanding tone had not dissipated. If anything, it had sharpened, grown more insistent.

"Of sorts. The groom from the Hawksmouth Inn dumped me and my trunk on the side of the road and went back to town."

"Why?"

"Apparently he took offense at something I said."

Looking her up and down, he said, "I can imagine." The brute swung out of the saddle.

She was tall, but he was taller. He must have been six foot two in his stocking feet, and he had that kind of massive, bulky build that some men worked hard for and some men were born with, and she was willing to wager he'd been born with his. She hadn't felt threatened before. Not really. But now thoughts of rape and murder rampaged through her mind, and for the second time in as many weeks, she wished she had learned a few more tricks to discourage a forceful suitor. She'd poked Mr. Wordlaw's Adam's apple with her fingernail, and he'd backed off in a hurry. She didn't think that would work with this chap. "Who are you?" she asked again.

She might not even have spoken. "Have you got papers to prove who you are?"

"I have a letter from Lady Bucknell."

"Show it to me."

"It's in my trunk." And she was glad, too. Even if it made trouble, even if he tortured her because he didn't believe her, she wanted to thwart this man who threatened and frightened a defenseless woman on the road to nowhere.

He hovered over her and stared as if he could decipher her thoughts.

Which she knew very well he couldn't. Every second the darkness thickened, the kind of dark she'd never seen before, untouched by city lights.

Stars popped out like tiny embers on a vast black hearth, and he loomed like a shadow. Nothing could stop her shudder.

"Where are you from, Miss Prendregast?" His rich voice taunted her.

She fingered the straps of her reticule. "London."

"You've never been outside of London, have you?"

"Never." Tensely she waited for him to proclaim some kind of atrocious initiation for country newcomers.

He only laughed, a laugh that mocked her ignorance. "You'd better be a first-rate governess."

She stiffened. "I am."

"Good." He strode back to his horse, mounted, and rode into the woods.

She stared after him, relieved, amazed . . . alone. "Wait!" she shouted. "You're supposed to rescue me!"

No reply, only the fading sound of a horse crashing through the brush.

"Something might eat me! How far is it to Silvermere?" she yelled. "Could you tell someone I'm out here?" In a quieter voice, she said, "Ye blackhearted lout, at least leave me a stick so I can fight off the bears."

Not likely. She was still stuck out in the middle of the wilderness, walking toward a house miles away, where cows slept in the bedchambers and the people slept on the dirt floor. With a sob, she rubbed her knuckles into her burning eyes. Then she squared her shoulders and marched on.

In London it was never quiet. Carriages always rumbled by, or children cried, or music and brawling spilled from the taverns.

Here, the hush pressed in, broken only by the occasional flap of wings overhead or a rustle in the brush, and she thought she would give anything for some kind of sound to break this dreadful, unnatural silence. Then, far in the distance, she saw the muted flash of lightning and heard the first growl of thunder. "Be careful what you wish for, my girl," she muttered to herself. "You're in for it now."

Tiredness dragged at her limbs, making each step an ordeal. She tripped on the ruts, tripped on the rocks, but not even exhaustion could convince her to walk in the grass beside the road. Snakes. She knew there must be snakes. And the lightning got closer and closer, shocking her eyes with each flash, and threatening with each rumble.

At first, she mistook the sound on the road for thunder. Then she realized . . . she thought . . . it almost sounded like . . . She stiffened. She squinted into the darkness.

Two lanterns appeared in the distance, swaying on . . . a coach! Lightning flashed—and she was right! It *was* a coach. If she hadn't been so exhausted, she would have shouted with joy. Now if she could get the coachman's attention.

The conveyance moved toward her, dipping and swaying. As it closed on her, she moved to the side of the road and yelled and waved her arms. And in the first piece of luck she'd had since her horrendous encounter with Mr. Wordlaw, the coach stopped. A footman jumped down and opened the door. She gave him her hand and he helped her into the luxurious interior. "I'm going to—"

"Silvermere. Yes, Miss Prendregast, we know." He shut the door.

She sat blinking in the darkness. Her hand caressed the rolled upholstery, and she wondered what . . . how . . .

That man. He'd been too lazy to rescue her himself, but he must have sent these fellows.

The coach turned around, then set off with such speed Samantha fell back against the seat. And was too exhausted to do more than rest there. She wondered if she should worry that she was being kidnapped, and decided kidnapping was a small price to pay for the chance to sit down.

They rode for long enough that she drifted into sleep. Then the coach slowed to a stop, and she jerked awake. The door opened, the footman thrust his hand in, she took it and stepped out onto the step.

And looked up, up, up at the magnificent mansion that rose like a monolith before her.

❧ Chapter Three ❧

Samantha woke to the clatter of dishes at her bedside. She pushed her hair out of her eyes and watched as the plump young maid drew the olive and gold brocade curtains. Morning sunlight poured in, and Samantha blinked.

"Good morning, miss," stated a black-and-white–uniformed maid cheerfully before curtsying briskly. She couldn't be more than fifteen, a child of nature who reeked of health, fresh air, and starch. "I'm Clarinda. I've brought yer breakfast."

"Thank you." Samantha pulled herself into a sitting position. "What time is it?"

"Gone past seven, but ye were tired after yer walk last night."

Samantha looked around the room she'd so briefly glimpsed the evening before. Her second floor bedchamber was large and spacious, surely a guest room. As did everything in this house, it glowed with prosperity. The dark oak furniture was carved and heavy, and her bed was wide, with a down comforter atop her and a feather mattress beneath. Most important, she had a separate dressing room with running water, drawn from a cistern on the roof.

This was the hovel that she feared would house livestock as well as six children and a hulking colonel?

"Here ye are, miss." Clarinda placed the tray across Samantha's lap and lifted the domed, silver cover. Steam rose from the golden fresh eggs, the spicy sausage, the buttery crumpets, the bowl of oatmeal, thick with honey, and a poached pear sprinkled with cinnamon. "Cook didn't know what ye like, so ye've got a smidgin o' everything."

"It looks wonderful." Samantha took a deep breath and realized that, for the first time since she'd left London, she was hungry.

Clarinda poured the tea. "Ah, it's a beautiful day, miss."

Outside, Samantha saw, the day was bright with sunshine. Great trees swept her windows with green, and through the branches she could see the sky, so blue it almost hurt her eyes. Nary a cloud dimmed the brilliance.

Going to the old-fashioned fireplace, Clarinda added logs to the flames. "The men picked up yer trunk off the road last night." Clarinda patted the black painted wooden box with its leather straps and heavy lock. Under her mob cap, her light brown hair sparked with liveliness, and her brown eyes snapped with interest. "Shall I unpack it?"

"Yes. If you would. The key is . . ." Where was her reticule?

"Here, miss?" Clarinda picked up the black velvet bag from the dressing table.

"Yes, thank you." Samantha extended her hand, grateful that she hadn't lost it in her exhaustion.

She wondered if she had hallucinated the whole episode the night before. The walk into the darkness. That man, crashing through the bushes. Then, just when she was relieved to be rescued, and by a gentleman, he barked questions at her like a barrister and took her purse.

All right. So he hadn't kept it. But he'd ridden away without offering a crumb of assistance. What a blighter!

Although . . . well, how had the coach arrived so propitiously?

It had all seemed too fantastic to be real, except that her feet hurt, and she would never forget the shock of stepping out of that coach and seeing the mansion that was Silvermere. The broad, four-story building rose into the darkness above the carriage portico. Light shined from every window on every level. The wide double doors stood open, and Mrs. Shelbourn, the dignified, elderly housekeeper, had gestured her in. "Hurry, my dear, we have a hot meal waiting for you."

Samantha hadn't been able to eat much of that meal, but this one filled the empty corners nicely. Finished, she poured the rest of her tea into her cup and slipped out of bed. She walked across the rug and, when she came to the fringed edge, tiptoed across the chilly wood to the window.

She looked out into a park composed of great sweeps of lawn, grand old trees whose tops reached higher than her eyes, and here and there a gazebo or a garden of blooming flowers. A topiary, with bushes cut into the shapes of lions and birds, was off to one side. The grounds were beautiful, and more important . . . "I can't see the mountains from here."

"No, miss, but they're out there. The mountains embrace Silvermere like great arms. Beautiful, they are."

"Humph." Samantha turned her back to the view. "Did that storm bring rain?"

" 'Twas a grand thunderstorm with lightning flashing from peak t' peak and rain t' wash the brooks." Clarinda smiled at her, and deep dimples popped into the smooth, rosy cheeks. "You must have been dreadful tired t' have slept through it. When you're dressed, Colonel Gregory would like t' speak with ye."

"Yes. Of course. As he wishes." Would Colonel Gregory be as surprising as his home? Certainly Samantha no longer imagined a grizzled, hardened warrior. Whoever lived here must have some idea of comportment, for all that he spent years in India ratcheting about in the wilds and repeatedly impregnating his wife.

She handed Clarinda her key. "What is the colonel like?"

"Ah, miss, he's a good man." Clarinda knelt before the trunk and wrestled it open.

Samantha waited, but nothing else was forth-coming. "Is he very old?"

"Not very old. Not as old as me grandfather."

"Oh." Samantha was back to thinking him grizzled.

"But handsome, me mum says."

Very grizzled. Probably gray and steely-eyed.

"And too strict with the children by half, not that ye heard me say so." Clarinda pulled out the first of the gowns, a froth of pale pink chintz, and flung it on the chair. Next came the flowered lawn, and the sapphire poplin. Finally, she reached the dark green serge. "Miss, shall I have this ironed?"

Samantha considered her mental image of the uniformed soldier awaiting her. Crusty older men responded well to an appearance of charm and youth. "No, I think not. A better choice might be the pink."

Clarinda considered the gown, then considered Samantha. "We'll see." Gathering up the gown, she disappeared.

By the time she had returned, Samantha had finished her tea, washed in the sink in the dressing room, and donned her undergarments. As Clarinda slipped the gown over Samantha's head, Samantha asked, "Why is Colonel Gregory so strict with the children?"

"It's his military training. He wants them t' follow orders. T' march in drill. T' never get dirty, and if they do, t' clean their boots until they shine."

Samantha lifted her eyebrows. "These children must be saints. Why, I'll have nothing to do at all!"

Clarinda burst into laughter. "We'll see about that, miss."

"Psst!" the sound echoed up and down the second-floor corridor.

Samantha stopped on her way to meet Colonel Gregory, and glanced around. A door stood slightly open. Three young faces were pressed to the crack, and three hands gestured for her to come in.

"Did you want me?" Samantha pointed to herself. As if she didn't know.

"Shh!" The children put their fingers to their lips, then vigorously gestured again.

Amused and intrigued, Samantha entered a stark bedchamber. Three narrow iron beds, spread with quilts, stood against the wall. A rigid row of dolls nodded on the window seat. Neither toys nor a rug cluttered a hardwood floor. Plain curtains hung at the windows. The girls' room, Samantha realized, although it bore more resemblance to an orphanage than to the bedchamber of much indulged children.

Then, as six dark-haired children lined up before her, the ones at the door as well as the ones waiting inside, she realized—every one of these children were girls. The colonel had only girls.

She almost laughed. Since her conversation with Adorna she'd been worried about her responsibilities. Worried that, for the first time, she had taken on more than she could handle.

But aristocratic girls were sweet, modest, and easy to manage, and only a military man, trying to fit them into a military mold, could imagine this to be a difficult assignment.

"Greetings, my lasses! Are you my new charges?" Samantha asked merrily.

The tallest girl, a beauty with budding breasts and a officious expression, pulled a riding crop out from behind her back and slapped her ankle-high black boot with it. "You are the new governess?"

Taken aback, Samantha considered the lass, and the line of her sisters, all dressed in indistinguishable, plain, dark blue shirtdresses, cut to a child's shorter length, with a white pinafore over the top. Each child's hair was pulled back in a tight braid tied with dark blue ribbon. They all wore the same ankle-high boots, and they all wore identical expressions of distrust and aggression. "Yes. I'm Miss Samantha Prendregast." Some second, cautionary sense made her add, "You may call me Miss Prendregast."

"I am Agnes." The girl indicated the next oldest should speak.

"I'm Vivian." This child was as tall as her sister, strikingly handsome, with dark hair and brows that winged upward without curve.

Agnes pointed with her crop.

The next child, dark haired and blue eyed, announced, "Mara."

Samantha had caught on now, and smiled warmly. "Good to meet you, Vivian and Mara. How old are you, Vivian?" She pointed at the girl.

Vivian answered, "Eleven."

"And you, Mara?"

"Nine."

Agnes glared at Samantha. "*Don't* interrupt."

"You're young to be issuing orders," Samantha said softly. "You may want to think before you continue."

As if shocked at the soft reprimand, Agnes blinked, then recovered. "No."

Her tone reminded Samantha of someone. Samantha frowned. Someone she had met recently. But who?

Agnes pointed to the next girl.

"Henrietta." This child, a brunette with brown eyes, clearly didn't quite understand the scheme to intimidate the new governess, and she curtsied to Samantha.

Never one to follow orders, especially from ruddy-mouthed children, Samantha interrupted. "What a beautiful name, Henrietta. You're seven?"

Henrietta nodded, eyes wide. "How did you know?"

"I'm a good guesser," Samantha confessed.

Agnes slapped her boot to get everyone's attention, and pointed at a grinning, gap-toothed lass blessed with those same, unusually straight brows.

"Emmeline," the toothless one said.

"Are you five years old?" Samantha asked.

"Yeth," the child lisped, "and I losth my teeth."

"So you have," Samantha said, smiling. Emmeline was a pet.

With a scowl, Agnes pointed to the smallest girl, as dark-haired and dark-eyed as the older girls.

She stuck her finger in her mouth, and looked down at the rug.

With a sigh, Agnes said, "That's Kyla."

Kyla ran to Agnes and buried her head in Agnes's skirt.

Agnes stroked her head and glared at Samantha as if daring her to make a comment.

"Kyla obviously adores you," Samantha said. "And for good reason. You're the one who keeps the family in harmony, aren't you?"

"Yes. We don't need you." Agnes drew herself up. "We'll explain to you why you should go home."

Samantha drew herself up in imitation of Agnes. "I can't."

"Yes, you can! You have to."

"I have been sent to Cumbria with strict instructions from my employer to remain here and teach you and your sisters everything I know about geography, science, pianoforte, penmanship, literature, deportment—"

"I don't need that!" Agnes interrupted.

Samantha raised her brows. "I would say you do." Her gaze swept them. "You all do."

Mara thrust herself forward. She had a disreputable air about her. She wore the same clothes as the others, but the skirt was wrinkled. A large, pink wet spot covered the bodice of the pinafore. Her hair was dressed like the others, but wisps had escaped and curled around her face. None of which stopped her from saying, "Papa doesn't like governesses."

"Your papa hired me."

Vivian joined in the battle. "He fired the last five governesses, so he doesn't like them."

"How many governesses have you had?"

"Eleven," Agnes said.

"Eleven!" Samantha hated to sound impressed, but she was. If success could be measured by insolence, these children had a marvelous record. "What happened to the others?"

Mara stumbled on the fringe of the carpet. "They left."

Samantha caught her arm and steadied her. "Why?"

In unison, all six girls spread their hands, palms up, and shrugged their shoulders.

"Well. Eleven." Samantha took a breath. "But you needn't worry. Your papa will like me. Everyone likes me, especially children." And if ever there were children who needed a governess, it was these. She stepped toward Agnes, the obvious instigator of this little rebellion. "And if he doesn't like me, it won't matter—because you will."

Henrietta decided to insert herself into the situation. "No, we won't!"

"No!" Agnes's mouth firmed.

"I like her," Emmeline said. "She'th funny."

Samantha nodded at Emmeline, her newest ally. "I am, aren't I?"

Kyla pulled her head out of Agnes's skirt. "I like her, too."

Emmeline's little body stiffened with indignation. "No, you don't. Thshe's mine!"

Taking Emmeline's hand, Samantha soothed her. "It's all right. I told you, everyone likes me." She sat down on the wooden toy chest and gestured to Vivian. "That's why your papa won't fire me."

Vivian sidled closer.

Emmeline leaned against her.

"Besides, I'm from London, and I don't know anything about living in the country."

"Really?" Agnes asked.

Samantha could almost see the wheels turning in her head as she plotted mischief.

Too bad Samantha had different plans. "But I know heaps about fashion, and the uniforms you're wearing are dreadful."

Agnes and Vivian looked at each other, then at their clothes.

Samantha continued, "I've got some trim we could stitch on them to make them prettier."

"Oh, do you?" Vivian cried. "I'm sick of wearing this horrid old thing day after day."

"Mayhap your papa could get us some material for new gowns. As a sewing project, of course." She winked at Agnes.

Agnes glared.

Kyla hurried over, planted herself before Samantha, and asked, "Can I have a pretty gown, too?"

Agnes frowned and turned away.

She would have to fight for Agnes's loyalty, Samantha realized, as she smoothed Kyla's cheek. "Of course you can, pet."

Without warning, the door slammed open and smacked the wall.

Eyes wide, Samantha came to her feet, clutching Emmeline's and Henrietta's hands.

A man stood in the doorway. He was tall, broad . . . familiar. He sported a healthy head of dark hair, cut neatly around his face and ears. Stark cheekbones with shadowy hollows beneath them.

A square jaw, thrust forward and tight with determination. A thin nose. A long nose. Some might say a big nose, and one that quivered with disdain.

He swept the room with his gaze, lingering on each of the girls in turn.

They stared back, mute and defiant.

"Greetings, Papa." Agnes swaggered toward him.

Now Samantha realized why the girl's voice and manner was familiar. Agnes was just like her father. Imperious, determined . . . obnoxious.

The man from last night was none other than Samantha's new employer, Colonel William Gregory.

❧ Chapter Four ❧

In the daylight, Colonel Gregory looked even more appealing—and more dangerous—than in the dark. He wore black. Black wool suit. Black boots, polished to an eye-blinking shine. A white shirt, stiffly starched and ironed. And a black cravat, tied with military precision. All tailored to fit him like a glove . . . a very well-formed, masculine glove.

He was the kind of man who caught a woman's eye. He certainly caught Samantha's, and her response to him created a vague sense of discomfort. She wanted to rage at him for leaving her in the dark. She wanted to fade into the cream-colored wall and watch him until she understood this shaky feeling in her knees and the clutch in her abdomen.

Or rather . . . not her belly. The constriction was

lower, not painful, but . . . she didn't know what it was, she only knew she didn't like it.

The rage was easier to understand.

He stared at Kyla, who stood scratching her nose with her sleeve, and at Mara, who rubbed one foot against the back of her other leg. "Line up!" he ordered.

In a rush they formed a line, Agnes at one end, Kyla at the other. They stood at attention, like good little soldiers, shoulders back, chins up.

He strode to Agnes, made a right turn, and marched down the line. He stopped and indicated Emmeline should straighten her pinafore, and she did so at once. Then he marched back up and stopped in front of Mara. "Mara, what is that sucking sound?"

Mara looked around in confusion. "What sound, Father?"

"Oh, wait." He leaned down until he was eye level. "I know what it is. It's your boots sucking polish off of my boots."

Mara looked down at her boots, scuffed and dull. Then at her father's, with their shine that hurt the eyes.

As Mara's eyes filled up with tears, Samantha found herself saying, "Do you care for your own boots, Colonel Gregory?"

He looked around at her, his annoyance plain. "I am an officer. Of course I do not."

"Well, neither does Mara," Samantha said cheerfully. "It's something you have in common."

Samantha heard several moist bursts of laughter, smothered at once, and Mara drooped as if a weight had been removed from her shoulders.

Colonel Gregory was not amused. In his deep, irritated, *familiar* voice, he said, "Miss Prendregast, when I sent for you, I expected you to obey the summons with all due alacrity."

"In the future, I'll remember that." *You big bully.*

"In the future, I do *not* expect to find you lingering with my children and bribing them with cloth which you think to procure from me."

He'd heard that, had he? Looking him right in the eyes, Samantha asked, "To whom else should I apply for the cloth, Colonel?"

A harsh crimson rose to his cheeks and forehead, and he looked right back at her. "If cloth is to be had, it would come from me. Which it will not."

Agnes stepped beside her father, allying herself with him. "I told Miss Prendregast to go to you at once, Father, but she insisted on visiting with us."

Astonished and impressed with Agnes's ability to lie with a straight face, and in front of everyone, Samantha raised her eyebrows at the girl.

Agnes blushed fiercely.

Colonel Gregory watched the exchange. "I see." He waved a hand at the other children. "At ease."

The girls sighed and broke into three little groups, with Henrietta taking the opportunity to jab Agnes fiercely in the ribs.

Colonel Gregory turned his attention to Samantha, and Samantha wondered what she should say. What she should think.

Adorna would say he was like the mountains: magnificent, indomitable.

Samantha would agree, but she would add: hard, ruthless. His jaw was inflexible, his ears small and neatly set against his head, as if they'd been schooled to remain in their place. He held his full lips in a slight, smooth smile as he struggled to mask that scorn in which he held a woman who panicked at the onset of night.

She shivered. Night, in the wilds of the mountains. She was lucky to get here alive. Indignation flamed in her. Indignation that he, with a few well-chosen words, could have eased her terror. "Well." She put her hands on her hips and looked him over. "At least I know why the coach arrived to pick me up."

He made no excuse for his abominable behavior, but looked her over in return, his gaze lingering on the ruffles at the bosom and set into the sleeves at the wrists. "That gown is an unusual choice for a governess, Miss Prendregast."

Last night, Samantha couldn't see his eyes, but she could now. They were blue. Beautiful, deep, cobalt blue, and as cold as ice in the depths of winter, with dark brows that winged straight upward without curve, giving him a saturnine appearance. This was no elderly curmudgeon. He was a man in his prime, a man who ruthlessly passed on his physical characteristics to his children. No froth of pink could soften his demeanor. No wonder Clarinda had suggested the plain, green serge.

Emmeline ran to him and hugged his knee. "Father?"

He put his hand on her head and looked down at her. "Emmeline?"

"Everyone likthes Miss Prendregast, Father. She told uth thso."

"Did she?" Condescendingly, he stared down his noble nose at Samantha. "Then I'm sure you shall like her, too."

"And you, Father! You like her, too."

"I am certain I shall . . . provided she has the correct references, and provided she demonstrates she's capable of living in the country, and provided she teaches you children properly."

Mouth puckered, Emmeline considered Samantha. "She'd better," she said truculently.

For a moment, just a moment, Colonel Gregory's eyes widened, and Samantha thought he was going to laugh.

The moment passed, leaving Samantha wondering if she'd imagined it.

He gently removed Emmeline from his leg and sent her, with a pat, to Vivian. "Miss Prendregast, if you would follow me?"

She most certainly would. She trailed him out of the door, and she wanted to speak so badly she had to bite her tongue to contain the words. But glancing back, she could see the children peering out, and it took little to imagine how they strained to hear the next chorus.

She wouldn't sing for their pleasure.

The colonel descended the stairway ahead of her and past the double doors that led out to the back. They entered the grand foyer that rose two stories, past the second-floor corridors, above the marble floor. Built in the gallery style with large columns that supported the corridor above, the rectangular foyer was painted in shades of pale blue and gold. A huge crystal chandelier sparkled above them. Samantha glanced through the open doors, seeing a library, a game room, a ballroom. Colonel Gregory led her to one door on the left and stepped back to allow her to precede him.

She thanked him while cynically wondering if he was always so courteous to his servants, or whether he simply seized this opportunity to observe her backside. But when she glanced at him, his face was impassive. Apparently this prickly feeling along her spine was not his gaze on her, but her imagination, and this discomfort she experienced at being alone with him was nothing but a spinster's overactive imagination.

Had she passed into the realm of desperate old maid, spinning imaginary liaisons in between planning lessons and cleaning up spilled milk?

Oh, now that disheartened her.

"Is there a problem, Miss Prendregast?" he asked.

"Not at all, sir, why?"

"You sighed."

She supposed she had. "I was taking pleasure in the beauties of your home." In its way, that was true. She expected his study to be stark and military. Instead, an ornate sense of India pervaded the room. Colors of burgundy and jade decorated the walls and drapes. An elaborate carpet in the same rich shades adorned the hardwood floor. Large, plush chairs invited her to sit before the large, mahogany desk carved in rope designs. "Last night. Why didn't you tell me who you were?"

He stood before her, the epitome of haughty mastery. "What purpose would have been served?"

"I wouldn't have been so alarmed if I had known."

"I wanted you to be alarmed. I don't take lightly the occurrence of a strange young woman wandering about the district."

"Do you often feel threatened by strange young women?"

"It depends on how strange they are." He moved behind the desk. "Won't you take a seat?"

She had been insulted, and by a master. With a flounce, she seated herself in a cushioned chair directly opposite his.

He remained standing. "I must tell you, I was not impressed with your response to me when you thought me a robber. You are inexperienced in such matters—"

She couldn't contain a "Ha!"

Lifting a haughty brow, he said, "Beg pardon. I forgot. You're from London, a dangerous city indeed. Perhaps you do have experience with robbery."

Not with being robbed. "No, sir."

He scrutinized her as if she were an oddity. "As you say." He studied her yet more. "So I'll excuse you this one time, but in the future, if you're the victim of a bandit, do not fight. And of more importance in your case—restrain your impudence."

"Do you mean that I should hand over my reticule to any male who wishes it?"

"In the case of a theft, yes."

"No." She didn't care that what he counseled was prudent, or that she would give the same advice to another victim. "I've worked hard for what I have. I will not give it up lightly."

"Your possessions can be replaced. Your life can't."

"*Your* possessions can be replaced." And he would never be robbed. No self-serving thief would try their luck with someone so large. "*My* possessions must be earned."

"My possessions were earned also, Miss Prendregast. Although my family has lived here for three hundred years, I was a younger son. My father bought my military commission for me, but I supported myself and my family with my work. Now, of course"—he gestured about him—"this is mine, but I mourn my father and brother."

She couldn't blame him for having advantages she could scarcely imagine. At least he understood he lived a life of privilege, and took his responsibilities seriously. In fact—she considered his stern visage—a little too seriously. "My sympathies."

"My daughters are my whole family, and very precious to me."

"Your sentiments do you credit." Although she'd observed little sign of affection upstairs. "Are you greatly troubled with thieves in the district?"

"The area is wild. Bandits have haunted the roads since before the Romans."

With a flush of irritation, she said, "Then you shouldn't have left me there."

He stared at her as if she were speaking a foreign

language, and again, he didn't answer her. "I assure you, I will flush them out and finish them off, but until I do, I request that you remain on the grounds at all times unless accompanied by my men." He wrapped his fingers around the knobbed finial of his chair. "I make that request for your sake, but also for my children's."

"Yes."

Still he stared at her.

"Sir," she added. What had she gotten herself into? If something dreadful happened—and in all her experience, something dreadful always happened—she would be trapped on his estate, unable to escape to London. "I think I can safely guarantee I won't be wandering about the wilderness without the assistance of a strong, capable footman."

His mouth quivered once in what might have been amusement—in a less stern visage. "Because of the things that might eat you?"

So he *had* heard her as he rode away. "Do you consider large fanged creatures humorous, Colonel?"

"I consider them unlikely, Miss Prendregast, but if your belief in bears or wolves keeps you and my children safe, then I encourage you to imagine whatever you like." He seated himself. "May I see your references?"

Gorblimey, but he was irritating. He was proof positive that some handsome gents had faults that rendered them intolerable. Which was good, of course. Such faults kept a girl sharp. "I have the letter from Lady Bucknell." Delving into the pocket in her skirt, she brought forth the sealed document. "I had understood she informed you of my expertise."

"She was rather vague about the specifics."

With as much innocence as she could muster, Samantha widened her eyes. "I can't imagine why."

Breaking the seal, Colonel Gregory perused Adorna's letter. "No. I suppose you can't." As he reached the end, his eyebrows went up. All expression smoothed from his face.

Good heavens. What did that mean? "Is everything in order?"

He folded the letter precisely along the creases and tucked it into the inner pocket of his jacket. "Indeed, yes. Lady Bucknell seems quite fulsome in her praise."

Samantha was too good an actress to sag with relief, yet she wondered . . . what had Adorna said?

"I'll get right to the point. These are your duties. A schedule is posted in the schoolroom. Each child will conform to the times and studies listed."

She should start as she meant to go on, or a man like him would run roughshod over the top of her—as he did everyone. "I must insist on making improvements as I see fit."

"After you've demonstrated your competence, you may discuss improvements with me."

"Who decides I have proven myself, sir?"

His eyes hardened. "I do, Miss Prendregast. Make no mistake about that."

She nodded. At least he was interested in his children's progress, and in her experience such care was only too rare.

He continued, "The children go to bed promptly at nine o'clock. No exceptions. Each of my children has her own nursemaid, so after dinner you'll be released to your own devices. That time is not to be spent in frivolity and flirtation."

Did the man deliberately offend her, or was he just oblivious to the social niceties? She hated to guess. On the other hand, he freed her to speak as she wished. "With whom? The groom from the Hawksmouth Inn?"

Colonel Gregory hesitated, perhaps weighing the desire to reprimand her for interrupting him. But no, he truly was oblivious to the social niceties, for he answered, "I have spoken to the innkeeper in Hawksmouth. The groom has been released from his duties."

She clutched the arms of the chair. "What do you mean?"

"His duty was to bring you here. That he should abandon you, a fragile woman, in the road at the onset of darkness is criminal."

"Then you're a criminal, too?"

"Miss Prendregast!" He rapped on his desk with his knuckles. "You were never in any danger!"

"Except from the wild animals."

His lids swept down as if he needed a reprieve from looking at her. "Alert me if you're attacked by a rabbit."

"I'm pointing out that the young man is no more guilty than you yourself. In London, when people lose their jobs, the misfortune leads to the streets, to the workhouse, and all too frequently to death. I'm not particularly fragile." She showed Colonel Gregory a capable hand. "Surely a reprimand would teach him a sound lesson."

"Your charity speaks well for you, but no. You're a woman, you're a stranger, and what you said in ignorance could not be construed as an insult by anyone but a hot-tempered youth given to rash judgments."

"But—"

"Be at rest, Miss Prendregast. It was not his first transgression, and he will return home to live with his parents on the farm. After a few months of backbreaking work, I'm sure he'll see his way clear to apologize and return to the inn."

The depths of Colonel Gregory's ignorance took Samantha's breath away. In her experience, men such as the groom did not gratefully learn a lesson. They resented both the lesson and the teacher, and blamed anyone but themselves. But perhaps things were different here in the country.

The window rattled—but not from the wind. "What was that?" She stared out. Colonel Gregory's windows opened out onto a broad veranda, and beyond lay the park she'd viewed from her bedchamber.

"The breeze." Colonel Gregory didn't bother to glance over his shoulder. "It's frequently breezy up here in the Lake District. Sew on your bonnet ribbons tightly."

"But . . ."

He watched her with austere disdain. "Yes?"

"Nothing, sir." The tree branches weren't waving, but she wasn't going to argue with him. Not about *this*. There were other, more important things to argue about.

"We were discussing your evenings."

"So we were, sir." She would be a fool to cavil at so much free time, yet like the four pounds a week and the half day off, so much liberty seemed like a bribe. And since she'd met the children, she had to think it was.

She smiled. She wouldn't rebuff Colonel Gregory's offer, nor would she tell him she had taught worse hellions and to grand results. "What do you expect of me?"

"I expect you to read, to improve your mind, to write letters, to plan lessons." Colonel Gregory leaned back, his large hands at rest on the chair arms. "You will review those lessons with me once a week on Monday night."

"As you wish, sir." She'd found pleasure in saying that phrase, but so far, the interview had been . . . almost agreeable.

Of course, Colonel Gregory was insufferable. But then, according to a great many people, so was she. Either Colonel Gregory didn't notice or he didn't care—although that surprised her. In her experience, these stiff military types liked their due respect, and then some. Perhaps he was so desperate to keep a governess he was willing to put up with anything. Or . . . what *had* Adorna said about her in that letter?

"Very well. I have explained everything." He picked up a paper off his desk and studied it. "I'll expect to see you here at seven o'clock sharp on Monday next."

That was concise. Now she would be equally concise. "About the cloth for the children's dresses—"

In painstaking motions, he put down the paper. "What about the word *no* do you not understand?"

"They're girls, not soldiers."

"Those are serviceable clothes designed for the wear and tear of healthy children."

"Healthy girls also require pretty gowns for dancing and parties," she shot back.

"My children do not attend parties."

"Are there no children's parties in the country?"

He glowered, his blue eyes heating with annoyance. "No."

"If not, how do children learn how to behave?" Samantha shook her head reprovingly. "Colonel Gregory, you are—you must be—one of the foremost landowners in the district. It's up to you to set an example for the other parents. We should plan a party here at once."

"I have no intention of—" He stopped speaking and stared at her as if he'd had a revelation. More slowly, he said, "I have no intention of hosting a children's party."

"Then you may get me the cloth for the girls' gowns and once a week I will host a party, just for them, and teach them the intricacies of social encounters."

"A point to be considered." He stroked his chin.

Samantha could have sworn he was paying her no heed. She didn't know if that were good or bad, but she struggled on. "Agnes is not too many years off from her debut, and Vivian right behind." Rising, she walked toward the door, hoping to escape before his attention returned to her. "A different color for each girl, please. We want them to feel like individuals, important in their own right. No pattern, and for the material, jersey, I think, since you're correct—they are still children and likely to be hard on their clothes." She could see she hadn't succeeded.

He rose, also, a slow motion that somehow gave the impression of threat and dominance. "Miss Prendregast."

He was impressive. She *was* intimidated. She didn't show it. "Yes, Colonel Gregory?"

"Kyla is getting a cold. Please notify her nursemaid and have the child moved to a bedchamber separate from her sisters."

Samantha blinked. Whatever she had expected, it wasn't this. "Indeed I will, sir. But if I might ask, how did you know—?"

"She was scratching her nose. Mara has outgrown her boots. I'll order new ones, but they won't be here for at least a week. In the meantime, have her try on Vivian's old boots to see if they will fit." He clasped his hands behind his back. "In fact, check all the girls to see if they're in need of new footwear."

"Yes, sir." Samantha strained to remember what he'd seen that alerted him to Mara's problem. "Mara was . . . rubbing her foot against her leg."

"And refusing to care for her boots as I require. I have told her—told them all—they are to notify me at once when they outgrow their boots, but Mara refuses to speak to me more than the minimum."

Samantha didn't even try to contain her sarcasm. "I wonder why?"

He moved around the edge of the desk, walked up to her, and stood so closely her skirts brushed his boots.

She wanted to back up, but she never backed up. Her heart beat more and more loudly. Or maybe it always beat like that, but she was aware of her heart, and her lungs as she breathed in the clean scent of this healthy man, and the fine hairs on her body, which rose in some visceral response that embarrassed and excited her.

"Will next week be soon enough for the material?"

He enunciated each word carefully, and watched her so shrewdly she knew he knew he'd been manipulated. And he allowed it, although she dared not wonder why.

"I would get it sooner," he said, "but so few of our governesses last above a few days. A few hours, even."

He had challenged her, and she responded. "Colonel Gregory, I will be here to make the girls' clothing. In fact, I will be here in a year. No child has ever gotten the better of me, and I vow your children will not." Silently she added, *Nor will you.*

❧ *Chapter Five* ❧

Miss Prendregast strode from the room and snapped the door shut behind her. Standing, Colonel William Gregory went to the window, pulled it open, and waited while Duncan Monroe, the officer he'd met in India—and his loyal friend—climbed through.

"What have you got?" William asked.

"Caught another Russian last night." Duncan dusted off his rough wool trousers and straightened his brimmed peasant cap. "Robbed him of his wallet and sent him on his way."

"Anything interesting?"

Duncan emptied his little pull-string bag on the desk. A crumpled wad of pound notes. A pipe. A bag of tobacco. A letter . . .

William fished out the letter and frowned at the intricate Russian. "I'll send this on to Throckmorton and see what he can make of it." He thought nothing of the peculiarity of the relationship between him and Duncan. He played the peacekeeper for the Lake District while Duncan played the role of highwayman, each carefully eluding the other to patrol for English spies, Russian agents, and even the occasional, genuine thief. It was a game they'd worked out between them, and while playing that game they'd managed to uncover a range of information for the Home Office. But they hadn't been able to uncover why the Lake District was the center of activity.

Until today. Which reminded him . . . "What in hell are you thinking, rattling the window when I had someone here?"

"Someone? That was not a someone. That was a beauty." Duncan fluttered his eyelashes in mock flirtatiousness. "Colonel, I didn't know you imbibed."

"Imbibed? One cannot imbibe a woman. One can only imbibe a—" William saw Duncan's grin, and stopped.

Duncan's sense of humor was legion, his bravery equally famous, and Mary had called Duncan handsome, but William knew he could wipe away that smirk. "That woman is my children's new governess."

Duncan did a double take that almost snapped his neck and gratified William to no end. "Your children's governess?" Duncan hooted. "They didn't make governesses like that when I was a wee lad."

"She came highly recommended from a reputable agency. The Distinguished Academy of

Governesses, in fact." But William agreed with Duncan. What in the hell was Lady Bucknell thinking by sending such a governess to him? Or rather—to his children. Miss Prendregast had been sent to his children.

He poured two glasses full of whisky and handed one to Duncan.

Tall and lithe, Duncan took a drink, then rocked back on his heels. "All my governesses were old and cantankerous."

"As you no doubt deserved. Most of ours have been young and easily intimidated." Never had William thought he would look back on those silly girls with nostalgia. But never was one a woman like Miss Prendregast. Miss Prendregast, who walked like an Amazon, looked like an exotic priestess, and had a tongue like a . . . ah, but he mustn't think of her tongue. Her tongue made him think of kissing and other activities, so better to say she was insolent and leave it at that.

He took a sip and let the whisky burn all the way down. "That hair of hers . . . a wig, wouldn't you say?"

"A wig? Are you mad? No, it's not a wig."

"It's too blonde." Last night, strands had fallen about her cheeks, and in the dusk they had shone like moonlight. "It must be a wig."

"We both agree you don't know a damned thing about women, and you certainly don't know about their hair." Duncan slid into the chair vacated by the governess. "I couldn't see her eyes. What color are they?"

"Brown." William lifted his glass. "About this color. Very odd."

"You noticed her eye color." Duncan looked too damned satisfied for William's comfort, and swirled the whisky. "I can't wait to gaze into this young lady's eyes."

"You're not to seduce my governess," William warned. "Not unless you are prepared to take her place and teach my children."

"I wouldn't dream of seducing your governess." Duncan placed his hand on his heart. "Did you see the way she walks? Like a great, stalking panther, all oiled grace and elegance."

"She's too tall." William was used to petite women who looked up at him and, when he waltzed with them, felt slight in his arms.

"Can you imagine having those legs wrapped around your neck?"

All too easily. Did Duncan never know when to stop? "She's too thin."

"She's too tall, she's too thin," Duncan imitated William. "*You're* too picky, as well as being a poor, desperate widower who needs a wife to care for his children, but I like you anyway. Maybe this Miss . . . Miss . . ."

"Prendregast," William supplied.

"Maybe Miss Prendregast will fill the bill."

"No."

"No?" A lock of tawny hair dropped over Duncan's brow as he scrutinized his friend. "It's been three years since Mary's passed on."

"Since Mary was killed," William corrected.

As gently as he could, Duncan said, "Aye, but it wasn't your fault."

Of course it was William's fault. "A wife's safety is her husband's responsibility."

"We were off on a mission for the regiment. How could you know Mary would answer a call for help and step into a Russian ambush set for us?"

Guilt haunted William. "I should have sent her home. I should have sent them all home. We knew of the danger, so close to the mountains."

Duncan stood and put his hand on William's shoulder. "I know you loved Mary and your heart's broken, but—"

William shrugged him off, strode to the window, and looked out at the park. That was the problem. He had loved Mary, but . . . she'd proven something he'd suspected for years. No woman was as interesting as a military campaign. No woman was as exhilarating as a ride across the moors. No woman could possibly capture his heart, for he was a cold man, given to hot passions, but never to love.

That was part of the reason why he was so determined to catch the traitors responsible for Mary's death. She had loved him so much, and he had never loved her back with all the fervor she deserved.

It was remorse that drove him, but he could hardly tell Duncan that, or any of the romantics who imagined him haunted by his lost love. "We will have justice."

"We're achieving justice." Duncan subsided

back into his chair. "But you should find a woman. A man's got needs."

"You would know." William faced Duncan. He didn't envy Duncan's freewheeling reputation in the district. "You're fulfilling yours often enough."

"And I tell you that goes a long way to soothe a broken heart." Certainly Duncan had had success up the length and breadth of India among the officers' daughters, until he'd been fool enough to fall for Lord Barret-Derwin's girl. His lordship had not been amused to have a Scottish ne'er-do-well courting his eldest, and the girl had been returned to England in a hurry. Duncan had resigned, but he'd arrived in London only to hear of his beloved's marriage to the earl of Colyer. He had reacted with rage and recklessness—a boon for William, who needed a compatriot for his mission.

"Miss Prendregast brought me a letter." William dug Lady Bucknell's letter out of his jacket and tossed it at Duncan. "Ostensibly a letter of recommendation."

Duncan picked it up. "Ostensibly?"

"Read it."

Duncan scanned the first paragraph. " 'Miss Prendregast is well-trained, intelligent, resourceful . . . ' That's wonderful, Will, but—"

William saw when Duncan reached the pertinent information.

Duncan stiffened. Without looking up, he groped for the desk and set down his glass. "Lady Bucknell sent you this? Lady Bucknell works for the Home Office? For Throckmorton? Lady Bucknell is a spy for England?"

"I believe Lady Bucknell serves Throckmorton when she can. To call her a spy might be an exaggeration."

Duncan read quickly. " 'Throckmorton says . . . the Lake District is the center because . . . ' " He dropped his hands, with the letter, into his lap. "Lord and Lady Featherstonebaugh? That harmless old couple have been directing a spy network that covers England and most of the world? *Lord and Lady Featherstonebaugh?*"

"I've never known Throckmorton to make a mistake. He certainly would never make a mistake about anything as important as this."

"I'm not really questioning his information, but . . ." Duncan shook his head. "How?"

William had had a few more minutes to consider the matter. "They're welcome in every noble home in England. No one suspects them of anything more lethal than gossip. They could be caught with secret papers in their hands and be excused without misgiving."

"I'm reeling."

"This explains everything. The constant stream of strangers in the district—foreigners, women traveling alone."

"Yes, and the Featherstonebaugh estate stretches clear to the coast. There's a harbor there. They've got an escape route." Duncan read the letter again. "Throckmorton is herding Lord and Lady Featherstonebaugh toward us. He wants us to secure as much information from them as possible before he moves in to arrest them. How are we going to do that?"

"I have a plan." But it was only his first, spur-of-the-moment plan. Surely he could do better.

Duncan rubbed his hands in glee. "Will we torture them? Break into their manor? Ride them down like the murderous dogs they are?"

"No." William grimaced. "I'm giving a party."

Taken aback, Duncan repeated, "A party?"

"A house party. Think, man! It's what Lord and Lady Featherstonebaugh do. They visit the best homes in England. Lord Featherstonebaugh tries to kiss the debutantes. Lady Featherstonebaugh gossips. And apparently, all the while, they're eavesdropping. They're stealing information they can sell to the Russians. We would lure them here with promises of information, then catch them as they try to send it off."

"A house party. It is brilliant." Duncan sighed. "I suppose. But you don't give parties. Whatever made you think of this?"

"The governess."

"Little Miss Prendregast?"

"She says I'm scion of one of the premiere families in the district, and I'm neglecting my daughters' social education."

"I've been saying that for years. Why do you listen to her and not to me?"

"Because I'm doing it to catch Lord and Lady Featherstonebaugh in the act of spying."

"Oh. That's right." Duncan raised his glass to William.

William knew what he thought. Duncan

thought that William would take his first steps to re-enter society, a female of unimaginable virtue would catch his interest, and he would marry again. That was what Duncan hoped, for Duncan disapproved of William's lack of *joie de vivre.*

Duncan lolled in his chair. "But how . . . pardon me, my friend, but you have no experience in planning a party, nor has your staff, and Throckmorton hopes to have Lord and Lady Featherstonebaugh here by the first of September. How will you get ready in time?"

"I'll write the countess of Marchant and ask her to help me." William waited.

Duncan froze, then produced a crooked grin. "Dreadful Lady Marchant. Must we?"

William had never understood Duncan's antipathy, nor did he have much patience with it. "Teresa was a friend of Mary's. Lord Marchant was a friend of mine. And Teresa has repeatedly offered her assistance in anything I desire."

Duncan's restraint failed. "I'll wager she has. B'God, William, anyone but her! Don't you know what she hopes?"

"No." Of course he did. "What?"

"That you'll fall desperately in love with her and she'll have snared another rich, handsome husband who'll make her the envy of all the ton."

"You think I'm handsome?"

"I think you're—" Duncan leaped up and smacked William on the shoulder. "I think you're a jackass."

William cackled. "I'm trying to think of another

plan. Anything would be better than . . ."

Duncan grinned. "Than her? Aye, so I would suppose."

"I was going to say a party." William leaned an arm against the mantel and studied Duncan. "You might as well know. I believe I'll let Teresa snare me."

Duncan looked stunned. "No! Why?"

"I need a wife." William despised men who brooded over lost loves and moaned over opportunities lost. But the passing of Mary had scarred his children. The realization that he had failed her had marked him. So he coped in the best way he knew—with military discipline and exacting standards.

Somehow, in the past year, he'd seen discipline vanish and standards slip. Half the time he didn't know what was happening in his own house. The girls were growing up, and he didn't know what to do, how to handle them. "Although Miss Prendregast looks promising, the governesses have been nothing but a trial."

Duncan leered. "She looks very promising."

"But no governess can take the place of a mother in the girls' lives. They need stability, so I'll take a wife." He walked to his desk and picked up a sheet of paper. "I made a list of my requirements."

"A list of your requirements?" Duncan fought a grin. "What would they be?"

"Most are obvious. My wife must be of my social class. She must have a pristine reputation. She should be accomplished in the ways that will advance my family—she should organize parties and help my daughters prepare for their debut."

"Sensible."

"She should also be pleasant to look upon, with a well-modulated voice."

"Of course. For your sake."

"Yes." William knew Duncan would comprehend that requirement. "Teresa fills the demands of the list."

"Plus, you wouldn't have to put forth the effort to court her. She's coming to you."

"Precisely."

Deadpan, Duncan said, "You silly romantic. You'll sweep a woman off her feet using love words like that."

William didn't understand why, but restlessness seized him. He paced to the window and looked out into the park. "That's the point. A man doesn't choose his wife based on romance. He chooses his wife based on her background, on her suitability, on her position in society."

"The countess is more than just pleasant to look upon. She's very pretty." Duncan couldn't have sounded more bored.

"Yes, I believe she is, but that's not important." Nor did William particularly care one way or another about her dark and dramatic good looks or her petite figure. "What's important is that she's a model of integrity."

"Perhaps you're not as informed about the countess as you suppose."

Duncan's muttered comment surprised William.

"If you know something I should know—"

"No! No, I just . . ." Duncan waved a negligent hand. "It's nothing."

Duncan's attitude surprised William. "I thought you'd be happy I was considering marriage."

Duncan slapped his palm on the desk. "That isn't marriage, it's a bloodless union. There are times I'm glad I'm not wealthy. I'll marry for romance, and list be damned."

Sometimes Duncan alarmed William with his reckless disregard for good sense. "That's not a wise way to approach a matter of such importance."

"So it's not." With a hasty change of subject, Duncan asked, "You'll keep me informed about the plans?"

"You'll be an integral part of any move I make."

Cocking a thoughtful eyebrow, Duncan asked, "Is your governess one of Throckmorton's people?"

"No." Sometimes Duncan annoyed William. "She's my governess."

"Did she read this letter?"

"It was sealed."

"That's not a deterrent to the skillful."

Sometimes Duncan *really* annoyed William. "She didn't read the letter. Lady Bucknell vouched for her."

"All right! I was being cautious. *You're* cautious." Duncan took a drink. "And how are you going to sleep when you know there's a woman who looks like that down the hall?"

Sometimes Duncan deserved to be kicked into next week. William took care not to reveal his annoyance, for if he allowed Duncan one hint of his unwilling interest in Miss Prendregast, Duncan would harass him unmercifully. "There have been more handsome governesses." Certainly Miss Prendregast seemed to have no awe of him, nor any interest, either, and that was not in the usual run of things.

But good. It was good that she didn't care for him.

Miss Prendregast guaranteed she would remain here through the year, and he believed her. Yet he wondered—would he survive the torment of having her in the house? She had an air about her . . . defiance, as if she hid a secret. Determination, as if she could deal with every situation. A harshness, as if she'd seen the worst of men and expected no better.

And undermining all that, a sweet astonishment, as if she recognized the attraction she held for him and didn't know how to handle it. Oh, yes. He'd wanted to stand as they conversed, to intimidate her with his height. Instead he'd had to sit to disguise a rather basic, obvious, primitive reaction to an attractive female.

Duncan watched William as if William had blurted out his thoughts rather than carefully concealing them. "Your other governesses were twittering idiots. I listened at the window. I heard this one giving you hell. She's going to be tough to resist."

"I don't like women who don't know their place."

Duncan grinned again, but this time with bitter perception. "Tell yourself that. Keep telling yourself that."

❧ Chapter Six ❧

"My gracious, young man, you certainly know how to show an old woman a lively dance." Valda, the countess of Featherstonebaugh, leaned against the marble column in the Throckmortons' grand ballroom and fanned herself with her peacock feather fan. "I'll wager you're popular with the ladies."

The ridiculous Lord Heath smirked and handed the countess her cane. "Thank you, ma'am, I like to think I please them in my own way. Could I get you a refreshing ice or a lemonade? After such strenuous exercise, a lady of your advanced age must be exhausted."

She closed her fan and tapped it on his arm. "You charmer! If you would take one more moment out of your precious time to fetch me a lemonade, I'd be grateful."

"Yes, ma'am. Glad to, ma'am." He swept her a bow and walked off, a tall, dark, and almost handsome man.

Except for that horrible rash of disgusting pimples that so marred his features. Valda waited until he was out of sight, then she walked off, smiling and nodding as she moved like a she-wolf through the pack of bleating sheep. One of the young ewes wore a feather in her upswept hair and a simper on her dimpled face. Another wore a ball gown of shimmering gold silk which made her complexion sallow. Of course, the male sheep all dressed alike: dark coats, plaid trousers, shiny black leather shoes and snowy white shirts.

In her purple velvet turban with its diamond clip and her purple velvet gown with a pink silk overjacket that buttoned to the waist, Valda looked better than all of them.

She caught a glimpse of herself in one of the many mirrors which ringed the ballroom. Or rather—she would, if she weren't so old.

In her face and form, she saw the remnants of the beauty that had caught an earl. Tall, charming, elegant—she was still all those.

But old. So old. She hated this business of aging. She fought it, but she was losing, and to a woman of her breeding and intelligence, that was unthinkable. She had spent her whole life overcoming every challenge life offered. She had been genteel and poor. She had married noble and rich. Her husband had lost his money and she'd been exiled on his family's damned primitive Lake District estate . . . ah, getting out of Maitland Manor had been her greatest success. She had discovered a way to make more money than anyone could imagine, and at the same time she got to outwit the dogs that protected these finely dressed, vapid sheep who danced, laughed, and flirted, all unsuspecting while a she-wolf slunk undetected through their midst.

Valda liked being smarter than everyone else. But she hated the liver spots on her cheeks, the stoop in her back, the cane she had to carry. Most of all, she hated the way the pimple-faced young men condescended to dance with her. Thirty years ago they had begged for the honor. Now they did their duty by her—and dancing made her hip ache.

Featherstonebaugh, the old fool, could still gavotte. She stopped behind a tall vase filled with magnificent flowers and watched Rupert prance about the floor with young Miss Kaye. He was spry as ever, chasing after girls who weren't half as pretty as Valda had been. If he could, he would have abandoned her completely, except she tied the purse strings around her arthritic fingers. And lately . . . lately, she thought she made him a little nervous. Perhaps, after all these years, he had begun to realize he had married a she-wolf who could turn on him and rip his throat out.

She rather enjoyed having him afraid of her, but it wouldn't do—more's the shame. For if he betrayed his wariness of her, people might start wondering if they really knew her. They would look deeper, and that would be unfortunate. After all, she knew everyone in English society, and they thought they knew her.

No, if she came under suspicion, there would be trouble. In her business, trouble was followed by more trouble, and usually death provided by a bullet between the eyes. She'd ordered that solution often enough herself. So she would have to be nicer to Rupert and stop treasuring thoughts of killing him. A widow didn't get invited to parties. A widow was expected to mourn, and if Valda couldn't go to parties, she couldn't collect the information these nicely dressed sheep provided so freely.

"Lady Featherstonebaugh."

She jumped at the sound of young Throckmorton's voice. She hadn't heard him walk up behind her. She was getting a little deaf—also a liability in her business.

He stepped before her and bowed.

Some women thought him handsome. Valda didn't see it. He was too tall, too broad, too serious, and his stern gaze could poke holes in a woman's composure if she wasn't careful. "Garrick, lad, it's good to see you. Got any of that important business information about where I should invest my spare coinage?" *May I sit in your office, and send you off to get me a drink while I rummage through your desk drawers?*

"Not tonight." He held out his hand, and that gardener's daughter he'd been dunce enough to marry stepped up and took it. "Celeste and I wanted to thank you for gracing our first party with your presence."

Valda smiled at them in benign, if false, delight. "My dears, we wouldn't miss your little celebration." With hidden maliciousness, she added, "Why, Rupert and I practically united you two lovebirds!"

That girl, that slut, that Celeste, didn't even have the grace to blush at the reminder of the disgraceful scene in the conservatory. She just opened her hazel eyes wide and said, "I feel that way too." Taking Valda's arm, she squeezed it in a comradely manner.

Valda wanted to pull her arm away and snap out an insult. But that didn't fit her role of benevolent family friend, and if ever a family had been rich in international information, it was the Throckmortons. They had made spying a tradition, and she hoped to extract another nugget from young Throckmorton this very night.

He thwarted her with another bow. "If you don't mind, my lady, I'll leave Celeste in your care. I've had a messenger arrive with news of great importance for my, er, my import business, and I must speak with him at once."

Valda wanted to shake off Celeste like a flea. Instead she brandished an admonishing finger at young Throckmorton. "What's up, dear boy? If this is an investment opportunity, you should tell your dear friends Lord and Lady Featherstonebaugh."

"Not exactly an investment opportunity." He tugged at his collar. "Rather, we've suffered great losses from the deprecations of, er, rats, and I have been told we've discovered who the main breeding rats are. If you'll excuse me."

Valda stared after him as he strode toward his office. A rat? Was that code? Was he talking about them? About her? Surely not. She wasn't a small, furry, disgusting rodent. She was a wolf—and a wolf who had better discover, and immediately, what was happening in that office.

She turned to Celeste, who was still smiling that inane smile. "I know you don't want to care for a silly old woman when you could be dancing."

Celeste blinked. "Oh, Lady Featherstonebaugh, I most definitely enjoy getting to know an *old* and honored guest."

The little bitch had definitely emphasized the word *old*. Valda's hand twitched. She wanted to slap Celeste.

As revenge for Celeste's insolence, Valda caught her husband's eye. She snapped her chin up.

He scuttled across the dance floor to them.

To Celeste, she said, "You are too kind to me, my dear." She placed Celeste's hand on Rupert's arm. "Our lovely young hostess is without a partner."

Rupert couldn't believe his good luck. He'd been trying to get his paws on the new Mrs. Throckmorton since the first time he'd seen her, back when she was newly returned from Paris and flaunting her seductiveness in front of any man who showed interest. Now he wiggled his eyebrows, bowed, and led her onto the floor.

Valda stayed long enough to see that they were well and truly occupied, then she made her way to Throckmorton's office.

A voice came from the antechamber. Throckmorton's voice, raised in loud disbelief. "This is outrageous. I don't believe it. Who made this accusation?"

Valda strained to hear as another voice, low and indistinct, answered.

"I assure you, he hasn't the intelligence to fool me for so long," Throckmorton proclaimed.

Valda took a long, silent breath. Clutched at her silk-covered chest.

The low voice answered again.

Valda crept closer.

"How likely is that? She's old." Throckmorton sounded as if he were sneering. "Furthermore, they are revered Throckmorton family friends!"

Valda had heard enough. They were talking about Rupert . . . and her. Before long, Throckmorton would be convinced, and she . . . she would be dancing at the end of a silk rope.

She walked away from the door toward the ballroom. Once there, she swept the room with her gaze. The old fool, Rupert, was standing off to the side by himself, clutching his hand as if he were in pain.

Apparently, young Celeste had not been amenable to his groping.

Valda glared at him, caught his eye, and again jerked her chin. She watched as he tottered toward her, a bony, long-chinned, disreputable old man who she longed to leave behind. But as always, he hung around her neck, a burden dragging her down.

He knew too much. He scared too easily. He had to go with her . . . back to the Lake District and Maitland Manor. Back to the place where she'd hidden their cache of gold and jewels.

Once there, she would set their escape plan in motion, and they would disappear from England.

She rubbed her aching hip. If only she were still young enough to enjoy the adventure.

Chapter Seven

"Those children are monsters."

"Aye, miss."

"I treat them with respect, and all I want in return is a little respect for myself."

"Aye, miss."

"Yet they continue to sulk, to refuse to cooperate, and to pretend they don't understand their lessons when I know very well that they do."

"Could be worse, miss."

Samantha raised her drooping head and stared at Clarinda. "How could it be worse?"

"Fer Miss Ives, two governesses ago, they filled a bag with manure, lit it on fire, and put it by her desk, and when the governess tried t' stomp it out—"

Samantha lifted her hand to stop Clarinda's

recitation. She sat in her bedchamber, the room that had become her refuge, taking her luncheon on a tray while the children took their luncheon in the schoolroom under the supervision of their nursemaids. Her own cowardice shamed her, but after four days she was bone-tired and for the first time in her career, unsure how to proceed in the face of such unending hostility. "How do they get away with such tricks? Is everyone in the household in on their pranks?"

"In a manner o' speaking, miss. They get more attention from their father when they've got no governess, and that's why they misbehave. Not that ye heard me say so. So we . . . help them along sometimes. Especially the nursemaids. They've got a bit of power now, and 'tis going t' their heads. Not that ye heard me say that, either." Clarinda put the fork into Samantha's hand. "Ye'd best eat, miss, ye'll need yer strength."

After she had eaten, Samantha climbed the stairs to the classroom on the third floor as she considered the information Clarinda had given her. No wonder she had failed to charm the girls. They had been aided and abetted in their defiance by their nursemaids and, indeed, by the whole staff, and if Samantha were going to succeed she would have to take drastic action.

She had to get the girls away from the house. Away from any support.

She heard the girls' animated chatter before she opened the door, but they quieted at once and turned eager faces toward her.

Perhaps, while she had been resolving to fix the problems of her situation, the children had been realizing how unkind they had been and deciding to do better.

She smiled at them.

They smiled back.

"I hope you had a pleasant lunch," she said.

In unison, they replied, "Yes, Miss Prendregast."

"We'll study our mathematics now." They really were chipper. A niggle of unease crept up Samantha's spine, and she considered them with misgivings. "If you would get out your books—" She opened her desk, and looked down into the drawer.

A mass of green snakes slithered in every direction, but mostly—toward her. She'd never seen a snake in her life. Hoped never to see one. But she knew what they were. Blinded by panic, by the image of those flickering tongues, the smooth scales, and those lidless black eyes, she screamed.

The children hooted in derision.

The snakes dropped onto the floor, writhed across her desk, glided over her chair.

She shouted, "Ruddy 'ell!" The children. Dear God, the snakes were going to bite the children. Gathering her courage, she ran to Kyla and Emmeline, grabbed them around the waists, and carried them out into the corridor. Heart pounding, she placed them on the floor and ran back for the others.

They'd stopped laughing.

"Come on!" She gestured frantically. "Before they bite you."

Agnes stood up at her desk and in a tone of withering scorn, said, "They're just grass snakes. Don't you know a grass snake when you see one?"

One of the dreadful creatures slithered across the floor right between Samantha and the children, and she took a running leap over it. Grasping Henrietta by the arm, she said, "Come on."

"They're just grass snakes," Agnes said again.

"I don't like this anymore." Henrietta came with Samantha out in the corridor.

The two younger children stood wide-eyed.

The other children traipsed out of the classroom now and joined them.

"They're grass snakes." But Agnes had realized she'd gone too far, and her defiance turned to open hostility.

Samantha led them to their bedchamber and found a gathering of nursemaids waiting for them. When she stepped through the door, the merry talk stopped, and they looked so guilty Samantha knew the information Clarinda had given her was correct. These maids had egged the children on. In a tone so quiet they had to strain to hear her speak, she commanded, "Get them dressed for a walk. I'll be back to fetch them soon. And you"—she looked at each one of the six maids—"all of you. Make sure the snakes, every last one of them, are removed from the classroom before we return."

The quieter she spoke, the angrier she was, and they must have realized the depths of her rage, for the nursemaids nodded and scurried to do her bidding.

Samantha stalked to her bedchamber. She looked out her window where the sun had broken through the clouds at last. She smiled evilly. Standing, she divested herself of her mauve gown, changed into her green serge and sturdy walking shoes, then went back for the children. She found them alone together, huddled on the floor of their bedchamber, whispering to one another. Samantha pretended not to notice. She clapped her hands to get their attention. "Come, girls. Let's go walking."

Six faces turned her direction. "Why?" Agnes asked.

"So you can tell me what you know. I've been boring you with things you've already been taught. That has to change."

"We're supposed to study now," Mara said.

"We're getting to know each other." Samantha glanced out the window. "The sun is shining, but if you'd rather stay inside . . ."

Emmeline leaped up and ran to Samantha. Kyla followed. The others rose more slowly, and viewed Samantha with suspicion. Agnes and Vivian exchanged glances. Henrietta and Mara nodded knowingly. They'd had time to regroup. To replot their defenses. She could hardly wait to see what scheme they'd cooked up now, nor did she doubt she could counter it.

She shuddered. As long as it didn't involve snakes.

Everything in the Gregory household was about to change. Turning toward the door, she said, "This is the first sunny day since I arrived, and I've seen little of the country. You can show me your favorite haunts."

Agnes clapped her hands. "Let's show her the rope bridge!"

"Yay!" the others cried. Even Emmeline and Kyla laughed and jumped up and down.

"That sounds wonderful," Samantha said. *That sounds fishy.* Or terrifying. A rope bridge. Over a canyon, no doubt, where they hoped she'd fall to her death.

She saw Emmeline's and Kyla's shining eyes, and corrected herself. Where they would jiggle the rope and frighten her.

"I have my bonnet and gloves." She showed them. "Get yours."

They rushed to comply.

Their hats were as ugly as their gowns, and their gloves were ... well, at least half of them were missing.

Samantha stood with her hands on her hips. "It's good to see you girls are average."

Agnes's head whipped around. "What do you mean?"

"You lose your gloves. You like to play outside. You remind me of my other charges."

"Well, you don't remind me of our other governesses. They were smart," Agnes snapped.

"They couldn't have been too smart or they'd still be here and I'd be in London." A fate to be devoutly desired. "Vivian, where are your old boots?" By the time she had Mara fitted in Vivian's footwear, everyone was ready to go, and Samantha held the door. "Come on. Step briskly!"

The children lined up like little soldiers, Kyla in the front and in size stair-stepping up to Agnes. Then they marched out, their arms swinging, their heels tapping. Suffering in equal parts amazement and amusement, Samantha followed down the stairs, through the lofty foyer, and to the back entrance—and that entrance was grand enough to warn Samantha of the elegance that awaited her.

A footman opened the double doors. The children stepped out onto the broad veranda that ran the length of the manor. Samantha followed them and, for the first time, a great panorama opened up before her gaze, filling her eyes, her mind, overwhelming her senses. Her jaw dropped and, stunned, she walked to the broad stone railing and gripped it hard.

She had known it was here. She'd even seen parts of it on the day she arrived. But from the veranda, everything seemed so . . . big. The sunny swathe of scythed lawn sloped down to a sprawling, azure lake. The still water mirrored the peaks that rose in gray crags and dips of pale stone and emerald meadow. Here and there in the depths of shadow drifts of snow lingered, even in the heat of the summer, and in the lower reaches, stands of ash, elm and hazel stood together like noble soldiers awaiting battle. Birds—huge birds—floated in lazy circles in the blue sky.

Overcome, Samantha covered her mouth with her hand.

Emmeline tugged at her other hand. "Miss Prendregast, why do you look so funny?"

"I . . . just . . . I've never seen anything like this. It's so . . . wild. And . . . horrifying."

Agnes strutted forward. "I'll tell Father you said so. He loves the mountains above all else."

Samantha tore her gaze away from the vista to look Agnes in the eyes. "Your Father already knows what I think about the wilderness. I told him."

"You . . . did . . . not." Agnes was wide-eyed and incredulous. "No one tells Father things he doesn't want to hear."

"I do." Samantha surveyed the veranda made of polished granite, with chairs and tables placed here and there below broad canvas sunshades. "This looks very comfortable. Why don't we stay here?"

"No! No!" Henrietta jumped up and down, fists clenched. "We want to take you to the m—"

Vivian slapped her hand across Henrietta's mouth. "To the rope bridge. We want to take you to the rope bridge."

Samantha looked from one to the other, then around at all the girls. "To the rope bridge?"

They nodded in unison.

"Then certainly to the rope bridge we must go." Samantha gestured to Agnes. "Lead on, Macduff."

They took the stone path that curved along the lake, then left it behind and led into the trees. The oak trees were at first part of the park, with smooth lawns beneath them and benches placed here and there for a walker's comfort. But soon the children veered off into a wilder part, clambering over drystone walls, strolling along dirt paths worn into a wildflower meadow.

Samantha slowed. "Are we still on your father's land?"

Agnes turned to face her. "Why?"

"Because your father requested that we remain on his estate."

"Why didn't you tell Father you didn't want to?" Agnes asked snidely.

"Because I do want to. I want to remain safe, and I intend that you should be, too." She held Agnes's gaze until Agnes looked away.

The ground rose beneath their feet. They walked around puddles and through patches of under-brush. In the steep parts, Agnes had to help Kyla, and Vivian helped Emmeline.

Agnes took a moment to glance back at Saman-tha. "Are you able to walk so far, Miss Pren-dregast?"

"Even though I am quite advanced in years, I find I am managing tolerably."

Agnes caught Samantha's dry tone, although Samantha doubted the others did, and shot her a first shocked, then malicious look.

Oblivious, Mara offered her hand. "I'll help you, Miss Prendregast."

Samantha took it and delighted in the trusting way the little fingers curled in hers.

"It's not far," Mara assured her.

The rope bridge was just what they said, a bridge made of thick rope knotted around slats to form the narrow footpath. Here there were no trees, only a few tufts of grass surrounding a hollow over which the sagging bridge crossed. Black, thick, oozing mud filled the hollow. The ends of the bridge were looped over stakes driven into the ground.

There were no handrails. Naturally.

Agnes stood with her hands on her hips and challenged Samantha. "I wager you're afraid to cross that."

Samantha had to play this very carefully. The others were children, credulous in the way of most children. Agnes, however, stood on the cusp of adolescence, and she had been in charge of their successful little rebellion for too long. Samantha leaned over, grasped the rope, and flipped it. The bridge rose and fell in a wave. She made a show of looking into the hollow. She backed up and shook her head. "I'm afraid."

Agnes looked startled. "You're . . . afraid? None of the other governesses have been afraid."

"I've never been out of London before. I've never crossed a bridge like this. It's too difficult."

Vivian frowned. "No. No, it's not. It's easy!"

Samantha put one foot on the bridge.

The children looked delighted.

Samantha pulled her foot back. "It's too hard." She waved her hand. "This place is wild. I want to go back to the house."

Henrietta took the bait first. She ran out into the middle and bounced up and down. "Look. It's fun!"

"Be careful!" Samantha injected the right amount of concern into her voice.

"She's not going to fall," Agnes assured her. "She'll come back, and you can cross."

"I'm too heavy. The bridge might break," Samantha said.

"Look!" Vivian walked out, wrapped her arms around Henrietta's waist, and they both jumped up and down.

Mara tugged at Samantha's hand. "C'mon, I won't let you fall."

"You go first, honey." Samantha urged her forward.

Mara went, and the rope bridge flailed back and forth and up and down under the influence of three leaping children.

"Doesn't that look like fun?" Agnes asked.

Samantha shook her head. "I'm afraid of heights."

"Even Emmeline isn't afraid of heights," Agnes said.

Emmeline ran right out and started jumping, too, and squealing and laughing.

"Don't let her go out there alone!" Samantha cried. Somehow she must have generated enough authority to get unthinking obedience, for Agnes ran and grabbed Emmeline's arm.

Samantha caught Kyla before she could join her sisters. "Stay here, sweetheart." Kneeling, she grasped the rope loop in both hands. She heard a screech as Agnes realized that she'd been duped. Looking up, Samantha smiled right at the girls, a pleasant, satisfied, toothy smile, and pulled the rope free.

Legs and arms flailing, they tumbled into the thick, rich, black mud with a series of moist plops that satisfied Samantha's vengeful soul. Agnes went in on her face. Vivian managed to land on her feet, then lost her balance, splatted on her rear, and started to sob. Samantha watched Emmeline carefully—the little girl went over with a shriek, and came up at once, laughing. Henrietta sat, her eyes wide and startled. Mara pushed her bonnet off, and fell back with an expression of bliss. One by one, they floundered to their feet, slipped, grabbed at each other, fell again.

Kyla stomped her foot, yelled, and pointed. "I want to!"

"You do?" Samantha laughed. She loved little children. They had no pretensions. They knew that mud was fun and didn't care a whit about the trouble involved in bathing and cleaning their clothes. And Kyla did not like being left out.

Picking her up, Samantha placed her on the rim and let her slide down into the mucky wallow with her sisters.

Kyla screamed with joy as she catapulted into Emmeline and they went down together.

Samantha let the girls reel about for a few minutes, laughing or crying as their personalities demanded. Stepping to the edge, she placed her fists on her hips and for the first time, she used her schoolteacher voice. "Young ladies!"

The girls quieted. They recognized that tone.

"I'm smarter and bigger and sneakier than every one of you, and if you continue to fight me, you'll continue to lose. Perhaps you'll believe me now, and treat me with the respect I demand. Or"—she stared at Agnes, who wiped the mud from her face and flung it away in jerky, furious motions—"you will not. Make no mistake, you will still lose. I am not one of your former governesses, wan and frightened. Not one of you is as tough and as devious as I am."

Mara guffawed and turned to Vivian, who stood unsteadily on her feet. "I knew she would be fun."

"I promised your father I would be here for at least a year. I mean to keep my promise." Samantha gazed at them all. "Are there any questions?"

"Yeah." Agnes dragged herself to her feet and staggered toward the rim. Her skirt and petticoats were heavy with mud, and Samantha could only imagine the ire on her mud-encrusted face. Reaching up her hand, she asked, "Would you help me climb out?"

"I'd be delighted." Samantha put her hand down, and just before Agnes grabbed it to pull her in, Samantha drew back her hand.

Agnes tumbled over backwards, sliding into the depths of the mud pit so rapidly she left a wake.

Samantha leaned over the pit and enunciated very slowly. "Listen to me, Agnes. I'm sneakier than you are. Give up now." Without waiting for Agnes to answer, or even recover herself, Samantha said, "All right. I'll give you ten minutes to play in the mud, then everyone out and we're going back."

Vivian started crying again. "Father will yell."

"I'll take care of your father." Samantha seated herself on a broad stone and pulled her watch from her watch pocket. "Play. I'll let you know when it's time to get out."

Mara pushed Vivian down. Vivian stopped sobbing, grabbed Mara's head, and pushed her under.

"Don't drown your sister, please, Vivian," Samantha called. Seeing Agnes plowing her way toward the side, Samantha added, "You might as well enjoy yourself, Agnes. You're not leaving without me."

Agnes hesitated. Samantha could almost see her turning over her options in her mind. Coming to a decision, she used the tufts of grass on the edge of the hollow to pull herself out, then stalked to a rock and sat down, back to her sisters, arms crossed across her chest, bottom lip thrust out.

Satisfied that she would remain until they were ready to go, Samantha turned her attention to the party below. Mud flew, children rolled, and Samantha watched with amused approval.

It smelled good here, like freshness and mint. Plucking the leaves from a short plant, she brought them to her nose and rolled them between her fingers. That was it. That was the odor. Like wintergreen. Perhaps the flavor came from a plant.

And perhaps the plant disguised itself with a pleasant smell to lure unwary visitors. She dropped the leaves and brushed her gloved fingers against her skirt. She hoped the scent wasn't lethal to inhale. She should have brought a book from the City, one that warned of the natural hazards of the mountains—like snakes in her desk.

Pushing her bonnet back, she lifted her face to the sunshine. She shouldn't, she knew; to be so bold was deadly to a genteel complexion, but the sun never shone so brightly in London. In London, the coal dust always coated the air, and she had never seen a sky this blue. If only . . . well, there was no use dwelling on the *if onlys*. She was in exile from her beloved London, and she had promised Colonel Gregory to stay at Silvermere for a year.

It was a safe promise. Lady Bucknell wouldn't allow her to return until she'd proven she could live with a family without meddling in their affairs for at least twelve months. And by then, surely the society matrons would have forgotten any malicious accusations Mr. Wordlaw had made, and she could secure a different position. In the meantime, though, she had a year to get through . . . a year spent dealing with young Miss Agnes and her sisters. A year spent laboring under the heavy hand of Colonel Gregory's authority.

She glanced at her watch and called, "Ten minutes are up!"

Black ooze covered the girls. They climbed out, helping each other, laughing, and looking so little like the grim little group she'd met in the morning she couldn't help but reflect she'd succeeded already.

She glanced at Agnes's huddled figure. Except with her, of course. Agnes was a challenge. Colonel Gregory was a challenge. But what was life without its challenges?

Chapter Eight

"We can't eat like this." Henrietta spread her mud-encrusted skirt for display.

"After you're cleaned up, you can eat," Samantha promised. "Let's go, now, fleet feet make short work of a journey!"

Agnes followed the hooting, chattering group at a dignified distance, and when Vivian tried to include her, Agnes shook her sister off.

Samantha was going to have to do something about her, and soon. Just as she was going to have to do something about Colonel Gregory and his insistence that the children be kept on a rigid schedule regardless of their age or temperament. But Samantha couldn't knock Colonel Gregory into a mud puddle.

"Why do you children do these dire things?"

Samantha had a pretty good idea of the answer, but she asked anyway.

Henrietta giggled. "What dire things? Like dropping our governess in the mud?"

"Or slipping spiders in her pockets?" Mara asked.

"Or putting thnakes in her desk?" Emmeline piped up.

Samantha glared.

Emmeline's lip trembled.

Vivian intervened. "Everyone says Father's so heartbroken because of the death of his dear wife . . . but that's not true. He was never home, he was off running the perfect regiment." Her resentment bubbled over. "*We* lost our mother, *we're* the ones who miss her, *he's* selfish and mad because he has to stay home now with us instead of going off and fighting with his soldier friends."

"And every night after we're in bed he sneaks away on his horse," Kyla said.

"Does he think we don't notice?" Agnes asked.

Samantha wasn't surprised by the comments, but she was very surprised by their vehemence. Something had to be done, and soon, but what to do? She had to be confident that a proper course would present itself.

"Miss Prendregast!" Emmeline pointed across the lawn toward the lake. "Look!"

Oh, no. A proper course needed to present itself *now*, for there stood two footmen with buckets full of water, and beside them, Colonel Gregory, his face like a thundercloud, slapping his boot with a riding crop.

"So that's where Agnes gets that disagreeable

habit," Samantha muttered, and pulled her bonnet up to sit properly on her head. She needed inspiration to get through the coming scene. She had none.

As they drew closer, she saw Colonel Gregory observe his children, muddied from head to toe. His blue eyes chilled. Those straight, saturnine eyebrows lifted.

He spoke to one of the footmen, who put his bucket down and ran for the house.

The children clustered behind Samantha for sanctuary and scurried behind at a distance.

Lacking inspiration, Samantha hoped confidence would take its place. As they came within hearing distance, Samantha fixed a bright smile on her lips. "Colonel! What a fortuitous meeting. I was going to come and find you at once." Not a lie, really, for the definition of "at once" surely varied from person to person. "The children had a bit of an accident and . . . er . . . fell into a puddle."

"So . . . I . . . see." Slap. Slap.

"But no one was hurt, and no harm was done."

Slap. Scowl. Slap. "They seem to be covered in mud."

"Really?" Samantha kept her gaze firmly fixed on his face. "I hadn't noticed."

"Their clothing is ruined." His eyes, Samantha was alarmed to see, had warmed to the temperature of blue hot coals.

"A little soap . . . a little cold water . . ."

He stepped around her to scrutinize his children, who one by one tried valiantly to look at him, but one by one failed. "The morning Miss Prendregast arrived, I told her what I expected of her. I expect her to follow the schedule." He slapped his boot, and in a whiplash tone, he said, "I expect the same thing of you. And what does that schedule say you should be doing now?"

Emmeline squirmed toward the front. "Father, we were getting to know Miss Prendregast."

He ignored her. "What does the schedule say you should be doing now?" He looked at them all, one by one. Each head drooped, and no one would speak. "Agnes?"

"Agnes, don't!" Vivian admonished in an undertone.

Samantha turned to look at the girl. The temptation to take control of the situation with a combination of spite and honesty must have been almost irresistible, but Agnes glanced around at her sisters. They stared at her with expressions varying from threats to pleading, and apparently she recognized the danger, for she muttered only, "We're supposed to be in the classroom."

"That's right." Slap. Slap. "Studying. And why aren't you?"

Mara worked up the nerve to say, "Miss Prendregast wanted to know what we'd already learned so she wouldn't repeat it."

Emmeline rushed toward him, dripping mud with every step, and stopped only when he held out an arresting hand. "Please, Father, don't make her go away."

He walked toward the mud-encrusted little group. Hand to chin, he considered them. "I am not happy about this. I have a schedule, and I expect you children to follow it."

Agnes opened her mouth.

He turned on her. "Yes, Agnes? You wanted to say something?"

With a furious scowl, Agnes reported, "Miss Prendregast doesn't like the mountains."

Agnes wouldn't stop making mistakes. In a voice as cool as a mountain stream, Samantha said, "I like the mountains almost as little as I like children who tattle to their papas."

"Miss Prendregast has stated her dislike for wild creatures and wild places, but I consider her attitude a matter of ignorance."

Samantha took a breath to retort, then let it out. Some matters weren't worth fighting over.

"We'll teach her differently." He strode along and surveyed the children once again. "Your clothing will never be the same."

They looked down at themselves.

Mara muttered, "A little soap . . . a little cold water . . ."

Colonel Gregory turned quickly, and Samantha feared he caught her smirk before she wiped it away.

"Perhaps a little soap and cold water will do the trick." He gestured to the line of servants, footmen and maids, coming down to the lake, each with a bucket in both hands. They were snickering, all of them. The butler and the housekeeper stood on the veranda, staring toward them with incredulity. "I have good news for you. I have ordered the material for your new gowns."

"Oh, Father!" The children clasped their

hands together or jumped up and down.

"The material arrived today." He smiled with more charm than Samantha had yet seen. "Do you know why I ordered this material?"

"No, Father, why?" the children chorused.

"Miss Prendregast has convinced me you need them."

The children's muddy faces came alight with joy. Their eyes glowed. As one, they gave a shriek.

Samantha realized what was coming. She held her hand out to stop them. "No. No, no!"

They rushed at her. She backed up, but nothing could halt them. They surrounded her and enfolded her in their muddy arms, smeared their muddy faces against her skirt, stroked their muddy hands on her arms. Sincere gratitude sounded in their piping voices. "Thank you, Miss Prendregast, thank you!"

She hugged them back, stroked their muddy heads, and glanced at Colonel Gregory. He was grinning—a grin that disappeared so swiftly she might have been hallucinating. But she wasn't. He'd set her up. He'd set her up! So she said, "Don't thank me. Your father ordered the material."

That high, little-girl shriek sounded again. His daughters wheeled around and leaped toward their father, and he was engulfed in muddy embraces.

Samantha stood back and smiled, arms crossed across her chest. "A thoroughly touching display of filial affection."

He heard her. His gaze met hers, rueful, intent,

and for the first time in her life she recognized a kindred soul. A man who hid his true self behind a façade of austerity. A man at war with his own nature.

She was like that. Proper. Sensible. When all she wanted was to run, to dance, to sing. To take joy in life in all its guises.

Surely she was wrong. Surely he wasn't like her.

They stared for one, very long moment, and Samantha grew warm and flustered.

Hastily, she looked away. Flustered! Nothing flustered her. Never. She was the calm one in every situation, the one who stood back and observed, the intelligent one. She didn't like this breathless sensation, and she really didn't like this impression of intimacy.

"All right. All right!" He shooed the children away, and they left behind mud on his dark blue trousers and mud on his shining black boots. Mud on his cream-colored waistcoat and mud on his dark blue jacket.

Samantha enjoyed the sight more than she should.

"Children, go stand in the lake and let the servants splash you with buckets of water," Colonel Gregory said.

"It's cold," Vivian whined.

He bent down to her level. "That is the punishment you get when you fail to dunk your governess in the mud."

Samantha caught her breath. No wonder he'd been waiting with servants and buckets. He knew the children's game. He'd let them play it—but why?

He had betrayed himself, but he didn't seem to care. He sounded military and precise when he said to her, "When a man has six daughters, he must be prepared for all eventualities."

"I see he must." She cleared her throat. "When one is a governess, one must also be prepared for all eventualities. That's why I believe it's time the nursemaids were replaced."

"Indeed?" His expressive eyebrows rose. "Is that your sincere recommendation?"

"It is."

"Consider it done."

Samantha wanted to cheer. Sometime during this long, difficult day, she'd won Colonel Gregory's respect.

His daughters gave a groan.

He turned to them. "If you want to argue against the change, you must be able to tell me why it's not a good idea."

The girls exchanged glances, then shook their heads. They were in far too deep for such contention.

"When the mud is washed off, you'll go upstairs. I'll send the housekeeper to supervise your baths. Don't be late for dinner, I have an announcement to make." He gestured at Samantha's mud-covered skirt. "Miss Prendregast, you should probably stand in the lake, also."

She looked pointedly at his encrusted trousers and grubby jacket. "I will if you will."

"You're a very insolent young lady." He offered her his arm as if it were a challenge.

She took it in the spirit in which it had been offered. "You are a very perceptive man."

Together, they walked to the house, starting rumors that would be impossible to quash.

❧ Chapter Nine ❧

In the elegant dining room, at the head of a long table, Colonel Gregory carved the roast into thin slices. Seated on either side of the table, the children watched with voracious attention.

At the foot of the table, Samantha sat dressed once more in her pink ruffled gown, trying to behave as if she'd done this a hundred times before. In fact, this was her third night to participate in a family dinner; all of her previous employers would rather dine alone than to dine with their governess, and most certainly they would never dine with their children. So with the amazement of someone who had never before participated in a domestic dinner, she observed every expression, every nuance, trying to comprehend how the family worked.

Tonight, the children were hungry from their

adventure, and she felt both sympathy and empathy. The scent of the food made her own mouth water.

As the long knife sliced into the crusty brown meat, Colonel Gregory announced, "Miss Prendregast has pointed out to me I've been lax in my duties, so I have decided to host a party."

Nothing else could have distracted the girls, but that did. Every eye turned in his direction, every mouth hung open.

And Samantha thought, *No wonder he will allow me the material to make the girls new dresses.*

Then she looked at him, at his jaw, so firm it looked as if it could shatter. At his form, hard, muscled, without an ounce of fat, and held with military rigidity. At his cold, cold eyes, rimmed with dark lashes. She didn't believe for a minute the man was acting on her advice. So why *was* he hosting a party?

Catching her eye, he lifted his brows in a parody of innocent inquiry.

She responded with exactly the same expression, and didn't know which one of them would have looked away first, but all the girls recovered their power of speech at the same time. "When, Father?" "Who's coming?" "For how long?" "Will there be children to play with?"

Mitten, the butler, directed the servants to bring the bowls of parsleyed potatoes, the steaming peas, tiny dark green brussels sprouts, the savory pudding and the golden loaves of bread. The footmen circulated as Samantha helped Kyla and Henrietta, seated on either side of her, to load their plates.

.

Colonel Gregory filled a platter with meat as he answered the questions succinctly and in order. "The invitations will go out at once, for the first of September. I'll invite everyone in the district, and as many old friends from abroad and in the service as I can find. They'll be here for three days—like old fish, after three days guests begin to stink."

Mitten accepted the platter, and served the older children.

Kyla's forehead wrinkled. "Can't they take a bath?"

Samantha flashed a glance toward Colonel Gregory and met his mirth-filled gaze. Warmth suffused her; she unfalteringly ignored it and patted Kyla's hand. "It's an adage, dear. They can take as many baths as they want. They won't really stink."

"Adults always say peculiar things like that," Vivian loudly whispered to Kyla.

Mitten brought the platter to Samantha, then put it down hastily to catch Henrietta's fork before it hit the floor. Samantha served herself, then helped Henrietta wipe the potatoes off her bodice while the footman brought new silverware.

Dinner with the children was always an adventure.

Round-eyed with dismay, Agnes said, "The first of September is only a fortnight away. How will we get ready in time?"

Colonel Gregory helped Emmeline cut her meat. "Three days ago, I sent a letter to the countess of Marchant requesting her help."

A groan like an a capella chorus rose from the children.

Swiftly he looked up, his eyes at their most glacial.

At once the children busied themselves with their plates.

He dismissed the servants, waited until they had bowed themselves out, then in clipped tones, he said, "Lady Marchant is an accomplished hostess, and we will all be glad of her assistance."

Samantha didn't know what was going on, but she certainly understood the need to smooth things over. "I'm sure that's true. Just as I'm sure she'll be of great assistance."

Agnes blinked rapidly as if the mere mention of the lady made her want to cry.

Samantha forked a small mouthful of peas into her mouth, chewed and swallowed. "When can we expect her ladyship?"

"With any luck, if she has no other engagements, she'll be here within the week," he said.

As if she couldn't hold it back, Henrietta released a huge sigh.

Samantha pulled Henrietta's plate toward her. "Let me cut your meat."

"Oh!" Mara covered her mouth in dismay. "How will we get our gowns done in time for the party?"

"I've hired seamstresses," Colonel Gregory said. "Your lessons will be temporarily suspended."

The children cheered.

"Temporarily," he emphasized. "You'll be busy getting ready to perform."

Agnes didn't even bother to conceal her hostility. "Perform *why?*"

Colonel Gregory looked sharply at her. "For our company, to display your accomplishments."

"That is what young ladies do," Samantha said.

The color washed out of Mara's face. "But . . . I can't do anything."

"You have a good voice," Colonel Gregory said. "So you will sing."

"I can't sing in front of . . . people," Mara cried.

"You sing like your mother," he answered.

The color returned to Mara's cheeks in a rush of pleasure. To Samantha's surprise, Colonel Gregory occasionally said the right thing. "Did Mrs. Gregory have a beautiful voice?"

"Very beautiful," Colonel Gregory said. "All of the children sing well, but only Mara has the purity and tone of her mother."

"I'll t . . . try," Mara stammered.

"You will sing, and you will sing beautifully," Colonel Gregory retorted.

He spoke in such a decisive tone, Mara nodded and looked as if she believed it.

He asked, "Now, what about the rest of you? Agnes, have you been practicing the pianoforte?"

Agnes pushed back her chair so violently it tipped over backwards. Bursting into tears, she ran from the room.

The other children looked from side to side, trying to comprehend what had happened.

Samantha started to rise, but Colonel Gregory said, "Sit, Miss Prendregast, and finish your meal. You're the last person she'll wish to see."

Samantha sank back down. She supposed he was right, but at the same time she hated to leave the child alone and sobbing.

"The housekeeper will give her warm milk and toast and put her to bed." Colonel Gregory poured a dab of sauce on his meat.

Henrietta's lip wobbled, too. "But Agnes has never done that before."

"No. But she's never had a governess like Miss Prendregast before, either, to teach her a much-needed lesson." Colonel Gregory swept the children with a glance that informed them he knew of their shenanigans.

Vivian and Mara blushed. Emmeline and Kyla scrunched down in their chairs. Defiant to the finish, Henrietta crossed her arms over her chest.

"Don't worry. Every soldier must learn to accept defeat graciously, and when Agnes does, all will be well." As he spoke, Emmeline reached for her milk and knocked it over. He helped her mop it up, and when everyone had settled down again, he announced, "That's enough about personal matters. You children know the rules. We use this time at dinner to discuss a matter of interest to all of us, and tonight that topic is—the wildlife of our area."

Samantha stopped eating the parsleyed potatoes long enough to glance sharply in his direction. Was he trying to educate her?

"But, Father, that doesn't interest me," Vivian objected. "I want to know the newest styles in gowns."

"Then you should be quiet, because everyone

else here is completely interested in the wildlife of our area," he said.

Up and down the table, the heads shook *no*.

"Anyone who is not interested in the wildlife of our area can leave the table." His cold blue eyes grew glacial. "I understand Cook has made a strawberry trifle for dessert."

The heads shook *yes*, and for the rest of the meal, even though Henrietta also spilled her milk and Emmeline dropped pudding on the sculpted oriental carpet, Samantha learned about roe deer, badgers, and squirrels. She did *not* say she was uninterested, although the subject engaged her only when they discoursed about creatures that might eat her. She adored trifle too.

When the trifle was consumed and the children stood and asked to be excused, Colonel Gregory allowed them to go with a curtsy to both him and Samantha.

When they had gone, he said, "Stay, Miss Prendregast. Have a glass of ratafia—or port, if you'd rather—and tell me how things are truly proceeding."

It wasn't really an invitation. She didn't think he knew how to issue an invitation. But it was a politer command than he'd previously delivered, and Samantha wanted to stay, far too much, and that was a reason to go. "I should prepare the lesson for tomorrow."

"Perhaps you could teach them about snakes."

She sat hard in her chair. "Do you know *everything* those children are up to?"

He didn't smile, but those azure, sapphire, cobalt

eyes—my heavens, they were most constantly changing blue!—contained a sleepy warmth that heated her muscles and left her knees weak. "Not everything. Not always. I'm usually a step behind and an hour late."

She had to stop fooling herself. She wasn't leaving the table. She wanted to sit and talk with another adult. She wanted to talk about the children, the weather, the party.

She wanted to talk to Colonel Gregory. "Port, please."

Standing, he poured two glasses, and placed one full of tawny liquid before her.

She sipped, and scarcely restrained a shudder. Port tasted like tar and burned like kerosene. "Who would drink that?" she asked hoarsely. "At least . . . on purpose?"

He grinned. "That's one kind. Let's try you with this. It's sweeter." He placed a glass of a ruby red liquor before her.

Cautious now, she sniffed it first. Rich, warm, heady. She sipped. "Oh." The liquid rolled across her tongue. "That's good. I think I like it."

"You've never tried port before?"

She couldn't keep the sarcastic tone from her voice. "Most employers don't encourage their governesses to drink with them, and all rather forcibly discouraged me from raiding the liquor cabinet on my own."

"So you haven't got a drinking problem?"

She chuckled, then realized he looked somber and inquiring. Hastily she sobered. "No, not at all. Why do you ask?"

"In India, my wife bought me a bag made of skins in which to carry liquid. The natives all used them when they traveled, and I've carried it in my nighttime rides about the countryside."

She cradled her glass in her hand. "Full of port?"

"Whisky, Miss Prendregast. I require my men to leave their homes and travel with me in the cold and the dark. Occasionally, I share refreshment with them."

She almost smiled at his haughty tone, but this was serious. "Someone drank the whisky?"

"Someone took the skin," he corrected. "The night after you arrived."

Carefully, she placed the glass on the table. She'd been accused of robbery many times before, and she couldn't bear to have *him* think that of her. "I don't drink on the sly. Nor do I steal."

"No, of course not. You have Lady Bucknell's confidence. She knows, as I do, that once a thief, always a thief."

Rage ignited and blazed behind Samantha's eyes. Rage . . . and fear. Did he know about her checkered past? Was this his less than subtle way of keeping her on edge?

But no. Not Colonel Gregory. He had not a subtle bone in his body. The man reeked of righteousness. So why was he so attractive?

He said, "I flatter myself that I can read a man's character—or a woman's—and you're not the kind of woman to choose such an easy, sordid way of earning a living."

"A wonderful compliment indeed, Colonel."

She'd heard such blathering before, from men who had never faced starvation, who had never known a moment's want, who never faced an upraised fist or an unwanted baby. After today, she had imagined, hoped that Colonel Gregory would be different . . . but Adorna had warned her, and really, why would he be? He was a landowner. A *man*. She knew better than to expect anything different from him, just because he was from the country. Just because he had blue eyes and hair the color of midnight.

"What's wrong?" he asked.

Whatever else could be said about him, he was astute. Probably the result of leading English troops through the lost lands of the East. She said flatly, "You probably misplaced the skin. That's the usual situation in these cases."

"Probably you're right." Pulling out the chair to her right, he seated himself.

This strong, law-abiding, tradition-following officer seated himself at the end of the table beside a servant. Why?

She pushed her chair back a little.

What did he mean by his familiarity? Should she be apprehensive about her past . . . or her virtue?

He stared with a little too much discernment for her comfort. She didn't want him making inquiries about her past. She didn't want him asking her questions she would find too difficult to answer. She had sentenced herself to a year in this place. She had to fulfill her promise.

So she asked, "Why do you let the children get away with such mischief as mud baths and snakes in the desk? You'd have better luck keeping a governess if you put a stop to them."

Still he considered her.

She tried to stare him in the eyes. But she couldn't quite; her past, her disillusionment with him, and most of all this continuing, discomfiting attraction she felt, made her glance down at the table, up at his right shoulder, sideways at the gold-framed mirrors that decorated the dining room, and back at his chin. She fixed her gaze there, and watched his lips move as he answered her. "I'm frequently away, and if the governess can't handle any situation that arises, she's of no use to me."

"I suppose." She considered the stains on the white tablecloth, stains put there by his children. "Who is the countess of Marchant?"

"Teresa is a lovely lady, a friend of my wife's." He twirled his glass and smiled fondly into the port as if he were looking into the countess's eyes. "She's been a great help to me since my return to England. She's been urging me to get back into society, so I know she'll be glad to assist with this party."

"Oh." A chill slithered through Samantha, and she straightened in her chair. She had known there had to be an ulterior motive to giving this party. He'd given her one she could understand—he had decided to court Lady Marchant and was going about it the best way he knew how, with the gift of his home as an enticement. This certainly explained why the children were unhappy. They would welcome no one to take their beloved mother's place.

That didn't explain why Samantha was unhappy, but she wouldn't think about that. "Will the children eat dinner with you when the countess is here?" Taking another sip of port, she savored the aromatic flavor.

"Not during the party, but otherwise . . . of course." He managed to look blank. "Why wouldn't they?"

She didn't know exactly how to explain the obvious. "They . . . spill milk."

"Of course they spill milk. My daughters spill milk all the time. The house is awash in milk. I'm surprised we haven't floated away."

Samantha gurgled with surprised laughter. "Which is why most gentry don't dine with their younger children."

"So why do I?" He placed his palms flat on the table and leaned toward her. "Is that your question, Miss Prendregast?"

No wonder he'd managed to hold her so firmly that night on the road. He had the most masculine hands she'd ever had the pleasure of observing, long-fingered and broad-palmed, and the nails were clean and shaped. The back of his hand was large and heavy, sprinkled lightly with dark hair and invested with authority and power. She could see the might of him in the veins and sinews, and she suffered that annoying curl of sensation in the depths of her abdomen. A blush climbed her cheeks to her forehead. She, who had never before blushed. What did it mean?

An inner voice mocked her. *You know what it means.* But fiercely she turned her mind away. She was far from home, among strangers, and she saw in one man security and strength. That was all. "Most gentry don't allow their children to learn their manners with them."

"I'm a busy man. I don't get to see my children as often as I wish. I can almost always eat dinner with them, and there is no one better equipped to train them than their father."

"Unique," she whispered.

He did as he wished, not as everyone else did, and that made him dangerous to her, for whom family union was a shining beacon that beckoned like a chimera. She'd spent her early life peeking into candlelit windows at families like this one, gathered around a table, eating and laughing and talking. It was a vision she'd decided was not for her. Many times she had decided that, but always the desire to be part of a family had returned to haunt the periphery of her mind.

How could he take her from disillusionment to a grudging admiration in so short a time?

"You have developed a tan, Miss Prendregast, and"—his fingers brushed the tip of her nose—"a bit of a sunburn."

She seized the chance to get away from the table. From him. From the questions and the unwanted intimacy. Leaping to her feet, she went to a mirror. He was right. She did have color in her face, and red tipped her nose. "Lady Bucknell tells me I must never go without my bonnet, but I couldn't resist today."

"It's charming." Then he spoiled everything with autocratic impertinence. "Why aren't you married?"

Samantha swung around. "What kind of question is that?"

"You're attractive, you're young. Probably you're on the lookout for a husband, and you'll be here only as long as it takes you to find one."

Now she understood. Colonel Gregory was worried that, no sooner than she settled the children, she would leave and he'd be without a governess again. Pure self-interest prompted his inquiry, and she understood self-interest. "If I were on the lookout for a husband, I assure you, there are a bounty of men in London." She seated herself again. "I have no interest in marriage."

"You would rather care for someone else's children than have the security of husband and a home of your own?" His tone made his disbelief clear.

How much to tell him? Enough. Not everything, by any means. "I didn't come from a settled home. My father had me supporting him in his dissipations by the time I was twelve." She tasted the port again, but the flavor had gone flat.

"To guide your life by one man's influence—profound, to be sure, but only one man—is irrational."

She didn't know why she answered him. Maybe it was the way he cocked an eyebrow, as if insinuating she, a woman, could be nothing but irrational. Maybe, as she grew older, she grew less patient with men and their everlasting superiority. "When I was fourteen, my best friend was madly in love with a young lord, and he madly in love with her. But when the babe grew in her belly, he—and his affection—disappeared, never to be seen again. I helped deliver that baby, and bury it, too." As she stared at Colonel Gregory, she wondered why she had ever thought him appealing. "Tell me, Colonel Gregory, what is the advantage marriage gives to a woman?"

Like the pompous jackass he was, he said, "A good man does not stray, treats others with honor, and supports his wife."

"Find me a good man, and I will wed him." She indicated her profound distrust of men—and him—with a patently artificial smile. "Perhaps."

Colonel Gregory did not smile back, or scowl at her for her bluntness, or tell her she was a woman who should be guided by him and every other male creature, regardless how pitiable their brain. "Your father is dead?"

"Yes." And that was all she would say about that.

"And your mother?"

"Gone." So many years before, and on a cold night she would never forget.

They might have stared at each other, neither giving ground, forever, but Mitten entered with a sealed envelope on a silver platter and presented it to Colonel Gregory. "Sir, this was delivered from London."

Colonel Gregory opened it, skimmed the message, then stood and bowed to Samantha. "I have to go out. Please tell the girls I won't be in to wish them goodnight."

"I will." She hesitated. "Is it the bandits?"

His eyes turned chilly. "What I do, Miss Prendregast, is never your concern."

❧ Chapter Ten ❧

Duncan raced his stallion along the twilit road. He'd served with William in India, and now for two years here in England, and he'd seldom received such a summons from William. Terse. Unrevealing. *Send for the men. Come at once.*

William was the consummate warrior. He took command easily, and once assuming command, expected to be obeyed. Yet he respected Duncan's army experience and paid him his due in explanations and consideration. But not now. Not tonight.

There was only one explanation. Matters were at last coming to a head.

Slowing Tristam, Duncan turned him onto the side path through the trees until he reached the clearing. William sat astride his ridiculously staid gelding, and Duncan moved to William's side. "What is it?"

"I've had a letter from Throckmorton." The half moon shone on William's grim face. "Lord and Lady Featherstonebaugh have left society and are fleeing north."

"Will we be ready for them?"

"The invitations have been sent out. The important people have accepted. Have been told to accept. General Wilson. Secretary Grey."

Impressed with the guests, Duncan whistled. "Wives, too?"

"Of course." William continued, "There's a ship which leaves the local harbor for Ireland every fortnight. It's that ship which Lord and Lady Featherstonebaugh plan to catch. But whenever they arrive at their estate, I've arranged that they receive word the ship will have just left—"

Duncan gave a bark of laughter.

"—and they'll be stranded in their home, waiting to escape, while only a few miles away, I'll be having a party loaded with my friends who know every secret England possesses." William's smile swept over his face like the north wind across a wintry moor. "Oh, yes. They'll want to bank more secrets for the future. They'll come."

"You're diabolical," Duncan said with admiration.

"Determined," William said. "They're moving slowly toward Hawksmouth."

Startled, Duncan said, "Slowly? Why?"

"They're visiting people who might have information, staying overnight, and taking care to leave the impression of casual travel. They're zigzagging across the country, probably in the hopes of throwing any pursuers off the scent."

Tristam moved restlessly, responding to Duncan's dissatisfaction. "But if they think there are pursuers, aren't they afraid those pursuers will arrive at their home before they do?"

"They have many homes. Perhaps they hope Throckmorton won't realize where they're going." Before Duncan could object, William held up his hand. "From discussions overheard, Throckmorton believes Lord Featherstonebaugh is balking."

Duncan had met Featherstonebaugh. He was a silly, arrogant man, given to gossip and lechery, and Duncan still couldn't imagine how the fellow managed to fool the best of England's spies. "Balking? About what?"

"He doesn't believe they're in danger."

Now that Duncan could believe. "He's been selling secrets to the enemy for thirty years and he doesn't believe he's in danger?"

"He's an aristocrat of the old school. He considers himself to be above the law."

By the time Duncan had recovered his breath, William continued, "The manner of their leaving has caused gossip. Gossip encouraged by Throckmorton and his network in hopes of flushing out the Featherstonebaugh allies." William grasped Duncan's arm. "Count Gayeff Fiers Pashenka has left London."

Duncan very well understood the import of that information. "Pashenka, eh?" Pashenka was an elegant man, a man popular in the ton, especially with the ladies, and a foreigner who had moved among English society for years, dining out on his sorry story of being unjustly stripped of his lands in Russia. Apparently the account had been nothing but a Russian fairy tale. "Is he on his way here? Do we hunt him tonight?"

"It's Throckmorton's opinion that Pashenka is escaping to the Featherstonebaugh estate, and from there to the sea." They heard the sound of hooves on the road. The men were arriving, and William lowered his voice. "Soon we will capture not only the traitors to England, but if we manage things correctly, we will also have Pashenka, the ringleader to whom they report."

"That's clever." Duncan smiled as he made the suggestion that he knew would delight William. "But wouldn't it be better to give him false information and send him on his way?"

William took a hard breath. "By damn, Duncan! Now I remember why I keep you close. You're too brilliant to lose."

For the third night in a row, the clear deep call of the owl floated across the cloudless midnight sky. William's men were returning to the clearing, and William waited, his horse calm and steady beneath him, to hear their reports.

Hawksmouth's mayor, Dwight Greville, arrived first, his horse picking its way along the moonlit path. " 'Tis quiet to the north, sir, all the way to George's Cross." His nose quivered with rabbitlike caution as he sniffed the breeze. "But I don't like it. My wife's left eye is twitching, and that's a premonition of trouble if I've ever heard of one. Yes, Colonel, a dreadful premonition indeed. I tell you, there's something in the air."

"Until there's something on the ground, we've nothing to worry about," William answered. Greville constantly foretold danger, afraid that somehow the tranquility of Hawksmouth would be tarnished during his jurisdiction. William spent most of his evenings reassuring him that all would be well.

Duncan rode in on that damned stallion of his, a thoroughbred beast more enamored of rearing and pawing the air than of getting Duncan from place to place in a reasonable manner. "'Tis a quiet night," Duncan announced. "No traffic to the south."

The other horses moved restively, responding to Tristam's wildness. Even Osbern, William's own stolid gelding, tossed its head and danced sideways.

But it was more than Tristam's presence that worked on Osbern. It was the moonlight and the hint of a breeze, the sprinkling of stars and the scent of the grass crushed beneath his hooves. It had to be, because William felt just as restless. Just as moody. For the first time in years, he could almost hear his blood surging through his veins. Feel his heart beating, taste the excitement in the air. He told himself it was because his goal was in sight. The beasts responsible for his wife's death were almost within his grasp. Soon, he would have justice for her.

But it was more than that. Ever since he'd met Samantha walking down the road, he'd wanted . . . something. Something different.

Duncan, that knave, had seen the difference at once, and correctly attributed it to Samantha. William told himself he suffered from a basic need, one he'd denied too long. But if that were the case, why didn't he think of Teresa with desire? She was an excessively attractive woman, a widow from his class, a model of elegance and grace who knew her place and never corrected him, or chided him, or insinuated that he did anything other than what was right. That was what he wanted.

Not a fast-talking, forward-thinking young woman of unknown origins. A woman who manipulated situations to suit herself and dared chide him for his treatment of his children. A woman who made clear her disdain—indeed, her fear—of his beloved countryside.

A woman who kept him awake because she slept right down the corridor.

Zephaniah Ewan rode in next. Sober, thoughtful, the young farmer watched the road that ran past his land and had an uncanny knack of knowing who should be left alone and who should be detained. He patted his horse's neck as he gave his report. "The road to the east is empty, sir, but for an encampment of gypsies."

"Gypsies?" Greville's voice vibrated with excitement. "Everyone knows gypsies are trouble."

"Not these gypsies," Ewan said. "They come through every year on their way to the fair. Keep to themselves, they do."

"We're not hunting gypsies," William said. "We're hunting strange foreigners and Englishmen, and -women, who have no business in the district."

"We could keep the traitors out if we caught a few and strung them up as an example," Greville said.

"We aren't trying to keep them out. We want them to come and curse the highwaymen, as part of the price they pay to play a dangerous game."

"Not anymore, though, right?" Greville's eyes gleamed in the moonlight. "Now we're catching them all and holding them because . . ." His voice trailed off. He didn't know why, and William wouldn't tell him any more than necessary.

"That's right," William said. "We're holding them all." Searching their belongings, their clothing, their shoes. Anywhere they could be hiding vital correspondence. Lord and Lady Featherstonebaugh were on their way home, and William's plan was now in action.

From far away, William heard the gallop of hooves on the lane. Someone was riding hard, and together the four men left the clearing and moved to the shadow of the trees alongside the lane.

It was young Milo, bent over the neck of his horse.

William moved into sight.

Milo pulled up, and gasped, "A carriage! With a crest! On the main road out of Hawksmouth, traveling west."

"What crest?" William prepared to ride hard.

"I couldn't see, sir, in the dark."

"Now? Tonight?" Greville stammered.

William, Duncan, and Ewan didn't waste time

with questions, but cut across country toward the main road after Milo. Greville followed at a slower pace.

Was it possible? Had Lord and Lady Featherstonebaugh arrived already? As they reached the rise in the road, they drew their hats over their eyes and wrapped scarves around their mouths. They became the dread highwaymen of the Lake District.

The coach rumbled forward. They moved into position across the road. William shot into the air while the other men pointed rifles at the coachman. The coachman pulled up the four matched horses.

William shouted, "Stand and deliver!"

Duncan rode to the door and jerked it open. "Get out!"

And a warm, rich, amused female voice said, "This is the kind of welcome a lady loves to tell her friends about."

William was glad his scarf covered his mouth, for his jaw dropped. Teresa? Teresa was here already? She must have rushed to answer his invitation.

She stuck her head out of the door, and in the moonlight her handsome features appeared thin and sharp. She smiled, but William thought the smile was more annoyed than pleasant. Descending the steps, she stood on the road, her cape gaping at the top, showing the gleam of a handsome bosom. The sight drew every masculine eye, and William had to admit that, in the moonlight, she looked petite and comely. "A handsome highwayman stops me to divest me of my jewels. Wait until I tell my host, Colonel Gregory. He'll be most entertained . . . won't he?"

Duncan must have been startled by her appearance, but he smoothly moved into his role as rogue highwayman. Putting his pistol back in its holster, he swung out of the saddle, stepped close and bowed to her with an elegant sweep of his hat. "My lady, whom do I have the privilege of addressing?"

"The countess of Marchant, and you're going to be sorry you did." Grabbing his hair, she twisted and in a swift move, brought him to his knees. Slipping his pistol from his belt, she held it to his head, and with a smile that chilled William's blood, looked toward him and the other *faux* highwayman. "You will let me pass unharmed or I'll shoot him in the head."

Greville bleated like a sheep.

Ewan moved his horse back.

Teresa looked small, determined, and ruthless. William signaled, and the men backed their horses into the woods.

She called, "My footmen have their firearms out now. If you come after us, they'll shoot you all."

William watched through the branches as Duncan tried to rise. Without even glancing at him, she smartly kneed him in the face.

This was a side of Teresa he had never seen before. Always she had been perfectly coiffed, smiling, and fashionable. Not capable of foiling a robbery attempt with her own delicate hands.

With the pistol still pointed at Duncan, she stepped into the coach and swung the door closed. The coach rumbled away toward Silvermere.

On the road, Duncan staggered to his feet. He held his hand over his nose, and he stared after the coach with killing fury. In silence, William caught Duncan's horse for him and held it while Duncan mounted. "Broken?" he asked.

"I don't think so." Duncan blotted his face with his handkerchief. "But I'll have two black eyes in the morning. You'd better ride hard to beat your guest home—and if that's the woman you've decided to take as your wife, be careful when you kneel before her to propose. That knee is wicked."

"Sir!" The vicar, Mr. Webber, rode toward them from Hawksmouth, waving his arm. "There's a foreigner at the inn, apparently quite a wealthy gentleman. Before he went to bed, he asked for directions to the Featherstonebaugh estate. Should we detain him?"

"Indeed we should." William turned his horse toward the village. "He's about to receive a visit from the most audacious robbers ever to hold up an inn."

Duncan blotted his nose. "And if we don't find anything?"

"We'll let him go onto the Featherstonebaugh estate, and while he's there we'll see that he gets the most secret of information about the English government it is possible to have." William smiled coldly. "It's too bad that when he returns to Russia with it, it will all eventually prove false."

In a falsely surprised voice, Duncan said, "That would be the death of him."

❧ *Chapter Eleven* ❧

The next day, at the stroke of noon, Teresa descended the stairs. In the daylight, she looked completely different, smiling, with wisps of dark hair curling about her thin cheeks, sparkling hazel eyes, and wide skirts of striking rose satin that rustled as she walked. "William, how good to see you once again." Extending her hands, she smiled with a carefully crafted combination of reservation and winsome pleasure.

Not at all like the wide, gamin grin which signaled Miss Prendregast's merriment.

Taking Teresa's extended hands, he said, "Thank you for coming at my request. I'm sorry I was out last night when you arrived."

"And I needed you so." She pouted with reproach. "You won't believe, darling. Robbers attacked me!"

Never had he been so aware that acting was not his forte, yet he hoped he managed to look surprised and appalled. "What? Where?"

"On the road not far from here."

"How dreadfully bold. You're not hurt, I pray?"

She clutched his arm. "My servants bravely chased them off, but I was terrified!"

Now he hoped he *didn't* look surprised. "Poor dear. Could you . . . identify any of them?"

"I knew you would ask me, but no. They wore masks, and anyway, darling, you mustn't risk your life for me. They stole nothing." Putting the back of her hand against her forehead, she pretended a faint. "Except . . . my peace of mind."

Was she jesting? Or lying? He'd seldom seen a female acquit herself as Teresa had. "I do apologize. The safety of the roads are my responsibility, and I fear I've failed you."

"You positively reek with conscientiousness, darling, but you're a landowner, not a thief taker. No one expects you to ride the highways at night searching for villains."

"Nevertheless—"

"Although I do wonder where you were last night. No! Never mind." She gave a throaty laugh and waved a dismissive hand. "Don't explain. Boys will be boys, and if you had a less than noble reason to be out at one in the morning, I don't want to know it."

He bowed slightly. Amazing. She'd accused him of being worthless, unable to ensure the safety of his district, and given him permission to be a libertine. How dared she presume so? "I am a noble man," he answered with stiff indignation.

Tucking her hand in his arm, she smiled up at him. "I know you are, darling."

And he realized how pompous he sounded. If he'd said that to Samantha, she would have snorted. Teresa soothed his masculinity so slickly, he wondered what she thought of him. Did she think him easily demoralized, uncertain of himself, in need of reassurance?

Yes. Of course she did. Teresa thought that of all men, and she liberally applied her flattery to ease her own way, and told lies to make herself look more vulnerable. He knew that; before, he'd never thought anything was wrong with it. Now, as every day he faced Miss Prendregast's straightforward candor, Teresa's cajolery seemed almost immoral.

"What's the matter, darling? You look quite odd." Teresa stared into his face.

He shook off his peculiar musings. "It's your news. I'm shocked." Or perhaps it was the successful evening spent breaking into Pashenka's room at the inn. Pashenka hadn't been easy prey—he had held Ewan at gunpoint until William had taken him down from behind. The pistol had gone off, grazing Duncan's arm.

Rotten luck for poor old Duncan.

They tied up Pashenka, searched his belongings, and stole a variety of things, including the money and letters he had sewn into his greatcoat. Even now the letters were on their way to Throckmorton, and with the help of the innkeeper, Pashenka was on his way to Maitland, where hopefully he would hide until Lord and Lady Featherstonebaugh arrived.

William didn't need Teresa's reassurances. He would, at last, have revenge for Mary's death.

"So we're going to give a party?" Teresa looked around the tall foyer, then hugged his arm, pressing it against her breast with such ingenuousness he almost believed she didn't realize what she was doing. "I'm so glad that you called on me!"

"Who else could I call but Mary's best friend?" Leading her toward the door, he said, "I've ordered our meal served on the veranda."

"You're so forceful, darling." She hugged his arm again.

He freed himself to let her proceed him. He smiled to hear her gasp as the whole vista of the mountains rose before her.

"This is magnificent!" Hurrying toward the rail, she leaned against it and stared. "How could you bear to go to India?"

"You know. Younger son, army commission, no choice." He stared, too, allowing the crags and valleys to soothe his weary soul. "But you notice I managed to hie myself to the mountains of Kashmir. It was only after Mary was killed that I knew I had to come back to my home. I don't know that I could have healed without the sights and scents of Silvermere. I need this place."

She placed her hand over his on the railing. "Forgive me, my friend . . . I can call you a friend, can't I?"

"You can." He had thought he knew her so well, but now she seemed alien. *I should never have brought her here.*

"Thank you." Oblivious to his uneasiness, she lavished another smile on him. "We all loved Mary, and the circumstances of her death were loathsome, but she has been gone for three years. It's time you came out of mourning."

He smiled tightly. It rubbed him raw to hear her give such advice. She might be the primary candidate to be his wife, but she would have to learn her station.

Rubbing her hands together in a workmanlike manner, she asked, "How many people will we have at this party?"

"I've invited about thirty."

"Thirty?" She blinked her wide hazel eyes. "You've already invited them? I thought I would look over the list and let you know who—" At last she realized she had overstepped the mark, for she said, "But of course, it's your party. I'm sure whomever you invite is perfect." She saw the footmen standing at attention beside a table set with a white cloth and fine china, and lavished that calculated smile on him again. "Oh, William, how beautiful your breakfast chamber is! I believe I shall make this my study while I plan this party."

"As you wish, my dear." Leading her to the table, he pulled out her chair. "We'll have their children and their servants, too."

She paused in the process of sitting. "Children? You want to invite . . . children?"

"One of the reasons I'm giving a party, of course, is to teach my own children the fine art of entertaining." That was an absolute untruth, but he wouldn't dream of telling her his plan to flush out Lord and Lady Featherstonebaugh with the promise of a last, juicy, sweet capture of information that would set them up for life.

"Oh. Yes. What a quaint idea." She watched him sit, and her one cocked eyebrow managed to convey both confusion and condescension. "But your eldest is what? Eight?"

"Agnes is twelve." A most difficult twelve.

"Already! How time flies. I remember when Agnes was born. What an exciting time that was, when all of us were in India and you and Byron were in uniform, and so handsome. I miss him very much." She dabbed at the corner of her eye with her handkerchief. "And what was that other young man's name? The one who so disgraced himself with Lord Barret-Derwin's daughter?"

William looked at her sideways. Odd, to have her ask about Duncan the night after Duncan had held her up—and she had got the better of him. "Duncan Monroe, and he is a friend of mine still. You'll no doubt meet him during your visit here."

"Will I?" She smiled, a lopsided smile of catlike delight. "Darling, your loyalty is to be commended. Now. Have I told you how beautiful it is out here on your delightful veranda with its fabulous view of the mountains?"

Leaning back in his chair, he took a deep breath of fresh air. "I'm always willing to listen."

She, too, took a long breath. "I could stay here forever."

"Some people wouldn't. Some people don't like the country at all." Some people were named Miss Prendregast.

"La! I have trouble believing anyone wouldn't find pleasure in such surroundings."

He could have laughed when he remembered Samantha's conviction that bears prowled the forests and meadows. And how she minced through the grass as if fearing something would grab her by the foot. And he would have given a crown to see the look on her face when she saw those snakes in her desk.

Teresa watched him quite oddly. "Why are you smiling like that?"

He shook out his napkin and signaled to the footmen. "No reason. I'm just hungry."

He ate a hearty meal.

Teresa ate like a bird, pecking at her food and producing little chirps of conversation until he was finished. Then she leaned her elbows on the table and asked, "Shall we map out our party strategy?"

From inside the house, he heard a door slam. Boots clattered on the stairs, and Teresa jumped and put her hand to her chest. "What is that cacophony?"

"It's the children. I suppose they are taking a moment away from their lessons."

"A man like you shouldn't have to deal with such matters." Teresa pulled a long face. "You don't even know to set up a schedule."

"I have set up a schedule."

"Don't they follow it?"

He refrained from snorting, but barely. "We have a new governess. She is unique in her ability to disregard schedules and make it appear she is doing as she ought."

"I'm surprised at you!" Teresa tapped his hand reprovingly. "She must be an impressive old crone to have you so cowed."

He didn't even want to examine his own dark satisfaction when he said, "You'll see. Miss Prendregast and the children are coming down now."

One by one, the girls came through the door onto the veranda. Their chatter made him frown, yet they were lined up in the proper order, their clothing appeared neat and tidy, and all of them were smiling. All except Agnes, who looked as if that sour expression had taken permanent residence on her face.

He didn't understand the child. He used to; when had she ceased to sit on his knee and confide her joys and her woes? He eyed her height. For that matter—when had she gotten too tall to sit on his knee?

Kyla saw them first and stopped, her expressive little face screwed up in dismay. Emmeline bumped into her, Henrietta bumped into her, and the line staggered to a halt.

Miss Prendregast came around the corner, clapping her hands. "Girls, girls, don't stop now! We're going out so Mara can practice her performance for the mountains and nothing can stop—" She halted at the sight of Teresa and him, and for one moment her face wore the exact expression of Kyla's. Then her features smoothed, she moved forward to take Kyla's hand, and she led the children out to face their father and Teresa.

Miss Prendregast curtsied.

Agnes's lip was trembling again.

What was wrong with the child? She grew more and more emotional every day.

He glared at Agnes and at the same time, stood and performed the courtesies. "Children, you of course remember Lady Marchant?"

"Yes, Father," they replied in a chorus, and in unison they bobbed miniature curtsies. "How do you do, Lady Marchant?"

"Very well, thank you." Teresa relaxed back into her seat and spoke to Vivian. "So you're going to sing, are you, Mara?"

"I'm not Mara." Vivian pointed to her sister. "She's Mara. She sings like Mama did."

Teresa's mouth twisted in chagrin, and she didn't attempt another individual comment. "That's wonderful. I'm sure you're all very talented."

"Yes, Lady Marchant," they chorused.

Still on his feet, he said, "Lady Marchant, may I introduce our governess, Miss Samantha Prendregast."

Miss Prendregast bobbed another curtsy. "It's an honor, my lady."

Teresa swept Miss Prendregast a comprehensive look, and her smile chilled William's blood. "You're not quite in the usual manner of governesses, are you?"

Miss Prendregast didn't smile, didn't frown; her ready, expressive face showed no expression. "Lady Bucknell is my patron, my lady." As if that explained everything, she curtsied yet again. "If you would excuse us? We have so little time before we must be back in the classroom and learning our . . ."

"Mathematics, Miss Prendregast," Henrietta told her.

"Our mathematics," Miss Prendregast agreed. At a nod from him, she led the children off the veranda, through the topiary, and out of sight.

Teresa sat, arms straight at her side, fists clenched. "She's insolent."

"*Really?*" *You think that's insolent? You should have heard her the day she arrived.*

As if realizing how shrewish she sounded, Teresa relaxed and put her hand over his. "But it's so difficult to get good help these days, and at least she's young and pretty. The children must like that."

No man was accomplished in handling women, but William certainly knew better than to agree with any fervor. "Yes, I suppose they must."

"But so . . . sickly-looking."

"I thought she was rather tanned."

"Yes, her poor complexion." Teresa sighed pityingly. "A natural result of having to march the children about the grounds. She is a working girl, after all. We can't expect her to look like a lady. But I was referring to her hair. I wonder how she gets it that color."

"It's artificial?"

Teresa's laughter trilled out. "You didn't think it was natural?"

"I had wondered." Damn that Duncan. He'd said it was real.

"And I wonder what color it is that she thinks she should change it. Probably that infernal red that looks so dreadful. Well, some women aren't confident enough to handle the trials God gave them." Teresa shook her head. "I thought she was thin. Are you feeding her enough, William?"

"No doubt of that." He remembered very well the amount of food Miss Prendregast could put away. "She eats quite heartily at supper."

"She eats supper with you?" Teresa's voice took on a shrill note.

"As do the children." He smiled into her eyes. "Tonight you'll be with us, gracing us with your presence."

"Why, yes. Of course I will." She blinked, not that sexy flutter of lashes, but a startled blink. "The children? I always said you were an original, darling."

He wondered what she meant by that.

She smiled graciously. "Perhaps I could help next time you hire a governess."

"I thank you, Teresa, but Miss Prendregast has guaranteed she'll stay for at least a year, and I know I can depend on her." He raised Teresa's hand to his lips. "Wait until you get to know her. You'll see what I mean."

"I can't wait, darling. I just can't wait."

Rupert, Lord Featherstonebaugh, complained about the old-fashioned coach and the dust and the horses until Valda, Lady Featherstonebaugh, was ready to shriek, but shrieking wasn't her style. Instead, she turned to him in smooth savagery. "Would you rather have taken the train, dear?"

"It would have made sense!"

"It would have made sense to do exactly what the Home Office expects us to do? To take the fastest, most luxurious mode of travel? I heard them. They're on to us!"

"Pshaw." He waved a blue-veined hand. "Why should they be on to us after all these years?"

"Because we've been lucky beyond belief." With a considerable lowering of spirits, she added, "It was bound to happen."

"The coach is jarring my bones, and these roads!" Rupert peeked out of the curtained window. "They're filled with holes. The next time I speak to the prime minister I'm going to make it clear—"

"If you ever speak to the prime minister again, it'll be so he can pronounce your sentence. He wants to imprison us. They want to kill us." She was talking too fast, trying to convince him from sheer strength of will. Will had never worked with Rupert, so she slowed down and carefully enunciated, "And if the English don't kill us, the Russians will."

"Now, dear, you're overreacting." He patted her gloved hand. "Have you been suffering from those heat flashes again? Ladies of your age do suffer delusions."

Still she paced her words. "I do not suffer from

delusions. I heard them talking. I heard young Throckmorton. We're finished in the business. I've been planning for this moment ever since we started. We're escaping England and if all goes well—and it will—in less than a month we'll be living in a palazzo in Italy under false names."

"Well, you could have planned better. I don't like the coach." He folded his arms over his chest, his long wrinkled face drooping in a pout. "It's unfashionable."

Maybe shrieking was her style.

❧ *Chapter Twelve* ❧

A scratching at her bedroom door made Samantha lift her head from her lesson plans. Who would be out in the corridor at this hour? Darkness had fallen outside, the fire in her grate couldn't completely vanquish the chill of a mountain evening, and she was tucked up in her bed with the feather mattress below and the down comforter above. Her white cotton nightgown was buttoned up to her neck, her blonde hair was braided down her back, and she was loathe to crawl out and let whoever it was in. So in a none-too-gracious voice, she called, "Come in, if you must."

A long moment of hesitation followed, then the door slowly squeaked open.

Agnes. Agnes stood in the doorway, looking like a miniature version of Samantha in a plain white nightgown, her feet bare, her hair pulled back in a braid. She shivered convulsively, and her eyes were huge and frightened.

Samantha came out of the bed in a rush, her feet hitting the chilly floor. Then she stood there, not sure if she should hurry toward the child, who looked as if she were torn between bolting and staying, or wait until the girl came to her. In the end, she slipped the shawl off her shoulders and held it out to Agnes. "Come in, my dear, and get warm."

Agnes's face contorted. Giving a sob, she rushed into Samantha's arms and clung as if Samantha were the last port in the storm.

Samantha smoothed the hair away from Agnes's face. "What's wrong, sweetheart?"

In between sobs, Agnes said, "It's . . . awful. I don't know . . . who to tell. It . . . hurts. I'm . . . dying."

Startled, Samantha asked, "Dying? Why do you think you're dying?"

"Because I . . . because I . . ." Agnes dug her head into Samantha's shoulder. "It's . . . *so* . . . disgusting."

An awful suspicion bloomed in Samantha's mind. She took a breath. "You're dying, and it's disgusting?"

"I'm . . . I'm . . ."

The child couldn't bring herself to say it, and why should she have to? Someone should have already told her. "Are you bleeding?"

Agnes looked up with astonished, tear-damp eyes. "How did you know?"

Samantha calmed her own burgeoning anger,

and in a soothing tone, said, "Because that is what women do."

Sucking back a sob, Agnes asked, "All of them?"

"All of them."

"When?"

"Once a month."

Agnes thought for a moment, then burst into a fresh frenzy of tears. "That's . . . horrid."

"Yes, it is." By the time Samantha got Agnes calmed down, explained the facts, and helped her deal with her problem, she was both furious and comprehending. No wonder Agnes had been so emotional. The child had been suffering from the buildup to her first menstrual period, alone with her fears and her feelings and without understanding what was happening to her own body.

"Can I sleep with you?" Agnes asked in a tiny voice.

The children go to bed at promptly nine o'clock. There is no exception to that rule. Well, Colonel Gregory could go hang. He thought he was so incredibly efficient, and look what he'd done to his own daughter through sheer neglect and ignorance. Holding up the blankets, Samantha said, "Of course you can sleep with me. We're the big girls now."

Agnes clambered in. "Thank you, Miss Prendregast. I didn't want to go back to that bed." She shuddered. "Everyone's going to know in the morning."

"Scoot over." Samantha climbed in, too. "Only the women, and they'll welcome you into the sisterhood. It's not so bad, you know. Someday, because of this, you'll be able to hold a babe in your arms."

"Then it should wait until I'm married, thank you," Agnes said with a return of her previous tart tone.

Samantha restrained a smile. "Anyway, it's time to talk about the best way to put your hair up."

Agnes sat up, wrapped her arms around her knees, and sounded quite a bit more chipper. "And let my skirts down?"

"Not until you're fifteen. And I'll tell you the truth—long skirts look good, but they get in the way. Think how much trouble it would be to climb a tree in long skirts."

"I can climb up to this room holding a snake in a box."

Samantha caught her breath in horror, then turned a killing look on Agnes. "Don't . . . you . . . dare. I promise I would get my revenge."

"I know you would." A wicked smile curved Agnes's lips. "But I can get into Lady Marchant's room, too."

Samantha's heart made a quick, joyful jump. Then she frowned in the proper governess manner. "That would not be the proper thing to do."

"She wants to marry Father."

"You don't know that."

Agnes flayed Samantha with her scorn. "Didn't you see her tonight at dinner? She watches him like a spider watches a fly."

Samantha should have wanted to laugh. She

didn't, and that was bad. "I think your papa can protect himself."

"And she sat in your place at the table."

Funny. Samantha had resented that, too—being reduced to sitting among the children. Being cut out of the discussion, which, she noted, no longer included an educational topic, but now could be rightfully deemed a conversation—led by Lady Marchant, while Colonel Gregory looked on with a bemused smile. "It's not *my* place at the table. Lady Marchant is acting as your father's hostess, and the hostess sits at the foot of the table."

Agnes crossed her arms over her chest and lowered her chin. "She wants to be more than my papa's hostess."

No matter how much Samantha would like to grumble with Agnes, she had to remember her position. She had be the voice of reason. "Lady Marchant can't force your father to marry her."

"I think he wants to. I think he likes her."

"Then you should be happy for him. He can't mourn your mama forever."

"I know that. I don't even want him to." Agnes bit her lip. "I remember Mama really well. So does Vivian. We don't need another mother. But the others . . . a mother would be good for them."

Agnes sounded so mature, Samantha wanted to cry.

"But not Lady Marchant," Agnes added. "She doesn't like us. Me and my sisters. You know it, too."

Without thinking, Samantha answered, "It

would be better if you weren't girls. She sees her rivals growing up under her nose—" She stopped in horror. She had to remember that Agnes was not a friend, and certainly not her own age.

"She doesn't think we're rivals. She's old." Agnes wrapped her arms around her head. "Where's your mother?"

"She's in heaven."

"With my mama. Do you think they're friends?"

A lady and a street sweeper? Somehow, Samantha didn't think so. "Perhaps."

"I woke up one morning and they told me my mama was dead." Agnes wiped a tear on the pillowcase. "How did your mama die?"

"She got sick, and she didn't have enough food, so she died." In the cold on some rags on the floor, with her seven-year-old daughter huddled by her side.

"That sounds awful."

"Yes. She was really a nice woman. She wanted me to be . . . like her. Honest and hard-working. But—" Samantha caught herself. She couldn't confess her past to poor, unhappy Agnes.

"I like you, Miss Prendregast." Agnes gave her a timid hug.

Samantha hugged her back. "Thank you, dear. I like you, too."

Agnes yawned. "I'm so tired. My head hurts. My stomach hurts."

"I know, honey." And Samantha didn't want to talk about this anymore. "Roll over." Agnes flopped onto her stomach, hugged her pillow, and allowed Samantha to rub her back. In only a few minutes, Agnes was snoring heavily. "Poor little girl," Samantha murmured. She remembered the day she'd started her monthlies. Her father had dumped her in an orphanage while he went off with a lady friend. In a bored monotone, one of the other girls had told her what was happening and what to do. She'd cried herself to sleep, missing her mother as never before. No girl should face this day alone and scared.

A sharp rap on the door brought her head around. *Who now?*

She knew, of course. She could tell by that imperative knock that Colonel Gregory stood outside her doorway.

But she had to calm herself. She'd learned her lesson. She had to harness her temper, not allow it to rage out of control, or all the problems that had driven her from London and into this godforsaken countryside would visit her again.

Sliding out of her bed, she caught up her pale blue flannel robe. She slid it on, knotted the tie at her waist, and pulled open the door.

He was dressed in black riding clothes with knee-length black boots. Leather gauntlets hung at his belt. He looked as he had that first night she'd met him on the road, stern, upright, and angry, his straight-winged eyebrows giving him a devilish appearance.

So he thought to frighten her? Her fury leaped to meet him.

Grasping her arm, he pulled her into the candlelit corridor and quietly shut the door behind her. "Where is my daughter Agnes?"

He knew the answer. He'd seen the child, but if he wanted to play games, she could play with the best of them. "In my bed, sleeping, and do you know why?"

"Because my governess can't follow a simple command."

"Because her father isn't competent."

His blue eyes widened, then narrowed. "What in Hades are you talking about?"

"That child"—Samantha waved toward her door—"*your* child didn't know what was happening to her."

To his credit, he looked alarmed. "What *was* happening to her?"

She didn't give a damn about reassuring him. "She became a woman tonight."

He stared uncomprehendingly.

In a falsely patient tone, Samantha said, "She started her monthly bleeding."

He jerked backward. "Miss Prendregast! This is not a subject for me to discuss with you!"

How dared he? "Who should I discuss it with? Or perhaps, more to the point, who should you discuss it with? You're her father. You claim you take responsibility for everything concerning your daughters, but you ignore this basic function which each one of them is going to suffer?"

His mouth opened, then shut. For the first time since she'd met him, he didn't seem to know what to say. At last he managed, "I have not ignored anything about my daughters, but that is a natural function about which I'm sure one of their teachers has told them."

"It wasn't on the schedule." She leaned against the wall and crossed her arms to keep from shaking him. "Women are no different than men. No woman wants to tell a child that her happy, carefree life is about to change, that her body is progressing into womanhood, and that sometimes that progression is painful and messy. How dare you assume someone else is going to take care of something so important?"

"Miss Prendregast, you will not talk to me that way."

Her resolve to remain calm melted in a blistering rage. "Oh, yes, I will. Someone needs to talk to you that way. You go on your merry way, staying out all night, not knowing your children worry about you, not knowing your nursemaids are plotting against the governesses, unaware of Kyla's croup and Mara's fears, of Vivian's nightmares and Agnes's period. You think it's so democratic that you have dinner with your children, but you make sure the conversation isn't a conversation, but a guided tour through some subject of your choosing."

He stepped away. "The children are making good use of their time."

"You don't know your children, and you make sure they can't talk to you. You don't allow them to tell you their fears and their hopes, to ask you how to grow up. You never admit you were ever wrong and you certainly can't admit you might not know everything. You've proven you know a lot about the fish of the Lake District, and not a thing about your children. You're out every night chasing bandits." She pointed toward the front door. "It's time to stay home with your children."

"Miss Prendregast!" He reached for her with both hands, and stopped an inch away from her shoulders. Instead he pressed his palms against the wall on either side of her head, glared in her eyes, his chest heaving with fury. "You can pack your bags. You're leaving in the morning."

She pointed toward her bedroom, and her finger was shaking. Her voice was shaking. "Agnes thought she was dying."

He took a breath. The color rose in his cheeks, then drained away.

"She thought she was bleeding to death. If you feel I've said too much and you must send me away, I can't stop you, but Colonel Gregory, every one of your daughters is going to come to this moment, and I suspect Vivian will come to it before very many months have passed. You need someone to prepare them for the trials of womanhood. In not too many years, Agnes will find a man who wishes to marry her, and someone has to prepare her for the wedding night, and childbirth, and the realities that lurk beneath the fairy tale. Can you do that, Colonel Gregory?" She leaned toward him, close enough so he could feel the heat of her fury. "Can you really do that?"

His eyes sparked. His arms shook. "You don't

know when to shut up." Leaning his head down, he pressed his lips to hers.

For a moment, she was too caught up in her plea to comprehend what he was doing. Then—*he's kissing me. Colonel Gregory is kissing me.*

Anger. Confusion. Astonishment. She pulled her face away, pressed her hand against his throat where his cravat met his skin. "Are you insane?"

"What do you think?" He kissed her again.

She thought . . . she must be insane, too, for she liked it.

But they were fighting.

But she liked it.

But the children . . . and Agnes . . .

They were all asleep. There was no one to see. No one to care.

And she liked it.

That was bad. Very bad.

She pulled away again. "We shouldn't be doing this."

"No." But he didn't move away.

"You're who you are, and I'm who I am, and this is wrong."

"Yes." His face was close. So close. His breath smelled of port, sharp and rich, like the first opulent sniff she took from the glass. She could see the stubble on his chin, see the rich, smooth, sensual curve of his lips.

I've done a lot of daring things in my life, but this is the worst.

Grasping the ends of his cravat, she pulled him back to her.

His hands rested on either side of her head. His

body leaned toward hers. He touched her with nothing but his lips. If she passively stood here, perhaps he'd tire of kissing soon. Yet she would have sworn he blanketed her in his warmth. The scent of him was rich with leather from his boots and gauntlets. His lips smoothed hers, seeking the contours, the edges.

Her eyelids fluttered closed. Jewel colors swirled: ruby, sapphire, emerald. Beneath her fingertips, the pulse at his throat throbbed, and her own heart raced to beat with his.

So this was why men and women kissed. To see, to feel, to know each other in impossible, wonderful ways. She could stand here like this all night, and never tire of his tenderness.

Then his tongue brushed her lips.

Her eyes sprang open. His *tongue.* She wrapped her fingers around his wrist and tugged. His wrist . . . thick and gloriously rough with hair.

His mouth moved against hers, soft and intimate. "Open your lips."

She didn't quite understand him. She lifted her lids. "What? Why?"

His lids lifted, too, and he gazed at her, his face so close she could see each individual, dark, curling lash around his marvelous blue eyes. "Like this," he whispered, then his lids slid closed again and his tongue glided between her lips.

Her eyes shut. Her mouth opened.

The first kiss was only a preview, an exploration. Now his tongue moved in her mouth, exploring as if he found treasure within her, and he made her feel . . . different. Not so much the confident, inde-

pendent woman life had forced her to become, but
cherished, glorious, dear. Her blood thrummed in
her veins. Her breath caught and staggered. The
wall held her up, hard against her back, and she
wanted to kiss him back.

She'd never learned, never wanted to. But with
him . . . the strength of him appealed to her. Her
mind cast up scenes. Scenes that involved him
and her, bodies close together, his hands touching
her in places no man had ever touched. She imagined what he would look like without clothing,
muscled, hairy, strong. Imagined how he would
gaze on her. Imagined he would . . . do those
things she'd always disdained. For those things
caused a woman nothing but grief, and sounded
awkward and revolting. Except when she thought
of doing them with him, they sounded too wonderful, like fur stroking her skin or water after a
long drought.

He was gentle, but insistent. His head tilted first
to one side, then the other, tasting her, encouraging
her to answer him.

Her breasts tingled and she pressed her thighs
together, trying to ease the sense of swelling, of discomfort. It helped . . . and it made matters worse.
She wanted to stop, and she wanted to go on. She
wanted to snuggle against him, but some errant bit
of wisdom kept her back tight against the wall. His
wrists began to shake in her grip. His tongue thrust
at hers, and she answered him, awkward, eager,
amazed. His kissing progressed toward despera-
tion, insisting on more passion, pushing her to-

ward experience and teaching her a deeper desire.

She wanted him to say something. She strained to hear—

She jumped and gasped, pulling her face away from his.

Colonel Gregory straightened. "What? What's wrong?"

"I thought I heard . . . something." Something like the snap of a door shutting.

He looked up and down the corridor. "It's your imagination."

Grasping her shoulders, he smoothed them, but the moments of passionate madness had been vanquished. In a deep and ardent voice, he said, "Your eyes . . . such an unusual color."

"Just brown. Dirt brown." She scarcely knew what she was saying.

"No, tonight they're like honey, golden brown, wide and bemused." He cupped her chin and tilted her face up. "You have the most expressive eyes, did you know that?"

She shook her head.

"I can read your thoughts in your eyes."

"Oh. No," she choked. Her thoughts were far too often of him, and far too often illicit and wanton. She looked away.

He chuckled, a sound too content for reassurance. "You could seduce me with your eyes alone."

Troubled, she looked back at him. "I don't mean to."

"I know. That kiss . . . it was a mistake."

"Yes. Of course. It was."

Yet once more, he was rubbing her shoulders. "We shouldn't do it again."

"No. Never." Samantha looked down at her toes, bare on the cool, hard floor. She had never felt so self-conscious. She'd been kissing Colonel Gregory. Yes, she had wanted to. Secretly. In the darkest corners of her mind.

But to do it. And for so long, and with such detail. Moreover, she'd liked it. And he knew it.

How was she supposed to face him tomorrow in the daylight? Right now, she couldn't even look up at him.

"What were we talking about . . . before?" He still didn't sound normal. A wealth of affection lingered in his voice.

Her toes curled at the sound. But she had to be normal. "Earlier. You told me to leave." She hoped he hadn't noticed her bare feet. Lady Bucknell had never told her any rules about bare feet, but if a woman couldn't in all propriety bare her hand to a man, the rules against feet must be ferocious. "Did you want me to pack my bags?"

"No! No. That is . . . no, I was angry." He coughed. "I said things I shouldn't have."

She glanced up to see him observing her toes with a slight smile.

She inched them further beneath her robe and realized . . . she wore nothing beneath the nightgown. She was worried about her toes, and he must know . . . well, not that he could see anything. Her robe was tied, and the gown was of thick sturdy material, impossible to see through. But the thought of being out here, with him, when he could simply lift her hem and touch her bare skin, all the way up to . . . she pressed her knees together. And if he did, he would find that she was melting inside. She must be; she was damp and swollen.

"I would rather you stay. If you would." When she didn't speak right away, he straightened his shoulders. He eased his hands away and stepped back. "You don't have to worry that I will repeat tonight's indiscretion. I don't kiss . . . that is, I do kiss, but not my governesses. To force my attentions on a young woman who works for me is the act of a cad, and I realize that fully. I can't imagine what came over me."

Her face warmed. She could, only too well, and imagining gave her more than a little discomfort. "You didn't exactly force your attentions. I could have yelled, or . . . some such."

"Nevertheless, it is obvious you're a young lady of little or no experience in the bedroom arts—"

Dismayed, she blurted, "Was that kiss wrong?"

"No!" He smoothed his fingers over her lips.

She fought the urge to follow, to kiss them.

"No, not at all," he said. "I enjoyed it. It was everything I had dreamed."

He has dreamed about my kiss?

"But you didn't put your arms around me, and when at first I kissed you, you didn't kiss back." As though he relished the touch of her skin, he smoothed her lips again. "It wasn't resistance, it was more bewilderment."

"You could tell that from my lips?"

He fought a smile. "Couldn't you tell how I felt by mine?"

"Well." She looked down again, and fiddled with the buttons at her neckline. "Yes."

"Also." His gaze dropped to her fingers. "When a woman deliberately entices a man, she manages to slip her buttons loose in strategic locations to allow him a glimpse of her bosom."

She let loose of the buttons, caught the two sides of her robe, and held them together, for even though they were well-fastened, with the kind of attention he was paying, they might have been gaping.

"Do you know what you do to me when . . ." As if he couldn't contain himself, he slipped open the tie on her belt. Placing his palm on her waist, he slide it down over her belly and onto her thigh. "No. Of course you don't."

If she were wise, she'd slap him hard enough to make his ears ring. Instead, she leaned her head back, closed her eyes, and savored the press of his hand, the sweetness of his touch, so cherished, and too brief.

Lifting his hand, he looked down at it as if he could see the imprint of her skin. "Nevertheless, an honorable man does not seduce his governess." He straightened his shoulders, and his voice once more sounded crisp, as Colonel Gregory's always sounded. "As I told you, Miss Prendregast, there are still honorable men in this world, and I am one of them."

"Yes." She sidled toward her door. "I believe you. I'll send Agnes back to her room in the morning."

He watched her as if he wanted to follow. "I

bow to your superior wisdom in the matter of my daughters' physical well-being."

"Yes. Well. Thank you." She stood in the doorway and fumbled with the handle, so uncomfortable and embarrassed she wanted nothing more than to disappear in her room and hide under the covers. At the same time . . . at the same time, she wanted to stand here, to look at him, to try and stammer out a conversation about absolutely nothing because . . . well, she didn't know why, but that was what she wanted, and only a fool would want that.

Correct? She took a step backward into her bedchamber. Correct.

"Goodnight, Miss Prendregast." His voice was deeper, keener, and richer than she'd heard before, like chocolate cream and tawny port.

"Good night, Colonel Gregory." Slipping inside, she shut the door in his face, and felt as if she'd saved herself from trouble—and condemned herself to loneliness.

❧ *Chapter Thirteen* ❧

William threw his bedroom window open, leaned out into the early morning sunshine, and took a deep breath of the cool mountain air. "It's a grand day to be alive!"

"Aye, Colonel, that it is." His valet, tall, thin, and soured by exile away from the excitement of the military, couldn't have sounded more sarcastic. "Not a cloud in sight, nary a battle to be had; a man could die of boredom."

Boredom? No, not with Samantha living down the corridor. Who would have thought a woman of such bold words and direct glances could kiss with such shy and startled passion?

"Now come and place yourself in the bath before the water cools." Cleavers tested the water with his elbow. "It's the way you like it—hot enough to boil lobsters."

Leaving the window open, William sank down into the copper bathtub. "Perfect." The heat soothed the muscles made sore by late night riding—and last night's captures.

Matters were proceeding. His men had captured a Russian trudging on the road toward Maitland, and more important, they'd arrested two Englishmen and an Englishwoman, traveling separately, all spies, all intent on reaching the sanctuary of the Featherstonebaugh estate. The men had spoken in rough accents, servants who collected information and sold it for a price. But the woman had been a lady, sophisticated, beautiful, carrying letters concerning the deposition of English troops abroad and sure she could use her beauty to escape capture.

She had tried her wiles on William. He had not only been uninterested, he'd made sure her jailer was a female villager of high character. The lady would not escape.

Rising from his bath, William dried off and pulled on his trousers and his shirt.

Cleavers presented him with two coats. "Will you wear the bottle green tailcoat, Colonel, or the black?"

William had detained the spies, even the lady, in the village jail. He hoped to have similar luck tonight, for Throckmorton's plan to flush out the enemies was succeeding beyond anyone's wildest dreams, and his own plan to catch Lord and Lady Featherstonebaugh in the act of passing information was taking shape. "The black, of course. Why do you keep presenting me with such outrageous colors?"

"Because they're in your closet? Because gentlemen wear many such somber—not outrageous, but *somber*—colors? Because I hope someday to drag you kicking and screaming into the social scene, where you could possibly entice a female to wed you, and I would no longer have to pick out your clothing?"

Arrested by a thought, William stared at Cleavers. "Women like green?"

Cleaver placed the double-breasted green tailcoat back on a hanger. "Aye, Colonel, I've been telling you that ever since the missus passed on, like you ever listen to me."

With his usual decisiveness, without wondering at his motive, William made his decision. "All right. The green." Picking up the matching bottle-green cravat, he carefully knotted it around his throat. He slipped into a black waistcoat with bottle green embroidery on the lapels.

Still Cleavers stood there, jaw hanging slack, the black coat dangling in his hands.

"Hurry, man!"

With a start, Cleavers laid aside the black and helped him on with the green.

Cleavers handed William his good boots, shined to a blinding black, and William stomped his foot into first one, then the other.

Yes, the spy business was wrapping up at last.

Moreover, the new governess was working out nicely. Mind you, she had a tendency to be overly critical, and last night, she was insolent in her reading of his character. But, sadly, she had justification.

Luckily, she had soothed him in ways he had scarcely imagined possible.

While William waited impatiently, Cleavers adjusted the cravat and the seams of the coat. "Thank you, Cleavers."

Cleavers clasped his hands to his bosom as he scrutinized his handiwork. "You are welcome, Colonel." Quickly, slyly, he added, "I suppose this is in honor of Lady Marchant?"

William stared at him blankly. "Who? Oh. Yes. Lady Marchant."

As he strode down the corridor, Cleavers stepped out and watched him, and pondered. Perhaps the rumors flying about the household were true.

William hadn't realized that Agnes had grown so much so quickly. It had never occurred to him his daughter needed womanly assistance, and that, more than anything, indicated how the need for vengeance had overcome him. He prided himself on being prepared for any eventuality, and he had failed Agnes. Miserably. He did not tolerate failure, especially not his own, and he would make amends. Today. Now.

He turned the doorknob to the schoolroom.

His daughters sat in their desks, and William was surprised to realize that Samantha was teaching history. She was actually following his schedule, but at the same time, she taught with such animation the children watched her with shining eyes. An odd emotion squeezed his gut; for the first time in a long time, his daughters were together, happy, and in agreement—and Samantha had done this. She stood by the slateboard, a pointer in her hand. In the enthusiastic tone of an ardent admirer, she told them, "So you see, Queen Elizabeth united the nation while successfully avoiding a contract of marriage which would have subverted her independence and undermined her authority in the male-dominated government. Regardless of what men tell you, it is possible for a woman to flourish without the aid of a husband!"

William frowned. What was she teaching his children?

Seven sets of eyes turned his direction.

"Father!" Agnes stood.

The others began to follow suit, but he gestured. "Sit down, sit down." With a smile to Samantha, he walked quietly to the back of the classroom and leaned against the table. Crossing his arms, he indicated Samantha should continue.

She took up the pointer again, but now a beautiful blush lit her cheeks. She did not look at him.

Clearly, she was remembering the kiss.

He shouldn't be so flattered. He was, after all, encouraging Teresa to believe he would make her an offer. He knew, logically, that Teresa was the wife he needed. He also knew, logically, that this lust for Samantha that plagued him with increasing severity was deplorable on his part.

She said, "Good Queen Bess held off the Spanish attack for years by using a combination of guile and promise. A woman's weapons, to be sure, but weapons that worked when nothing else would."

Vivian had her chin propped in her hand, staring at Samantha. "What did she do, Miss Prendregast?"

"She promised she would *think* about wedding the king of Spain, knowing full well that if she did marry him, she would be subservient to him and England would be subservient to Spain."

Samantha's gaze skittered past William, scarcely touching his shoulder, his throat, his chest, and never coming near to his face. Ducking down, he caught her stare, and that made her blush yet more and stammer a little.

"B . . . by the time he realized she was toying with him and attacked our shores, England had built up her sea power and was able to defeat the Spanish Armada."

Samantha really was beautiful. Her hair a glorious pale blonde, her eyes such a warm brown. Tall, slender . . . some people would say too slender, but they would be wrong. He liked a woman whose curves didn't overwhelm her garments, and he imagined that when he ever had occasion to remove her bodice . . . no. That wasn't right. If he ever had occasion to remove her bodice . . . but no, that wasn't right either.

A man would have his fantasies, no matter how he denied them, and so he knew he could cup her breasts in his palm. And hold them, caress them, suckle them . . .

A sudden state of discomfort made him feel conspicuous, and he crossed his ankle over his knee.

The trouble was, Samantha wore a totally unsuitable gown of violet muslin trimmed in pink satin. Governesses didn't dress like that. They didn't teach with such enthusiasm. They didn't kiss . . . like startled virgins, with all the passion and vibrancy of their personality. Samantha should not be a governess. She should be an houri, or a courtesan . . . or a wife.

He stared at the floor. A wife. To some other man. Not to him. She didn't fit any of the criteria of his list. He didn't know her background. He didn't know her family. He *did* know her temperament, and no one could call it meek. They obviously had nothing in common. Yet still, he thought . . . she might be a suitable wife for him.

Which was patently stupid. He had brought Teresa with the intention of seeing how she fit into his household, and instead he was concentrating on Samantha? Had he lost his good sense?

Furthermore, the matter of Lord and Lady Featherstonebaugh should be consuming most of his attention. He could handle that matter while courting Lady Marchant. He could not while courting Samantha.

He snorted. Hell, he could barely stand while lusting after Samantha.

Looking up, he realized Samantha and the children were staring at him.

"Did you disagree with me, Colonel?" Samantha asked, a little too sweetly. She no longer avoided his gaze; she looked right at his face now, and her eyes slashed at him.

He looked at the children. He couldn't confess to

not listening. That would undermine Samantha's authority. But neither could he blindly agree to anything Samantha had said. Picking his words carefully, he said, "I was simply wondering how you reached your conclusions."

"That Her Majesty Queen Elizabeth was one of the foremost tacticians of English history?" Elbows akimbo, Samantha asked, "How, pray tell, would you frame an argument against that?"

"No, no! I agree. I simply believe that, like so many of our most exalted commanders, she achieved greatness by prudently choosing her councilors, listening to their advice, and usually acting on it." He could stand again, and he did. "Also, like so many of our most exalted commanders, she occasionally did as she thought best."

"A good point, Colonel!" Samantha lavished a smile on him. "Queen Elizabeth was an absolute monarch, and at the same time she was not a tyrant, like so many of our kings."

He smiled back at her.

The blush started in her cheeks.

It grew very quiet in the schoolroom as they looked at each other. Two people, with nothing in common and so much between them.

Then Emmeline asked, "Father, will you thstay for mathematith, too?"

Shaking off the enchantment, he went and knelt beside Emmeline. "Why mathematics, Emmeline?"

"Because thubtraction ith hard," she wailed.

"Not for you." In a voice guaranteed to carry throughout the classroom, he whispered, "You're my smartest daughter."

"No, she's not," Kyla yelled.

He held out his arms and let the children descend on him. It had been years since they'd hugged like this, a huge embrace of family affection, so long he could remember looking up and seeing Mary as she watched them with a smile. This time, when he looked up, he saw Samantha, and that was all right. Mary would approve of Samantha—of her kindness, her discipline, her love for their children.

Agnes stood off to the side, watching him watch Samantha, and he reached out a hand to her. His woman-daughter smiled and gave him her hand, and he raised it to his lips in an affectionate salute.

When he had hugged each child collectively and separately, and assured Kyla that *she* was his smartest daughter, except for Henrietta and Vivian and Agnes and Mara—and Emmeline—he walked to Samantha, dragging children all the way, and bowed to the only governess who had ever outsmarted his daughters. "You're doing a magnificent job teaching my children."

She watched him with odd solemnity. "Thank you, Colonel. They're a pleasure."

He looked around at the children hanging on him. "Are your dresses done?"

They all tried to talk at once. He shushed them, and pointed to Agnes.

"Not quite, Father, but almost," she answered. "We're having fittings all the time."

"They're boring," Henrietta said.

"I'll tell the seamstresses to stop at once, for my daughter is bored."

"No! No, I pretend I'm a princess who's going to my own ball, and I don't think about it." Henrietta pouted. "Except when they stick me with a needle."

All the girls groaned and agreed.

"I look forward to seeing all of you in them. Now I shall go plan the party, and you children shall learn mathematics." He stroked Emmeline's cheek, then Agnes's, and almost before he thought, Samantha's.

Samantha jerked her head back. "Colonel Gregory, I am not one of your children."

Her motion, her reprimand, aggravated him. "Nor have I mistaken you for one." He allowed a bit of the heat he felt to seep into his gaze, and willed her to remember as he remembered.

Color sprang to her cheeks, but she pressed those soft lips into a firm line and stared back, a woman would not be coerced except with the sweetest weapons.

"I give you good day. Miss Prendregast. Children." With one last, piercing stare, he left for the veranda.

Not one of his children? He would say not!

❧ *Chapter Fourteen* ❧

As William expected, Teresa sat enthroned beneath an awning. As she had promised, she'd made the veranda the center of party preparations. She had lists spread out on the table before her, with sketches and charts. She had a bell at hand she used to summon the servants, who came and went, receiving instructions and reporting they had carried them out; and a vase of carnations, white, pink, and red, nodded gaily in the breeze. Teresa, William had discovered, would have been a great general.

She *would* be a good wife for him.

"William, at last!" With a welcoming smile, she held out her hands to him.

He kissed them gallantly.

She withdrew at once and picked up her pen.

Clearly, he was nothing but a passing distraction.

Dipping the nib into the ink, she wrote a few words and announced, "I have decided. We'll put up tents on the lawn between the house and the lake, and weather permitting, we'll serve luncheon there all three days." She looked fresh and dewy in her yellow morning dress and wide-brimmed hat, her lips softly tinted and her eyes sharp.

"A tent on the lawn." That was the stupidest idea he'd ever heard. "Why, when we have a perfectly good dining room?"

She frowned at him with dainty ferocity. "You can't expect us to eat every meal there. That would be tedious. No, outdoors will provide the variety we require, and besides, it's fashionable to picnic."

"Then picnic we must." William had been out late last night, in the saddle, riding the roads in search of traitors. He hadn't the patience to cajole Teresa out of her wild ideas, but neither could he snap with impatience as he wished. She was, after all, doing him a huge favor. "I want to impress my guests." He wanted to impress Lord and Lady Featherstonebaugh.

"Of course you do, darling. This is your first foray in public for far too long." She patted his hand, lavished a smile on him, and went back to her lists. "The first day, we'll have a revitalizing repast laid out so as they arrive, they can refresh themselves from their journeys. We'll have chairs set up, of course, but only a few so they're forced to mingle. That night, we'll have an informal gathering. We'll have a card room, of course, and games, with music. The ladies can perform—"

"Don't forget the children."

"No. How could I forget them?" She visibly infused her smile with enthusiasm. "At that time, the children who are guests can smile politely. Then perhaps dancing, if people wish, and dinner at midnight."

It sounded much the same as any other house party, except for the tents, but he wasn't fool enough to say that. "Very unique."

"Thank you. The second day we'll set up tables and chairs and have a meal. I hope the weather's warm."

"If you command it so, I'm sure it will be." Not even God dared thwart Teresa in the matter of entertaining.

"Thank you! What a lovely thought." She scarcely paid him heed. "We'll serve jellied salmon, cheeses, cold venison pie, and ices . . . I'm so glad you have an ice house, darling."

"Very fortuitous in these circumstances. Don't forget my children will wish to entertain."

"Oh, dear."

She didn't sound as enthused as he might like. She hadn't yet learned their names with any success, and she seemed inept at making conversation with any of the girls. Did Teresa not like children? For that would pose a great setback in his plans to wed her.

She consulted her schedule. "I don't have time for them then. Rather . . . let's work that in late that afternoon, right before the tea. Then we'll send the guests up to change. That night we'll have the ball."

He thought perhaps he was supposed to express enthusiasm. Instead he scarcely restrained a sigh. Having fun was an ungodly amount of work, and his men would be patrolling the roads without him.

"I've ordered the orchestra already," Teresa said. "They'll be coming in from York."

He hoped Queen Victoria appreciated his efforts to keep her realm safe, for this was costing him a fortune.

Teresa must have read his mind, for she said, "Now, darling, you've got that *economy* expression on your face. Remember, you haven't given a party for three years, so you must consider this one will make up for the rest."

"Yes, and ever after each party will have to be bigger."

Plucking a carnation from the vase, she broke off the stem and threaded it into his lapel. She laid her hand flat on his chest, and looked into his eyes. "Most men don't realize that."

She touched him. She gazed at him. She spoke to him in her melodious voice. And he experienced not one smidgin of the excitement he enjoyed with a single word from Samantha. Samantha, with her snappy repartee and her tart observations . . . and her sweet mouth and long, slender body. "Right," he said gruffly, although he didn't quite remember what he agreed to.

"Don't worry about the ball. It will be grand and wonderful."

"I'm not worried about the ball." He was

worried that Lord and Lady Featherstonebaugh wouldn't come into the snare laid for them.

"That's the way!" She patted his lapel once, firmly. "We'll have a midnight supper. The last day . . . another repast in the tents, I think, or maybe on the veranda, and then they'll be on their way."

She was done. At last. "That sounds marvelous. I look forward to seeing it come to fruition." Although he didn't look forward to more parties, and more discussions like this one . . . if he made her his wife, as he was resolved to do. "Make sure there are lots of places for private conversation, where these men can relax and talk about business or pleasure."

"Yes. Yes, of course. But there won't be much pleasure with this gathering. William, there are more men than there are women." She tapped her long nails on the table in a sharp, rapid rhythm. "Many more men than women."

"Yes. Yes, I know." But only men were officials in the Home Office and in the military. Only men would attract important spies like Lord and Lady Featherstonebaugh. And frequently career soldiers were not married. "I don't know that many women. I've invited all of the neighbors with daughters."

"Which is why it would have been better if you'd waited until I got here to make out your guest list." Teresa made a visible effort to shake off her irritation. "But the damage is done. The few single ladies will be very pleased with the marked attentions."

It was odd. Teresa appeared to love his home, his lands, and be fond of himself. Yet she seemed out of place at Silvermere. She glittered like a diamond, showing different facets every way she turned, but he didn't know which ones were real. He had to wonder—what secrets did she hide that she so carefully concealed herself?

And why, he wondered, did he even care? All of the reasons for deeming her a suitable mate still applied. She was of his own class, she was gracious, a good hostess, dressed well, and could present his daughters into society. He was wasting his time trying to comprehend a woman. No man ever could. Yet that was the problem. Since he'd met Samantha, sometimes it seemed he did understand her. And the two of them had nothing in common.

He had to stop thinking such madness. He signaled the footman, then asked Teresa, "Have you had breakfast?"

"Yes, but you can order if you wish." She glanced at him piercingly. "Although I never knew you to be a slugabed. Were you out again last night?"

She'd given him permission to carouse, so he supposed there was no harm in admitting, "I left around eleven."

"Not until eleven, eh?" Picking up her pen, she dipped it in the ink, dipped it again, then threw it down. It landed with a splat on one of her lists, but she paid it no heed. "William! I must speak!"

He finished ordering his breakfast from the footman, then said, "Of course, my dear. What is it?"

Straightening her narrow shoulders, she said, "I know how much military people value confidentiality, and I feel speaking will violate that, but this concerns your children."

She had his full attention. "What is it?"

"Last night, late, I was wakeful. I heard voices in the corridor. I stepped out and I saw your Miss Prendregast—*talking* to a *man*."

He had spent years in the military, negotiating with distrustful natives, dealing with arrogant, ignorant officers. He'd learned to hide his thoughts, and never had he needed the skill as much as now. Talking? Had she seen Samantha talking to a man? To him? Or had she seen Samantha kissing a man? Him?

But if Teresa had seen them kissing, she would say so. There would no advantage to her in avoiding the issue.

And he would not repeat the experience, regardless of how pleasurable it had been. He respected Miss Prendregast. She might be stubborn, opinionated, and outspoken, but she was dedicated to his children. She deserved an award for being so outspoken last night, and he couldn't believe how shortsighted he'd been. "I was that man. Agnes was ill, and she'd gone to Miss Prendregast. I was angry and we had words." And more, but even if Teresa knew that, she wouldn't judge him. She had assured him of that.

"My goodness! You mean Miss Prendregast does not even have the evenings to herself?"

Teresa surprised him. He thought she would flay Miss Prendregast for immorality. Instead, she thought about Miss Prendregast's inconvenience. "My rules are that the children are to go to bed at nine and stay in bed."

"Obviously, Miss Prendregast has charmed them so much they feel free to intrude on her free time."

"Yes." He couldn't argue with that.

"Poor Miss Prendregast!" Teresa shook her head and sighed. "Anytime one of the children want her, they'll go to her bedchamber in the house. Aren't you afraid you'll lose her? She says she's from the Distinguished Academy of Governesses. Those ladies are much in demand. She doesn't need to remain in a place where she gets so little solitude."

He frowned. Teresa had a point, a good one. He didn't want Samantha to become dissatisfied and possibly leave . . . only because, of course, a suitable governess was a prize above all others. "Unfortunately, Miss Prendregast is so convivial I fear she'll welcome the children no matter what I say."

"She has such pretty manners, and is so well-spoken. She is a lovely woman. Lovely. Absolutely charming." Teresa tapped her cheek as she thought. "Perhaps a better plan would be to house her in one of the cottages where she could have time to herself."

He retorted without thinking. "No."

"Why not?"

Because he wanted Samantha under his own roof.

Clasping both of his hands in hers, Teresa looked into his eyes. "I know it's more convenient for you if Miss Prendregast is nearby in case one of the children takes ill, but darling, you must be fair to the poor girl. She's already so thin, if she loses sleep I fear for her health."

Alarmed, he asked, "Do you think she's ill?"

"No, I'm sure she's . . . well, she seems sturdy enough when she marches the children off to practice their singing. And as you said, she eats an *incredible* amount." Teresa pressed her fingers to her stomach. "One might almost worry she has a tapeworm. So no, don't trouble yourself about her health. Think about her well-being, and I know you'll make the right decision."

He hated to admit it, but Teresa was right, and this visceral reaction of his was wrong. All wrong.

In addition, this would get Samantha away from him at night, and much as he hated to admit it, while in his bed, he did think of her. That was wrong, for he was courting Teresa. Samantha distracted him, and while he had confidence he could overcome this ridiculous attraction to his governess, it would be easier if he saw her as little as possible. After all, he'd heard of a lord who, only last year, had gone half mad and married his housekeeper, but William could never lose his head over a woman. Especially not a woman who was most likely unable to fit into his society. "Thank you, Teresa. Miss Prendregast will move tomorrow."

"I think that's best." Teresa smiled vaguely, no longer interested now that the matter had been settled to her satisfaction.

Standing, he bowed and start to move away. And stopped. "I have a thought. You yourself said Miss Prendregast has pretty manners."

Teresa watched him warily. "Yes, so I did."

"Then Miss Prendregast will fill one of the female slots for the party. She'll help even the numbers." And what a test it would be, to see if Samantha moved with ease among his friends! "I'm glad I thought of it."

"Oh, I, too."

𝒫𝑒 *Chapter Fifteen* 𝒫𝑒

"Psst."

Agnes raised her head off of her pillow and stared into the darkness. "Vivian?"

"Yes, it's me. Let me in with you."

Agnes lifted her covers and Vivian crawled in. "What do you want?" She didn't really like having Vivian in bed with her now. She was still bleeding, and occasionally she wanted to cry, especially when she thought about Father hugging them all today. It reminded her of when Mama was alive, except Father had looked at Miss Prendregast in a way that made Agnes want to squirm.

In a singsong voice, Vivian said, "I know something you don't know."

Agnes tensed. Had Vivian realized how Agnes's body had betrayed her?

"Father likes Miss Prendregast."

Agnes sighed in relief. She didn't want to enlighten Vivian about the monthly bleeding. Bad enough she had to deal with it; she certainly didn't want to talk about it. "How do you know that?"

Vivian pulled her head under the covers.

Agnes joined her.

"Last night, when everyone was asleep, I got up to use the pot and guess what I saw in the corridor?"

"What?"

"Father was kissing Miss Prendregast."

"No!" No, Miss Prendregast had been in bed with Agnes.

"Yes. I tell you, I saw it."

Of course, Agnes had been asleep. Hard asleep until dawn, when Miss Prendregast had roused her and sent her to bed.

"He was kissing her like . . . I don't know . . . like . . ." Vivian was having trouble finding the words.

So with rising excitement, Agnes supplied them. "Like he liked her?"

"Yes! And she was in her nightgown!" Vivian sounded shocked. "What should we do?"

This was the way they always plotted to get rid of their governesses. In bed, together, heads under the covers. But this felt different. Different, and better. "Do you mean . . . to chase Miss Prendregast away?" Agnes asked uncertainly.

"No, dummy! To make sure Father marries her!"

Agnes relaxed into the mattress. "So we could be a family again."

"That's what I want."

"Oh, me, too."

Firm footsteps sounded across the wooden floor. A single candle brought its feeble light, and the girls slid the covers down far enough to peer over them.

The housekeeper stood there in her nightcap and gown, looking cross. "That's enough plotting for one night, girls. Off to sleep with you, now. Tomorrow's a big day, I'll be tired if I don't get my beauty sleep."

Both girls giggled, but neither one said what they were thinking—that a beauty sleep would do her no good. Mrs. Shelbourn was a kind soul, for all that she hated sleeping in the same room with them.

"Yes, ma'am." Vivian climbed out of bed. "What's happening tomorrow?"

"Why, there's only two days before the party, of course!" Mrs. Shelbourn took Vivian back to bed, then returned to smooth Agnes's forehead. "All right, dear?"

She meant, did Agnes need help with her period? Miss Prendregast was right. All the women had been very nice and very understanding of Agnes's ordeal, and Agnes didn't mind Mrs. Shelbourn asking. She made everything seem so matter-of-fact. Agnes shook her head and shut her eyes. And planned how to make Father marry Miss Prendregast.

No one seemed to know what the purpose of the meeting was. Certainly Samantha didn't have a clue.

Servants lined the walls of the foyer. The children stood in front of them, tallest to shortest. Samantha held Kyla's hand, and everyone watched Colonel Gregory.

He stood squarely in the middle of the foyer, clad in a conservative outfit cut from midnight blue cloth. His fists rested on his hips, and he gazed out at the household lined up before him through those remarkable blue eyes that sent a shiver down Samantha's spine—although she worried that it was no longer a cold shiver.

"I've brought you here for two reasons. One"— he held up a finger—"the guests will be arriving tomorrow, and I want everyone to know that if they see anything that gives them pause, anything at all, they should come to me."

Samantha had had experience with house parties, and bored guests of privilege, and what they did from pure mischief, so she knew what he meant.

Mitten did, too, of course, but in his ponderous tone, he said, "Excuse me, colonel, but for the edification of the newer staff, could you tell us what that might be?"

"I would not be happy if a guest pilfered the silverware." Colonel Gregory pulled a long face. "And unfortunately, occasionally . . ."

Mitten and the other servants nodded solemnly.

"Which brings me to my second point." He lifted another finger. "The miniature of my wife that I keep on my desk is missing."

Samantha's heart sank into her belly.

The servants gasped and looked from one to the other.

"I understand that sometimes accidents happen, and I surmise that while cleaning, perhaps an accident did happen."

Everyone looked at the downstairs maid. She shook her head.

"If one of you—any one of you—broke the frame, or some other accident happened, and you don't want to admit it, I understand completely." Colonel Gregory looked the role of the commander, his shoulders back, his feet braced, his blue eyes stern, but kind. "You can bring the miniature to me, and I promise there will be no repercussions. Or leave it on my desk, and I'll ask no questions. But please return it. It is precious to me."

Samantha glanced at everyone in the crowd, searching for the culprit.

The servants were now silent and stoic, or silent and upset. The children were wide-eyed and tearful; Agnes glared at everyone, and Mara was biting her lip.

Colonel Gregory, too, considered them all, and his gaze rested briefly on Samantha. But he didn't seem to be looking for the thief in her. No, the warmth of his gaze spoke of something else entirely, and Samantha found herself shifting her feet like someone who wanted to run away—or run toward. And everyone was here. Surely everyone saw the way the color rose in her cheeks.

She looked down. But of course, if they did, they probably thought her the thief. Certainly Colonel Gregory had accused her in the matter of the drinking bag, and that when he knew nothing of her past.

She squared her shoulders. She had to remember who she was, and what she was, and not be seduced by one man's brief interest.

A clatter sounded on the stairs, bringing everyone's head around. Lady Marchant stood there, small and exquisite in a morning gown of dark blue dimity sprinkled with silver flowers and a matching silver ribbon around her waist. "I'm sorry." She raised her silver-gloved hand to her mouth. "I'm interrupting a household meeting. I was coming down to breakfast."

"A fine plan." Colonel Gregory smiled at her as if she were his dearest friend.

Samantha set her jaw. She had to get over this irrational dislike of Lady Marchant. Lady Marchant barely knew she was alive, and there was a very good reason for that. She knew as well as Samantha—better than Samantha, apparently—that the governess was no threat to her position as Colonel Gregory's potential wife. Over the next week, Samantha would hardly see Lady Marchant, or Colonel Gregory, or any of the guests. Not unless she was accompanied by a bevy of children. And once Lady Marchant had assumed the position of William's wife, she would want to install her own servants here. Probably she would dismiss Samantha, and Adorna could not be disgruntled about Samantha's return to London for such a reason as that.

So Lady Marchant could become Samantha's liberator. Samantha should be grateful, and stop wanting to mockingly imitate her gliding walk and fluttering lashes.

Colonel Gregory continued, "Go on out to the veranda, Teresa. The footmen will be out with your meal soon."

Lady Marchant glided down the stairs and out the door like a sprite spreading fairy dust behind her.

Colonel Gregory turned back to the assembled servants. "That's all. We're going to have to work as a team to make this gathering a success, and I know we can do it—together." He clicked his heels. "Dismissed!"

Samantha was torn between being impressed at the dedication he inspired, and at the same time his military demeanor brought forth an irrepressible grin. They rapidly moved out. The most important last-minute work had yet to be done to prepare for the guests. Cook, especially, was beginning to wear a perpetually harried expression.

Samantha started to lead the children back to the classroom, when Colonel Gregory called, "Children, if you would please remain."

The children swung about in military precision and waited for his command.

Stepping close to Samantha, he spoke so only she could hear him. "Miss Prendregast, do I amuse you?"

"Not at all, Colonel."

"You were laughing at me."

She didn't know whether to look at him, or past him, or at her feet. She still remembered the sensation of his mouth on hers, the way he leaned toward her, surrounding her with himself, and she could scarcely speak for embarrassment and . . .

oh, why not admit it? Delight. She wanted to stand beside him, to listen to his voice, to imagine he wanted to kiss her again. "I wasn't laughing. I was just . . . you're very much an officer."

"Yes, I am. I served in India and in the mountains beyond for over ten years. Some habits are ingrained in me. Does that bother you?"

Amazed, she looked up at him. "Why would you care what I think?"

"I'm a very caring man." A smile played around his mouth, and he seemed so pleased with himself he looked like a lad deep into mischief.

Or as if he was laughing at her.

Her mouth firmed. He'd better not, or she'd . . . at dinner, she'd help Kyla spill milk into his lap. She relaxed. The revenge available to a governess was small and petty, but certainly enjoyable.

Turning to the children, Colonel Gregory said, "We're going up to the playroom. After me." He led them up the stairs.

Samantha stayed to the back, behind Agnes, and tried very hard not to notice the way his trousers clung to his thighs, or how his posterior swiveled with each step. The girls on the street had occasionally commented in ribald detail on the way a man's body looked and moved, but as Samantha had acerbically pointed out, so few men were worthy of notice, she had not made it a habit of looking.

Colonel Gregory proved the exception to the rule. Now she couldn't look away.

They climbed the second flight of stairs to the playroom. The children filed in. Samantha followed them.

And from the rocking chair in the corner, a tiny woman of about fifty rose. She had a round apple face, rosy cheeks, and a perpetual smile that gave Samantha a feeling of warmth.

The children smiled back, bewildered but somehow pleased.

Going to the sweet-faced lady, Colonel Gregory took her hand and led her to Samantha.

"Mrs. Chester, this is Miss Prendregast, our governess."

"Ah, Miss Prendregast, ye're famous already in Hawksmouth." Mrs. Chester beamed as she curtsied. "Fer taming these rascally hoydens."

To Samantha's surprise, the children shuffled the feet and grinned as if abashed.

"Mrs. Chester, these are my rascals ... er ... daughters." Colonel Gregory named each one, and while they curtsied they scrutinized Mrs. Chester.

Mrs. Chester's smile grew wider, and she clasped her hands together. "So ye're the dear children who I'll be tucking into bed at night."

Samantha looked at Colonel Gregory and found him smiling. She grew warm again; she had to stop blushing when he smiled.

"I'm yer new nursemaid, and we'll have a wonderful time together, I promise." Mrs. Chester's chirping voice vibrated with contentment. "I haven't had so many fine children to care fer since my own little dears grew up."

As one, the children looked to their father.

He said, "Mrs. Chester has agreed to be your nursemaid for as long as you need one, to take care of anything you need, especially this week during the party when we'll need Miss Prendregast to make up our numbers."

The silence was profound as the children turned to stare at Samantha.

Henrietta's eyes were wide with awe. "Oo, Miss Prendregast, you get to go to the party."

"Yes, Miss Prendregast, you get to go to the party"—Agnes looked significantly at Vivian—"with Father."

Vivian's eyes got round. "That's right! You'll get to dance . . . with Father."

"You'll be the belle of the ball." Agnes rested her hand on her father's arm. "Don't you think she'll be the prettiest lady there, Father?"

"All the ladies will be pretty." William answered diplomatically enough, but he gazed at Samantha with such an expression of keen anticipation, she suffered a palpitation.

This attraction between her and the colonel could not be good for her heart. As good sense returned, she swallowed in profound dismay. She was a well-known pickpocket, the daughter of a thief, a woman with a hair-trigger temper that went off at the first sign of injustice. Gorblimey! She didn't want to go to this celebration. "Colonel, you don't mean that. Your guests will hardly be happy to know they're associating with a governess."

"My guests are too well bred to complain about my other guests," he said.

"Miss Prendregast, you'll be the prettiest lady there," Mara said.

"Thank you, dear. But . . . I'm a governess." A *pickpocket*. But she couldn't admit that. She'd promised Adorna, and besides, she didn't want William to know. Not now. Not ever.

Mara hugged herself. "You'll be like Cinderella. You'll go to the ball, and you'll marry the prince."

"Yes, Miss Prendregast, you'll find your *true love,*" Vivian said.

"I would hope not," Samantha snapped. "I am too busy for true love."

Agnes and Vivian exchanged sly grins.

With a brisk impatience, Colonel Gregory said, "Most of the people at the party will be my friends from the military. There'll be a great many younger sons of noble families, and even some men who have earned their rank the hard way. The only thing they'll complain about is a lack of feminine companionship, and you're the cure for that."

"Sir, my background is not such that even younger sons or common officers would relish my company."

Colonel Gregory's annoyed gaze sent a shiver down her back, and this time it *did* feel like a trickle of ice. "Miss Prendregast, set your mind at ease. You're simply a warm body at the dinner table."

"All right," she muttered. "Don't say I didn't warn you."

"What?" he snapped. "I didn't hear you."

"Nothing, sir."

He scrutinized her with an irritation that scraped at her skin. "I'm going to leave you children here, with Mrs. Chester, so you can get to know each other." He took Samantha's arm in a firm grip. "Miss Prendregast will go with me and discover the extent of her new duties."

He pushed her ahead of him.

"Wait!" Samantha said.

He didn't.

Calling back over her shoulder, she said, "The children are due for a dress fitting at three o'clock."

"I'll take care of it," Mrs. Chester answered.

"They need to practice the piano and their singing."

"I'll make sure they do."

"Kyla's new shoes are the wrong size. The new ones are coming in on the mail coach—"

"Don't ye worry, Miss Prendregast. Between the children and I, we'll take care of everything."

Colonel Gregory pulled her into the corridor and shut the door between Samantha and the children.

She shook him off. "It is unnecessary to treat me like a recalcitrant child."

"It is when you act like one."

"I'm responsible for the children."

"I've relieved you of the immediate responsibility—"

She started to speak.

He stopped her with a gesture. "—and left a schedule with Mrs. Chester. Did you think I wouldn't?"

Of course. She needed to remember. This family wasn't hers to keep. The children were only hers to teach, and then she would move on.

Stalking ahead of him, she said, "It would be better if I remained in charge at least until after . . ."

"After what? The party was over?"

"Yes. My background—"

"No matter what your background, Lady Bucknell has taught you how to behave with courtesy and grace." He followed her down the stairs to the second story. "Do you think I would have tapped you for such a role if I hadn't already observed you at meals? During lessons? While you speak?"

Had he really been scrutinizing her so closely? "No, but you don't understand." She tried to explain without actually giving the details. "I have lost positions because of my past."

"And you have gained the position of chair filler because of your presence." He looked pleased with his pun. "I'm also moving you out of the manor and into a cottage."

"What?" She looked toward her room, and saw servants removing her trunk. "You can't do that. Who will the children come to if they're ill?" She knew the response as soon as she asked.

He answered anyway. "That is why I hired Mrs. Chester. Lady Marchant pointed out, and rightly, that with the children visiting you night and day, you have no time to yourself."

"Lady Marchant—" She couldn't say that Lady Marchant was a scheming Jezebel. "Lady Marchant is very thoughtful," Samantha ended lamely.

"In addition, we need the bedroom in the house for one of the single ladies we have coming to the celebration."

"A cottage seems so . . . isolated." And she wanted to stay here, close to him, although why she should was a mystery even to her.

"I wish you wouldn't question matters you don't understand," he said crisply.

"I understand. You're kicking me out of my bedchamber."

"Yes. Because you can't stay here and test my moral fiber. It's not as strong as I would like it to be, especially where you're concerned." He sounded emotionless, but his words made her recall the kiss. The passion. The great, devouring sense of togetherness that fed on itself and called for more.

"Oh." She moved her lips, but the sound scarcely escaped.

"Clarinda will stay in the guest house with you. None of the guests will bother you. You'll be well chaperoned." He stroked her jaw, a brief caress that brought goose bumps to her skin, and his gaze on her was heated, liquid, so filled with blue she wanted to float away.

Instead she pushed at him. "Don't."

Drawing his hand away, he looked at his fingers with what looked like profound misgivings. Then he transferred those misgivings to her. "So you see, Miss Prendregast, this move is for both of our sakes, so you'll accept graciously and without argument."

Clearly, he didn't trust her. And why not? Because she was not of his social class, and he feared she would use her wiles to trap him into a compromising situation. She had told him she wasn't interested in a man; like every man, he believed himself irresistible.

Very well. By her actions, she would make her feelings obvious. "I am grateful for your thoughtfulness, and glad to move. You're going to marry Lady Marchant." Then her temper took hold of her. "And I wouldn't want to be caught with my fingers in her biscuit tin."

With profound irritation, he said, "I am hardly a biscuit."

"Exactly."

"Come." He took her arm again, and marched her down the stairs and out the door.

❧ *Chapter Sixteen* ❧

Lady Marchant sat at one of the tables beneath a canopy on the veranda. Her pale skin was without mar. Her brown hair was perfectly arranged with ringlets at the sides and a knot at the back. As she sipped her cup of tea, her little finger was perfectly curved. With the faintest of clinks, she set her cup on its saucer and smiled at Samantha. "So, here's our little governess who will fill in our numbers. I certainly hope you appreciate the privilege Colonel Gregory has extended to you."

As William held her chair, Samantha seated herself. "I can't begin to express my appreciation."

At Samantha's tart tone, Lady Marchant blinked.

Samantha wanted to ask if she had something in her eye.

"She's afraid that our guests will be disgusted

by her background." William seated himself also.

"You are a sensible young woman!" Lady Marchant complimented her. "I did express that concern to you, William."

William filled the chair with stolid proportions, a large man who should have looked out of place in the delicate metal fancywork of the chair. Instead his body was perfectly erect and balanced, a compliment to the military and his heritage. "I know these men. They're both sensible and ordinary. They'll want to relax with the company of a beautiful, charming woman." He transferred his gaze to Samantha and watched her as if weighing her in his mind.

Against what, she had no idea.

He continued, "As you yourself said, Teresa, Miss Prendregast is both."

"Quite right," Lady Marchant said. "My concern is for Miss Prendregast herself. I don't wish her to feel . . . awkward. Out of place."

Crikey! Who did Lady Marchant think she was fooling? She would *love* for Samantha to feel awkward and out of place. Samantha said, "I've associated with men of good character before"—when she picked their pockets—"and I find they're much the same as men of bad character." She widened her eyes at William. "Easily manipulated."

Leaned forward, he projected an unexpected menace. "Have you found me easy to manipulate, Miss Prendregast?"

She met his gaze without flinching. "I haven't been interested enough to try, Colonel Gregory."

Seemingly unaware of the tension that simmered between Samantha and William, Lady Marchant laughed throatily. "Not all women are as intrigued by you as I am, William. And Miss Prendregast, the trick with manipulating men is to do so without their realizing."

"We allow you to think you've succeeded," William snapped.

Samantha could scarcely contain her irritation with Lady Marchant and her silly philosophy. "The trick is not to put oneself in a position where one has to bother with a man at all. A woman of independence is in the perfect position to please herself."

Lady Marchant blinked again. "How marvelously refreshing you are, Miss Prendregast. I applaud your autonomy. So befitting a servant. Don't you applaud her, too, William?"

"Indeed." He had the audacity to sound skeptical. "It's a rare woman who truly wishes to face the cold, cruel world alone."

Samantha answered him directly. "Only one who has seen how much more alone a woman is when faced with an indifferent mate."

Lady Marchant perked up. "You've been married, Miss Prendregast?"

"No." Samantha clipped the word. "Nor do I intend to be."

"Refreshing, indeed." Lady Marchant withered back into her chair. "Now, I think—"

William interrupted without appearing to notice. "A woman who declares herself free of any aspiration for union with a proper mate must be declared without sentiment or femininity."

What an exasperating man! "Are you calling me unwomanly?" Samantha asked.

"You're fond of children," William said. "Do you never wish to have one of your own?"

Which was no answer at all, but Samantha couldn't resist reacting to his taunt. "I'd love to have a child of my own, Colonel Gregory, but that would involve a husband, and that's a poor start for a family."

"William, let me pour you a glass of water." Lady Marchant picked up the pitcher and, in the first ungainly act Samantha had seen from her, slopped the first drops into William's lap.

Samantha almost laughed to see William's astonishment and indignation. Without a doubt, he knew, as Samantha did, that Lady Marchant had done it on purpose. Yet he could scarcely accuse his hostess of such clumsiness. So as she apologized, he brushed the water off and declared there to be no problem.

In truth, Samantha was glad of the interruption. She'd been so involved in quarreling with William, her heart beat faster, her breath whistled in her lungs. And why? He was nothing but a man. A man who attracted her, yes, she would admit it. But also a man who might wish to use her as her father had used her mother, and she was too proud to allow any man liberties with her person or her dignity. Taking the glass Lady Marchant now poured her, she toasted William's hostess. "Thank you, my lady. The water was just what I needed."

"Good." Lady Marchant settled back into her chair. "Now, I must think. Prendregast. Prendregast. I feel I know that name."

Samantha curled her hands in her lap. If Lady Marchant did know the name, her time as a houseguest was over before it started, as well as her time as the governess in the Gregory household.

"Are you one of the Somerset Prendregasts?" Lady Marchant examined Samantha. "I thought I knew them all, but I don't recognize your person."

The interrogation had started, the one that would stretch all the way through the party. "I'm from London, my lady."

As Samantha knew, Lady Marchant was not to be satisfied with that. "Only from London?"

"She is such a city girl, she fears everything about the country. She fears the mountains will fall on her"—William swept a hand toward Devil's Fell—"that a snake will bite her, or that a lake monster will swallow her whole."

Samantha's fingers fluttered to her throat. "How did you know about the lake mon—?"

He threw back his head and laughed, and Samantha realized he hadn't known. He had guessed, and guessed well.

"A lake monster?" Lady Marchant questioned. "Dear, you must be teasing."

"I am. I'm definitely teasing." Samantha wanted to smack him for making fun of her fears, but at the same time his foot was nudging hers beneath the table, a less-than-subtle caress right in front of the lady she thought, the children thought, the servants thought, he wanted to marry.

Samantha liked to know where she belonged. She liked to know the rules, because she'd discovered the penalty for breaking the rules was humiliation and exile. Now Colonel Gregory was breaking the rules. Except she could scarcely believe a man of such rigid values would break any rules. Perhaps he knew of different rules. Perhaps he was changing the rules. No matter what, she didn't know if she were on her head or her toes. Glaring at him, she tucked her feet tightly beneath her chair. "It's a frightening place here, Colonel."

"We'll teach you to love it." He sounded absolutely confident, a repulsive trait in a man.

Gesturing toward the peaks, Samantha said, "Everything's too big. The lakes are blue instead of brown. The air's so fresh I can't even see it."

"That's because there's no coal dust here," Lady Marchant explained.

Colonel Gregory allowed his eyes to twinkle at Samantha, and they shared a moment of ... oh, what to call it? ... camaraderie, perhaps.

Then Lady Marchant realized what Samantha had said, and gave an artificial laugh. "Oh. That's a jest. How funny. Now where do I know you from?" The lady was like a trained dog after a bone, relentless and politely savage.

"I've lived nowhere but in London, which is why this place is dreadfully odd, and I've been a governess for the past four years. Perhaps you saw me at one of my posts." *And perhaps you saw me at*

Newmarket picking pockets, but I'll not admit to that unless I'm forced.

Colonel Gregory watched the two of them, listening, weighing their conversation.

"I do know London very well. You could tell me who employed you and I—" Lady Marchant frowned and shaded her eyes with her hand. "Who's that young man coming from the stables?"

Samantha didn't know, but she already liked him, for he had rescued her.

A tall, handsome gentleman strode, dressed in a brown wool tailcoat, brown trousers, and a black top hat. As he climbed the stairs onto the veranda, the dimples in his tanned cheeks flashed. He removed his hat, and Samantha saw he sported two black eyes and a swollen nose. In a merry tone, the stranger announced, "William, I have arrived. Let the party begin."

Colonel Gregory laughed, rose and shook his hand. "Monroe, we've been waiting for you to start the festivities."

So Mr. Monroe was a friend of Colonel Gregory's.

"Oh," Lady Marchant said in a bored tone, and she barely glanced at him. "Duncan Monroe. It's you."

Apparently, Lady Marchant didn't care for him.

Colonel Gregory introduced Samantha. Mr. Monroe raised her hand to his lips, bowed, and scrutinized her in one all-encompassing glance. "I'm so glad to meet you at last. You've already gained a wide reputation for charm."

Samantha saw at once the kind of man he was.

Light-hearted, laughing, hiding a profound soul and a sharp mind beneath the façade of rake. "I do have that reputation, I admit—among the nursery crowd."

Even Lady Marchant laughed in genuine amusement.

Keeping Samantha's hand in his, Mr. Monroe said, "Has anyone ever told you you have the most unusual eyes? The color of whisky, I believe I've heard them called."

Frowning fiercely, Colonel Gregory said, "That will do, Monroe."

Samantha took her hand back. "Thank you, Mr. Monroe." From his tone, from Colonel Gregory's rejoinder, she knew who had said that. Everyone at the table knew who had said that, and Lady Marchant was not pleased. But for all that Samantha knew she was foolish, she couldn't hold back her happiness at knowing Colonel Gregory had spoken of her.

In a repressive tone, Colonel Gregory continued, "Apparently, Monroe, you've already met the countess."

Duncan bowed so elaborately, with such a sweep of his arm, that his hat swept the floor. "Lady Marchant. The pleasure is all mine."

Lady Marchant's expression resembled that of a woman who had bit into a insect. "Mr. Monroe. I hardly think that our party's success depends on you."

"Our party?" Duncan looked between Lady Marchant and Colonel Gregory. "It's our party now? Should we be expecting an announcement of betrothal soon?"

Samantha caught her breath. Lady Marchant and Colonel Gregory were well suited—him so tall and dark, she so petite and brunette. But two nights ago, he had kissed Samantha, and for some reason, she felt that gave her some right to him. To his body. To his mind.

This had to stop at once. She glanced at him.

He was watching her. He wasn't fondly gazing at Lady Marchant. Neither was he correcting Duncan. He watched her as if gauging her reaction.

So she summoned her most polite, social smile, directed it toward him, then turned it on Duncan.

"I am the hostess." Lady Marchant batted her eyelashes at Duncan. "So yes, it is my party, too."

"That's right." With an insouciant smile, Duncan seated himself at the table. "You are always the hostess. I remember in India, you gave the finest parties. I met the most interesting people at your parties."

Lady Marchant replied with an open hostility that made Samantha raise her eyebrows. "You made a fool of yourself at my parties."

"So I did." Duncan tilted his chair back on two legs. "How kind of you to point that out."

Samantha didn't understand the relationship between these two people. They obviously detested each other, yet . . . they almost seemed to enjoy fighting like cats in a bag.

The full light of the sun struck his face, and for

the first time Lady Marchant really looked at him. "Wait a minute. Those marks on your face . . . How did you get them?" She struck the table with her palm. "You're the man who held up my coach the other night!"

Lady Marchant captured Samantha's full attention. "He held up your coach?"

"This is the man who stopped your coach?" Colonel Gregory asked. "I don't think that's possible. He wasn't even in the district."

"It is possible," Lady Marchant snapped at Colonel Gregory, and Samantha would have wagered for the first time. "I grabbed his hair and kneed him in the face. Look at Mr. Monroe! He ran into something."

"A door," Duncan said, but he grinned at the obvious jest.

"You dare smirk about this? I've accused you of being a highwayman!" She turned to Colonel Gregory and laid her hand on his arm. "I tell you, I'm certain of my accusations."

"But Teresa, you told me your coachman chased off the robbers." Colonel Gregory's voice held a tone of mockery Samantha hadn't imagined he would use with Lady Marchant.

Caught in a lie, Lady Marchant took a breath, then let it out in a sigh. "I fear I may have changed the facts an eensy bit."

"Something odd is going on," Samantha said. Something between the two men, and the facts didn't add up. "The first night I was here, Colonel Gregory stopped me on the road and went through my reticule. I believe he was looking for bandits, although why he thought I, a woman on foot, would be a highwayman, I still don't understand. Perhaps Mr. Monroe is working with Colonel Gregory."

The two men exchanged glances.

Lady Marchant bolted to her feet. "My heavens, that's it! Isn't it? You both look as guilty as two soldiers caught drinking on watch."

"Miss Prendregast is correct," Colonel Gregory admitted. "We roam the district at night to try and catch the bandits that continue to plague us." He bent a stern look on them. "But I'd appreciate it if you two women kept this quiet."

"You keep the district safe by robbing travelers?" Lady Marchant was clearly outraged.

"I didn't rob you," Duncan insisted.

"Because I held your pistol on you and threatened to shoot you in the head."

Samantha looked at the petite Lady Marchant with new respect. Perhaps she had misjudged the lady. She was both smarter and tougher than she appeared. It was something to remember.

Duncan continued, "I wasn't going to search you. We stopped you by mistake."

Lady Marchant still attacked him. "How could you think I, traveling in a coach with a crest, could be a bandit?"

"I assure you, Teresa, he's telling the truth," Colonel Gregory said.

Lady Marchant scrutinized him. Then her eyes widened. "You were one of the other men!"

Samantha enjoyed seeing Colonel Gregory squirm.

"Yes. I admit it. I was. And as I said—"

"I don't believe it," Lady Marchant said. "It doesn't even make sense. Will you ride out and rob your guests as they come in?"

"Not at all," Colonel Gregory soothed her. "Everything is under control."

Lady Marchant turned to Samantha and in the first gesture of female comradeship Samantha had seen, asked, "Do you understand any of this?"

"No, my lady, but I understand one thing." Samantha allowed her eyes to twinkle at Duncan. "If I were Mr. Monroe, I would be wary before I tried to hold you up again."

Duncan's eyes twinkled back. "In the future, I intend to take the greatest care of Lady Marchant."

At Maitland Manor, the Featherstonebaugh servants rose and fell in a wave of obeisance. Usually Valda enjoyed the sight, but now, livid with rage, she swept up the steps and past the line of servants without looking at any of them.

She heard the gasps and titters from the maids as Rupert tottered in behind her, pinching their cheeks—and lower.

Her eyes narrowed. The stupid old fool had even tried his moves on her, and she, like an idiot, had succumbed. Then, while she slept, he had attempted to sneak out and escape from her. He still didn't believe they were in danger. If only he didn't know so much, she would kill him.

She would enjoy killing him.

As she stepped inside, the butler followed and took her coat and hat. "My lady, we didn't know when to expect you."

She glanced around. Maitland was a beautiful home, a glorious eighteenth-century manor set in a jewellike valley, stocked full of great works of art and valuable knickknacks, and she would have to leave it all. It made her sick. "It doesn't matter. Nothing matters." Except for the map she'd stolen on her way here. A cretin named Captain Farwell had left it locked in his trunk, and while she didn't usually take things so easily traced, it no longer mattered if Captain Farwell knew where his map had gone, because she was taking transport to Ireland, and then on to Italy, and no one could trace her there.

The map showed the location and number of every English spy in Russia. She would sell it for a tidy sum, and that would be a kind of insurance in case something went wrong. It was just her old sense of caution flaring up; except for Rupert and his stupid antics, since they'd left Blythe Manor, everything had gone absolutely right.

It was enough to frighten a woman to death.

The butler continued, "But your guest did warn us you would be coming, so—"

She swung on him. "My guest?" The back of her neck prickled. "Who would that be?"

The voice she wanted least to hear—an accented voice, an elegant voice—echoed through the foyer. "Me, of course. Your dear friend, Count Gayeff Fiers Pashenka."

Unhurriedly, she turned back to face him.

Tall, handsome, austere, he stood with a pistol concealed—although not well—in his pocket. A pistol pointed right at her heart.

🍃❧ Chapter Seventeen ❧🍃

The guest cottage was very nice. Tiny, but nice. The perfect refuge for someone who wanted to avoid the guests pouring onto the estate.

Whitewashed inside and out, the cottage was on a single level, and set in a garden of white phlox and pinks, purple pansies and scarlet begonias. A covered porch led to the front door, with rocking chairs and a table in case the guest wished to sit and admire the view of the mountains.

Samantha did not, so she stayed indoors, wandering between the two rooms, wishing she'd been firm with Colonel Gregory about attending this party. She'd spent the night awake in her new bed, imagining the different kinds of disasters that could occur as she met and mingled with members of the ton. Adorna had sent her to Cumbria to get her away from notoriety, not to court it.

"Will ye be leaving now, Miss Prendregast?" Clarinda called from the bedchamber.

"Not yet." Samantha paced vigorously back and forth across the front chamber, swinging her arms like a soldier on parade.

Yes, this cottage suited her very well. The ceilings were high, with open rafters that rose right up to the thatching and gave an illusion of spaciousness. This room held a small table with chairs, ideal for two people should they wish to eat or play a game, and a cupboard that held dishes and blankets. A blue brocade sofa stood before the white stone fireplace in the inner wall, and that fireplace opened not only to the front room, but on the other side of the wall it opened into the bedchamber.

The bedchamber was ideal, with a dresser where Clarinda placed Samantha's unmentionables and a cupboard with hooks for her clothes. An oak-framed mirror hung over the dresser. The bed was smaller than Samantha's bed in the big house, but was sufficient for a single sleeper, and the brown-striped eiderdown was as thick and plush as the one she'd left.

It was the perfect, cozy spot for a romantic tryst. Her eyes narrowed. Was that the real reason he'd put her here?

But no. That was foolishness. He'd kissed her, yes, but she'd seen his distrust of her when he suggested the cottage. He obviously suspected her of some nefarious deeds. The theft of his wife's miniature, perhaps. Or perhaps he thought she wished to seduce him. He'd made his opinion clear enough yesterday. Women wanted security, and they'd do anything to get it. He suspected she would seduce him if she could, when in fact he had seduced her. Dreadful man, but typical, too, to blame her for his fault.

"Colonel Gregory will be wondering where ye are, miss," Clarinda called again.

And that was the problem, wasn't it? In between worrying whether she'd be recognized, Samantha fretted about Colonel Gregory. Blast the man! He made her so angry. It was bad enough that he'd kissed her. That was a single event, one she could have eventually dismissed as two people seeking to temper their mutual rage. But when he'd said she had to move out because she tempted him beyond sanity . . . well, she couldn't ignore that. Especially if she had to see him every day in a social situation where she was not his governess, but his equal.

She stopped and rubbed her forehead.

Clarinda came to the bedchamber door. "No wonder ye've been dragging yer feet, miss. Why didn't ye tell me the children were coming t' fetch ye?" Grinning, she wiped her hands on her apron. "They certainly look festive in their new gowns."

Walking to the window, Samantha parted the lace curtains. Colonel Gregory had cleverly sent the one command she couldn't ignore—one delivered by the girls.

They fluttered along, laughing and talking, the older ones holding the little ones' hands. Colonel Gregory had taken Samantha's advice, getting each one a different, solid color so they looked like a miniature ruffled rainbow of yellow, blue, red, violet, green, and pink. The little girls wore the darkest colors. Agnes wore the pink, and it matched the excited color in her cheeks. Even Mara managed to look tidy in her green gown with its modest lace collar. Their bonnets matched their gowns, each tied beneath their chins with contrasting ribbons.

For the first time during this day, Samantha smiled. "Didn't the gowns come out beautifully? Aren't the girls pretty?"

Clarinda crossed to her side. "Yes, miss, that they are. Ye've made them happy, no doubt about it. Been waiting fer someone like ye, they have." Firmly, she patted Samantha on the shoulder. "Remember that, miss, when ye're thinking ye don't belong amongst the noble folk."

Samantha looked sideways at Clarinda. "Have I been so obvious?"

"It's natural to worry when ye get pitched in among the gentry, but ye'll hold yer own. Why, Mrs. Shelbourn says ye've got as pretty a manner as any lady, better conversation than most, and ye fit right in anywhere ye choose t' go."

A warm tide of satisfaction swept Samantha. "Lady Bucknell says that, too. Thank you, Clarinda. I needed to hear it again."

"So go on, now, and meet the children, and let them take ye to the party."

And if someone recognized her . . . well, she would cope with that situation as it arose. That was how she'd always lived before, taking one episode at a time, and she would not allow Colonel Gregory to knock her so off balance. She couldn't blame the man for doing the right thing, after all, in putting her as far away from him as possible, and once the party was over she would return to being a governess. She had only to get through the next three days.

She wouldn't think about the rest of the year.

Decision made, she went to open the door.

Clarinda moved in front of her. "No, miss. Yer maid should open the door t' yer guests." Flinging the door open, she waited until the children pranced up onto the porch. Then Clarinda curtsied with great formality. "Whom may I say is calling?"

"It's us, Clarinda." Kyla sounded bewildered. "Don't you know us?"

"Sure she does, she's pretending we're real grown-ups paying a call," Henrietta explained.

"Ohh." Kyla lifted her chubby little chin in a superior manner. "I knew that."

Standing in the shadows of the front room, Samantha watched as Agnes lined up the children.

Vivian said, "We are the Misses Gregory, come to visit Miss Prendregast."

"I'll see if she's in." While the children squirmed, Clarinda stepped inside and announced, "The Misses Gregory, ma'am."

With a gracious smile, Samantha glided onto the porch. "It's so kind of you to pay me a call." Then the pleasure of seeing them caught up with her, and she clasped her hands together. "Don't you girls look beautiful?"

"Yeth, we do!" Emmeline shouted.

"So do you, Miss Prendregast." Mara sounded awed.

"Thank you." Samantha smoothed her skirt. Clarinda had taken one of Samantha's day gowns, a bell skirt of sapphire blue-and-gold plaid poplin, and added flat gold braid to the off-the-shoulder neckline. Adorna would have approved of the change, for it accentuated Samantha's long neck and slender hands, and gave Samantha confidence. "May I invite you ladies in?"

"No, Father sent us to fetch you." Henrietta planted herself before Samantha. "He said"—she deepened her voice in imitation of Colonel Gregory—"'Is she afraid to come to the party?'"

"I'm not afraid," Samantha said automatically.

"That's what I told him." Mara took Samantha's hand and swung it. "You're not afraid of anything, are you?"

If only that were true. "Everybody's afraid of something, Mara."

"What are you afraid of, Miss Prendregast?" Agnes asked.

Samantha could imagine only too clearly the scene she feared. Someone at this party would point a finger at her and denounce her as a thief. The children's faces would crumple. Colonel Gregory would show her the door, and she'd go, humiliated and furious. Adorna had warned her she could never escape her past. She thought she'd accepted that. But never had the stakes been so high. Never had she wanted so much to belong.

It was the Gregory family closeness that attracted her. The warmth of the children's affection. The jokes and the laughter. The tears and the hugs.

Nothing else. Certainly not Colonel Gregory himself. Absolutely not.

"Don't be troubled, Miss Prendregast," Agnes said. "We're on our best behavior."

"There is to be no mud," Samantha told them sternly.

"No, Miss Prendregast," they singsonged.

"And Mara is singing beautifully," Agnes continued.

"Bea-u-tifully," Henrietta agreed.

Emmeline planted herself before Samantha. "We're thinging bea-u-tifully, too."

"Yes, we are," Vivian said. "Since we're going to sing with Mara, she won't be so scared."

"I know she'll do wonderfully well. All of you will." Samantha saw a chance to stall a little longer. "In fact, shall we have a practice right now?"

"No. They're serving lunch in the tents, and there's a tent especially for the children with puddings and trifle." Mara tugged at her. "Let's go to the party."

Clarinda bustled out of the house where she'd been waiting. "Here's yer bonnet, Miss Prendregast." She tied the strings under Samantha's chin as Samantha pulled on finely made gloves of dull-gold kid.

"We should practice," Samantha argued.

"I'm supposed to practice at five o'clock, so I'm not practicing now. But you could come and help me then," Mara wheedled.

"A wonderful idea," Samantha said promptly.

By the time four hours had passed, she would be ready for a reprieve.

"And Mrs. Chester says I'm scheduled to sing tomorrow after luncheon," Mara said.

Better and better. "I'll be there then, too. After all, you must have your accompanist."

As they crossed the lawn, Samantha saw the three huge, colorful tents, pitched by the lake, open on all sides, and bright with flags. Inside the first, servants were setting up long tables and bringing out dishes to set on them. Inside another, a dozen children hopped and wiggled beneath the watchful eyes of their governesses and nursemaids. And in the largest, a crowd of well-dressed men milled about, with a few brightly garbed women among them, conversing in the manner of people greeting each other after a long absence. The sound of laughter and speech floated through the air, and Samantha found her throat tightening as she tried to identify the adult voices.

But she could pick out only one—Colonel Gregory's deep voice. She located him by his broad shoulders. He stood with Lady Marchant on his arm. Lady Marchant looked up at him adoringly as he spoke to a group of solemnly clad gentlemen and soldiers in uniform, who listened and nodded as if Colonel Gregory were an oracle.

Such attention wasn't good for him. He was already far too sure of himself.

The girls, their duty done, dropped Samantha's hands and raced to join the other children. "G'bye, Miss Prendregast. G'bye!" they yelled.

At the sound of her name, Colonel Gregory looked up—and surveyed her in a most flattering inspection. He didn't smile, but his eyes heated like blue coals.

Samantha blushed, and cursed her fair complexion.

If Lady Marchant noticed his interest, or Samantha's reaction, she gave no indication. Bustling forward, she took Samantha's hand, and drew her into the circle. "Here is our little governess, gentleman."

The solemn expressions lightened, and the men bowed with such delight Samantha realized Colonel Gregory had spoken the truth. These gentlemen didn't care if she were a governess; they longed for female companionship.

Lady Marchant took William's arm again. Any doubts she harbored about Samantha's presence were well hidden beneath a gracious smile. "Isn't she charming?"

A young officer with a truly magnificent brown mustache bowed. "Indeed, ma'am, I would be privileged if you would introduce me."

"Introduce you? Du Clos, you dog." Another officer jostled him aside. "She's going to introduce me."

Samantha chuckled, low and warm. "Indeed, Lady Marchant, introduce them all. I hear there's safety in numbers."

The men groaned, and lined up to greet her.

Lady Marchant waggled her finger at them. "Before I start, gentlemen, I must warn Miss Prendregast that you're all single and in want of a wife, and unless she wants to find herself settled with a staid husband, she should be very careful of your gallantries."

"Single and in need of a wife? Indeed, I will remember," Samantha promised.

Lady Marchant introduced the first of the somberly clad males, a man of perhaps fifty with drooping eyes and thinning hair. "This is Mr. Langdon, a gentleman most sought after for his charm and his dancing."

"I'm honored, Miss Prendregast." He kissed Samantha's fingertips in a manner that flattered and charmed.

"The earl of Hartun. His mother would like him wed and settled." Lady Marchant smiled at him knowingly. "I have promised her my help."

"Thank you for warning me. And, Miss Prendregast, it's a privilege to have you among us."

Lord Hartun wore his garments with a continental flare, but Samantha wanted to squirm beneath his steady, grave gaze. It was almost as if he knew she hid something, and he would ferret it out.

Lady Marchant indicated the mustachioed officer who wore his regimentals with such flare. "Lieutenant Du Clos from my husband's company. He returned from India this spring, where he was known for dashing ways with the ladies."

Lieutenant Du Clos also kissed Samantha's hand, but on the back, and with an intimacy that made her uncomfortable. His manner and Lady Marchant's warning clearly told Samantha he was a lady killer of unparalleled skill. She would take care never to find herself alone with him.

"Gentlemen, gentlemen!" Lady Marchant clapped her hands. "Try to contain yourselves. Miss Prendregast might be our newest belle, but she needs room to breathe. Perhaps a few of you could curry favor by fixing her a plate and bringing her a drink."

Other men clustered around, and Samantha assessed them, too. The skills she'd learned as a cutpurse stood her in good stead now. She didn't listen to their words, but watched their eyes and their gestures, seeking the truth of their characters in their expressions. She had only to keep her head, and she could pull this off.

Oh, and she needed luck, of course. A wise thief never dismissed the significance of luck.

⊰ Chapter Eighteen ⊱

"See, William, darling? You were right. Our little governess is doing very well." Satisfaction oozed from Teresa's tone as she took his arm.

William knew why. He was being pushed back further and further from Samantha's sphere, and that was exactly as Teresa had planned it. Make Samantha the center of attention, and Teresa would have William to herself. An admirable stratagem, one that benefited both Samantha and Teresa. Only William was left frustrated.

Although really . . . why should he be? He had hoped Samantha would prove adept in society. Not because he wanted her, but because such proficiency gave her confidence and made her a better governess, more able to teach his daughters such skills. He looked down at the crushed grass beneath his boots, and wondered why she didn't challenge the other men as she had challenged him. With them, she was all charm and ease. With him, she was nothing but a handful of thorns.

And the fact that Teresa felt she had to maneuver events meant he had not covered his interest in Samantha, and that was a disservice to them all. Even if he remained indifferent to Teresa as a possible wife, she nevertheless deserved his complete attention as his hostess. "Come," he said to Teresa. "General and Lady Stephens have arrived. We should greet them." He led her away.

Yet somehow, without trying, he managed to keep sight of Samantha as she basked in the devotion of a constantly increasing crowd of gentlemen, lords, and officers. She had even managed to attract and hold Lord Hartun, a man whose family was both ancient and moneyed. A man who, it was rumored, had connections deep in the secret recesses of the Home Office. Lord Hartun was one of the willing participants in the scheme to ensnare Lord and Lady Featherstonebaugh.

If not for Lady Bucknell's recommendation, William would be highly suspicious of Samantha's allure.

But how could he not be fascinated by her? She gestured openly, unlike the circumscribed ladies scattered throughout the crowd. Her slender fingers fluttered like birds. She was vibrant, blonde, unique in a way that the men here could scarcely fathom.

As William greeted the guests, chatted, and

smiled, he watched her. Watched her not because he feared she would falter. He watched because he couldn't look away.

Her throaty laughter rang out, bold, free.

The ladies' heads turned, then leaned together.

"Oh, dear." Teresa got that steely-eyed look that spelled doom for any feminine malice. "I must go visit with my dear friends."

"Of course." He watched her move into the group of ladies and with incredible charm, move them toward Samantha. She introduced her, and in a few moments everyone was laughing.

True to form, Teresa had saved the day.

"Lady Marchant is the perfect choice for your hostess." Mr. Gray, a gentleman whose appearance matched his name, spoke loudly. Then he glanced around at the four men surrounding William. When he was sure they were chaps of like mind, he lowered his voice. "Have the rats taken the bait?"

"Not yet. They're still in their rat hole. But I not only sent over an invitation with a personal message expressing my dearest wish that my neighbors attend and lend their elegance to our gathering, I also gave our spy among their servants a list of the guests. By now, Lord and Lady Featherstonebaugh know every name." William's gesture included the four gentlemen gathered close. "With you here, Mr. Gray, and Hartun, and General Stephens, and so many of the gentlemen deep in the government's confidence, I feel sure the rats will arrive soon." Teresa caught William's gaze; he smiled and nodded as if he were having no more than the usual well-bred conversation.

General Stephens, a clean-shaven, upright military man, said, "It's a damned risky plan. Someone could slip and give real information."

"It *is* a damned risky business," William agreed, "and none of these men got to their positions because they made a habit of slipping."

Lady Stephens joined them, and the gentlemen made way for her. She had won their respect; she spoke five languages and had such wide blue eyes she'd pried many a confidence from many a foolish foreigner. "You don't like having to travel so many miles in such a hurry, Henry. At least—not to a party. Now if it were a battle . . ."

All the gentlemen chuckled, then quieted as Teresa swept back in. "Excuse me for leaving you, William, but I wanted to tell the ladies why we have your governess at the party. I didn't want them to think us havey-cavey, as Miss Prendregast so quaintly says."

"Why *is* she here?" Lady Stephens asked.

"William invited disparate numbers of men to women, and Miss Prendregast has such lovely manners, of course we thought of her at once. But she's so modest, we quite had to cajole her into coming to the party at all." Teresa patted William's hand. "So you must blame William for Miss Prendregast."

"Give him a medal, rather," General Stephens said.

The other chaps laughed.

"Yes, she's certainly collecting more than her share of the gentlemen." Lady Stephens's cool gaze considered Samantha. "Do we know who she is?"

"Her people, you mean? No." Teresa pulled a long face. "She's an orphan, I believe, but she has Lady Bucknell's patronage."

"Oh!" General Stephens harrumphed. "Quite all right."

Lady Stephens's famous smile blossomed. "Yes, if Lady Bucknell says she will do, then she will do. Look! There's my dear friend, the ambassador from Italy. I must go greet him."

"Not without me, you won't. That chap's been infatuated with you since you came out twenty years ago." General Stephens chased after his wife.

Everyone laughed, and drifted toward different groups.

William turned to Teresa. "A fabulous performance with the ladies."

She tried to pull an innocent face, but gave up and chuckled. "I love making them do as I wish."

"You're wasted on society. You should be running the British Embassy in Paris."

Teresa, the sophisticated, actually colored. "I would like that. Why don't you recommend me?"

"Perhaps I shall." He'd left one element off his list of desirable traits in a wife—that he should like her. For all her foibles and wiles, he very much liked Teresa.

"Did you ever find Mary's portrait? The one you were seeking yesterday?" Teresa asked.

His pleasure in the day, in the plan, dimmed. "Not yet. I hate to think one of my servants took it, but I suppose that is the case."

"You don't have the time it takes to run a household properly." Teresa touched his cheek. "You need a wife, darling."

Her gesture was less than subtle, and that surprised him. Teresa was usually the soul of refinement. Looking around, he saw several smiling faces watching them. Duncan scowling. And Samantha had her back to them. Was Teresa trying to force his hand?

"Well!" she said brightly. "Perhaps you think you can get along without a wife. Certainly you have for a few years."

He hadn't answered, he realized. That was rude, yet . . . what could he say? He couldn't propose in public. Hadn't even thought about how to accomplish the deed . . . and that was unlike him. He was a man who planned ahead. Yet in this important matter, he was delaying.

Because of one kiss with another woman. Belatedly, he responded to Teresa. "I flatter myself I've done well with the servants—until now. I pray nothing else disappears."

He'd offended Teresa, for her mouth was puckered and she spoke too quickly. "I, too. Can I leave you to mix and mingle while I check to see if the silks I ordered for the ball have arrived?"

"Silks?" *How much did that cost?*

"To decorate the ceiling of the ballroom. Don't worry, your guests will be most impressed."

"I'm sure," he murmured, and tried to look as if he cared.

Apparently he didn't succeed, for she relaxed with a laugh. "I promise. I won't bother you with any more details."

"Thank you." As she strolled off, his gaze roamed over the crowd once more. His daughters had swept the visiting children, twelve in number, across the lawn to play croquet. The ladies had dispersed throughout the crowd, their higher tones adding a pleasant mix to the deeper voices of the men. Everything was perfect for a party—and for the baiting of a trap.

He met Duncan's troubled gaze. Lord and Lady Featherstonebaugh were not here. His men had reported their arrival at Maitland. His personal invitation had been sent over. Yet he'd had no reply, and his gut tightened. If this plan didn't work, they would have to arrest Lord and Lady Featherstonebaugh on an assumption of guilt, and that wouldn't be nearly as gratifying—or as undisputable—as first providing Pashenka with false information, then sending him on his way.

On the other hand—he straightened—since Lord and Lady Featherstonebaugh had failed to put in an appearance, he was free to go speak to Samantha.

The crowd of gentlemen around her had dispersed a little as three of the young officers tumbled away in a mock wrestling match. She didn't seem to notice William's approach, but when he spoke at her shoulder she smoothly turned to face him.

So. She had been conscious of him all along.

"You see, Miss Prendregast?" Aware of a dozen feminine pairs of eyes which observed his every move, he took care not to touch her. "I told you you would do very well at my party."

"Has no one ever told you that *I told you so* is a dreadful phrase?"

He caught himself before he laughed. "Only people to whom I say it."

She smiled, but without the open, gamine quality that always captivated him, and she didn't quite look at him. Rather, she looked past him, around him. To any onlooker, they shared nothing more than the bond of employment. "If you cannot be broken of the habit, I fear your chances for a waltz are much diminished among these lovely ladies."

"Yet I would have my waltz with you."

At his low-voiced declaration, her gaze sliced to his face, lingered for one long, shocked moment, then moved away.

He was content. With that one glance, she showed him her vulnerability to him, and her desire to be in his arms for whatever reason. And he, who had always hated to dance, fervently wished the ball was tonight so he could hold her against him and erase the remembrance of these besotted suitors who surrounded her.

Still she maintained her poise, and managed to sound prosaic and even slightly bored. "To answer your original comment—yes, I discover that I am rather good at this society whirl. It isn't difficult at all. I treat the gentlemen like small children, keep eye contact, pretend to be interested in their silly diatribes, and reprimand them lightly when their horseplay threatens to get out of hand."

"You're being sarcastic about my gender." Which he didn't really mind. He didn't want her to find traits to admire in the other men.

"Not at all. The gentlemen are very welcoming." She gestured toward the women. "With Lady Marchant's help, the ladies have been, too."

"How could they not be charmed?"

"Very easily, I fear. Ladies are not so distracted by a fashionable gown or a pretty accessory."

He wanted to laugh. Was she really so innocent? Yes, he knew she was. "Believe me, my dear, it is not your gown or your accessories that the men appreciate."

Her brow wrinkled. "You mean . . . they appreciate my figure? That's hardly likely. I'm quite thin, with scarcely a curve." She seemed to realize she'd been curt, for she added, "But thank you for the compliment."

If they had time alone, he could convince her of his appreciation. But the officers, the lords, and the gentlemen who had stayed out of their conversation out of respect for him found their respect wearing thin. They stomped and pawed the ground, grumbling under their breaths. After a glance at them, William gravely said, "Allow me to warn you. The younger officers are back from India, and rather wild after their return. Please view any suggestions to stroll in the garden or admire the stars with great suspicion."

"Unless I want to end in a wrestling match?"

Her eyes flashed with irritation, although how he'd irritated her, he didn't know. "Believe me, men in every class use the same sorry lures. I'm wise to them all."

Jealousy stabbed at him. "Have you had a great many men try to seduce you?"

"A great many, yes. None have succeeded. None will succeed. As I told you before, I am single, and pleased to remain so." Looking him over with withering scorn, she said, "Nothing has changed my mind."

She meant, of course, that *he* hadn't changed her mind. But she'd also inadvertently told him she hadn't found the other men attractive. He tamped down his satisfaction, but she must have seen it, for she stared, perplexed.

Duncan strode up. "Miss Prendregast, it's so good to see you again." But he wasn't paying attention to her, and Duncan always paid attention to women—unless he was working. "William, Lord and Lady Featherstonebaugh have arrived. You'll want to greet them yourself."

William swiveled to see Lady Featherstonebaugh hobbling across the lawn from the house, leaning heavily on her cane.

For the first time today, he touched Samantha. Just her gloved hand. Just once, lightly. A spark sprang between them.

Her brown eyes widened. She took a hard breath.

In a soft tone, he said, "Remember, you're not so experienced as you would like to imagine."

As he strode toward Lady Featherstonebaugh, he thought he heard Samantha murmur, "Nor am I as innocent as you would like to believe."

"Pardon me, gentlemen." After luncheon the next day, Samantha excused herself from the little group of gentlemen. "I have duties to perform."

"Colonel Gregory doesn't need you." Lieutenant Du Clos smiled gallantly, if a little edgily. He hadn't taken her determined indifference with any amount of grace. "He's talking with Lord and Lady Featherstonebaugh."

"It's not Colonel Gregory who needs me, but one of his children." Samantha curtsied and marched toward the house. Why did the lieutenant think her duties concerned William? Had she somehow betrayed her interest in Colonel Gregory? Had she smiled too sweetly, gazed at him too fondly?

She rubbed her head. This being in love was a difficult business to handle.

In love.

She tripped on the step going into the house. The footman caught her arm. She thanked him and kept walking, putting one foot in front of the other, hoping there were no more obstacles, glad no one remained inside the house, for right now she could no more navigate difficulties or make conversation than she could fly.

In love. With Colonel Gregory? It wasn't possible. That would be the height of stupidity.

All right. She admitted it. She was *attracted* to him. She found his figure alluring, his conversation stimulating, and the way he kissed inspiring. But that was all it was. A pathetic fascination with the way he kissed. That was why she watched his lips when he spoke, and imagined them on her skin. That was why she fretted half the night over what to wear on every occasion. She was trapped by his magnetism, nothing more. This constant heartache, this irresistible desire to dance in the sunshine, this need to see him night and day—this was not love. Not with a man so far above her station. Not with . . . not with any man. She knew better. She *did* know better.

Entering the empty music room, she went to the pianoforte. Opening it, she ran her fingers over the keys. When played as a background, the magnificent instrument blended in divine harmony with Mara's voice. Colonel Gregory would be proud of his daughter tomorrow. Her voice was everything he had promised.

Samantha frowned. But Mara herself . . . the child seemed distracted. Frightened. Overwhelmed by the challenge of singing for so many people.

Samantha understood. When Samantha's father had first decided she should earn her living, she had been four years old, standing on the street corner, grease smeared on her face to make her look more pathetic, singing for her supper. She'd been so frightened her voice had quavered, and no one gave her money. And she starved that night, for Da wouldn't feed a parasite. She'd gotten over her stage fright in a hurry, but she'd never forgotten the soul-shaking fear.

Her father. Yes. Whenever she imagined herself

in love, she should remember her father. Half Welsh, half mad. Those nights when he drank, and came in to fall unconscious on the bed. The days when he was sober and surly, searching for tuppence for his gin. The times when he was smiling, clean, well-dressed, bringing presents to his daughter and his wife. As a little child, she couldn't understand why her mother cried when he was so wonderful. Only later did she understand he'd found a woman, a rich woman to cajole and pleasure. He'd been handsome, her father, charming when he chose to be, and when she thought how he had ended . . . she put her hand over her eyes as if to shut out the memory.

Yes. When she softened with longing toward Colonel Gregory, she would remember Da.

She heard the clatter of boots on the hardwood floor, and hastily she lowered her hand.

Mara appeared in the doorway, cheeks flushed. "I'm sorry I'm late, Miss Prendregast, but a team of us were playing ball."

"That's why you're wearing your old clothes."

"Mrs. Chester insisted. She's already had to mend a tear on my new gown when I put too many rocks in my pocket and tore it loose." Mara appeared remarkably unrepentant.

Colonel Gregory had been right about Mrs. Chester. The little lady held absolute control over the children, no matter how many children there were, and her practical sense had proved infallible. Samantha no longer worried about Colonel Gregory's daughters; they were in good hands, at least for the duration of the party.

Samantha ran her fingers down the keys. "Shall we sing?"

Coming to the piano, Mara warmed up, then launched into a rendition of "Barbara Allen." Her voice was high and pure, singing the old ballad with touching innocence. Then, in the middle of the second stanza, she stopped and faced the piano. "Do you know where my father goes at night?"

Samantha dropped her hands into her lap. Her heart sped up. What did Mara mean? Had she seen William kissing Samantha? "Have you seen your father go somewhere at night?"

"Yes! Father rides out on his horse every night."

"Oh." Samantha's breath calmed. "You mean—when he catches robbers."

"No—worse than robbers." Mara sounded absolutely matter-of-fact.

"Who could be worse than robbers?"

"I don't know, but he caught one last night."

He'd caught more than a robber. He'd caught Samantha. *In love.* She was a fool. "Good for him," she said to Mara. "It's wonderful that your papa is so brave and keeps us all safe. You must be very proud of him."

Mara shrugged. "Yes, Miss Prendregast." The child watched her, head tilted, toe tapping.

Samantha's suspicions stirred. "How did you find out about your father?"

Mara lifted her chin. "I was hiding under the desk in Father's study, and I heard him and Mr. Monroe talking."

"This morning?"

"Yes."

Times like these tested a governess to her utmost. Samantha held out her arms. "Come here, dear." When Mara came and nestled next to her on the piano bench, she embraced the child and smoothed her hair back from her forehead. "Do you know you're not supposed to eavesdrop?"

"Yes, but I wasn't supposed to be in the study, either, so I had no choice." Mara shrugged. "Father would have yelled at me."

That made absolute sense to the child and, sadly, to Samantha. "Yes, well . . . don't hide like that anymore."

"I promise."

"It would be best if you didn't tell anyone else about your papa's activities. That would be dangerous for your father." Samantha's mind swiftly built a scenario in which William confronted a robber, was caught off guard, shot, writhed in the dirt of the road while the robber lifted his other pistol—

"I know that," Mara said scornfully. "I only told *you*. I can tell you anything. Can't I?"

Mara's quavering voice yanked Samantha's attention back to the girl in her arms. She recognized trouble when she heard it. "Absolutely. Did you want to tell me something else?"

"Yes . . . no."

"Do you want me to guess?"

"No." Pushing her way out of Samantha's arms, Mara took her place beside the piano. "I want to sing."

There was no forcing the child's confession, but

when Mara had finished the melody, Samantha tried to reassure her. "You'll sing tonight, and you'll be the hit of the party. I promise. And your father will be so proud of you."

Mara's face fell. "Miss Prendregast?"

"What is it, dear?"

"About . . . about . . . it's about . . ." Mara took several audible breaths.

"When you sing tonight, you'll forget all your fears and your troubles, and you'll be transported to a different plane."

"Yes, ma'am, I believe that, but . . ." Mara looked at Samantha with hopeless eyes. "It's not that."

"Then what?"

"Miss Prendregast, I can tell you anything." Mara's voice rose an octave. "Can't I?"

The same question. Samantha stood and wrapped her arm around Mara's shoulders. "Absolutely."

"Even if it's—" A stampede outside the door stopped Mara. She stared at the door as the other Gregory children burst in.

"We've come to practice our song," Agnes said.

"We're going to practice! We're going to practice!" Kyla and Emmeline jumped up and down and clapped their hands.

Mara broke away from Samantha. "Yes, I love to practice our song!"

Samantha wanted to call her back, but . . . she looked all right now. Hopefully everything would work out for Mara, for Colonel Gregory—and for Samantha.

Samantha had only to remember who she was, and where she'd come from, and never, ever admit her love for the children's father to anyone.

Including herself.

❧ *Chapter Nineteen* ❧

That evening, in the music room, as those horrible Gregory children sang some pitiful song, Lady Featherstonebaugh nodded agreeably and tapped her toe. A wolf in sheep's clothing, that was she. A woman of wit disguised as a dear old grandmotherly type. At least for now. She touched her split lip. At least until her bruises healed.

She hated Pashenka with all her heart. If not for him, she would soon be in Italy where she had money in the bank, a false identity, and the sunshine to heat her aching bones. Aching because he'd knocked her down, the blackguard, trying to force information from her.

It had taken a long, painful half hour before Pashenka had revealed his hand. There was a party over at Colonel Gregory's. A party of high-ranking military men, ambassadors, and even an official from the Home Office or two. Pashenka, the weasel, didn't want to take a chance that someone knew of his defection. He wanted her to go. She and Rupert. He promised that if she did this, and came back with enough information, he would allow her to live.

So here she was, sitting in the back row, listening to a bunch of children caterwaul while their father beamed proudly. Today she had sat all alone in a comfortable chair in one of the alcoves in the great hall, and sat alone in an uncomfortable chair in one of those stupid tents for luncheon. After supper, she would don a handsome ball gown so she would have the privilege of watching other people dance.

Her split lip and aching hip kept her smiles to a minimum, and that was unusual for her. Usually she flattered and smirked and socialized with the best of them, and always kept her ears open while she did. Now she had to sit like an old woman and wait for people to come close, and speak of matters better kept secret.

And actually . . . they did. As always, the generals and the diplomats failed to realize her canny intelligence and saw only an old woman who frequently nodded off, and never seemed to hear well. They spoke of troops in Crimea and Egypt, of spies, of explosions and munitions. In their words she heard the clinking of gold. Or she would . . . if she could safely escape from Pashenka.

Rupert sidled down the row of chairs to her and sat down so closely, his leg rested on her posh lavender velvet skirt. Damn the man. He could always be depended upon to call attention to himself—and to wrinkle her clothing. In a stage whisper, he asked, "Valda, where's that map?"

Incredulous, she stared at the line of people sitting before her. Quietly she commanded, "Cease your blather. We can't talk here."

"No one can hear us. The children are singing."

She stared at him in disbelief. That was why he'd never become a preeminent spy. He saw what he wanted, acted as he pleased.

His voice rose a little. "I'm your husband. I'm the man, and I say you should give that map to Pashenka."

"For pity's sake." Lady Marchant sat in front of them, and three of the other decorative women. "They can hear you."

"They're not paying any heed, and even if they were, they wouldn't understand."

As if she were listening to some husbandly wit, Valda curled her lips at the corners and kept her voice low and well modulated. "Never underestimate the power of gossip. If, in their ignorance, they repeated this conversation, we would have trouble."

"I don't care." But Rupert lowered his voice. "Just give Pashenka the map, or there'll be more trouble."

"For whom?" She examined him: his hooked, thin nose, his long fingers, his skinny calves in their old-fashioned hose. "And why? He doesn't know about the map."

Rupert opened his mouth, then shut it.

Grasping his arm, she dug in her fingers. "Does he?"

His eyes shifted from side to side.

"You told him?" Her voice rose.

"If you give him the map, he won't hurt you again." Ever since Rupert had seen her slammed against the wall, he'd been more sober, more aware of the danger stalking them. Oh, he would still abandon her in a minute if he thought he could flee without repercussions. He wasn't clever enough to do it, and so he played his part for Pashenka. He watched her, for if she escaped without him, he was dead.

"No," she said sarcastically, "if I give him the map, he'll kill me . . . us."

"No, he won't. He promised he wouldn't."

She smiled in chilly disbelief. Sliding her hand into her pocket, she fingered the pistol she'd stolen from Colonel Gregory's collection, and thought how grand, how much gratification she would get, from shooting Rupert. "Until I set foot on Italian soil, I am a walking corpse—and I'll take you to the grave with me, Rupert, so don't betray me."

"Where is the map?" he whined.

So Pashenka was in contact with Rupert, pulling his strings, trying to make her reveal her secrets. Did Pashenka think her stupid? Once she'd given him the map, he would kill her and escape from England, and use the knowledge she'd obtained to secure his own safety.

So. She had to make yet another plan. When she returned to Maitland, she would promise Pashenka the map. Maybe even give it to him, if he threatened her. But she would keep the secrets she'd learned at this party in her head. She'd say she would only speak to his supervisor—in Russia.

Nonsense, of course. His supervisor would kill her with even less emotion that Pashenka, but she had to buy herself some time. Time to hatch an escape plan. And what better way to spend her time than listening to English military secrets?

No matter what the challenge, she had always survived and thrived. She would do so again.

She smiled. And winced as her healing lip split.

William stood, arms folded, and listened as his children sang for the guests. They wore their jewel-toned gowns, stood with their toes on an invisible line. Lovely in a satin of so pale a pink it matched the color on her cheeks, Samantha played the piano in accompaniment, a faint smile on her beguiling countenance. When the girls had finished, they curtsied and posed while the other parents clapped, and murmured words like, "Charming," and "Delightful." Every one of them was beaming, seeing in the colonel's children the promise of their own.

At Samantha's whispered instruction, Agnes and Vivian pushed Mara to the forefront, and Mara bowed by herself. The clapping increased, and through a haze of fatherly conceit, William heard calls of, "Brava!"

Before the cheering had completely died, Samantha herded the girls from the music room, holding Emmeline's hand so she couldn't throw kisses to the crowd.

"That was charming, Colonel Gregory," Lady Blair complimented. "You have extremely talented children."

"Of course." He grinned as if his daughters were the finest choir in the world . . . which he was convinced they were. "They have an extremely talented father."

Everyone laughed. They were pleased with the entertainment, with the food, and with the wine. They were pleased with Teresa's place settings and decorations. And those who knew the real purpose of the party were ecstatic about the presence of Lord and Lady Featherstonebaugh, as well as the attentiveness Lady Featherstonebaugh showed whenever people of importance stood near her and spoke in "confidence" about English troop movements, about plans for sabotage, even of ways to infiltrate the Russian embassy in Paris.

Yes. Everything was proceeding as William had planned.

Everything except his courtship of Teresa.

Outside the door, he saw Mrs. Chester take the children under her wing, and gesture that Samantha should return.

He cared nothing about marrying Teresa, and all because of Samantha. It was her fault that he was distracted from his duties. Her fault he viewed an appropriate marriage with such indifference.

As always, Samantha's presence brought a buzz of excitement. This time it wasn't only from the young men. More than one parent was eyeing Samantha avariciously, and would try to steal his governess when they left.

As the guests drifted back toward the repast the servants had set up in the dining hall, Duncan raised his glass to Samantha. "The girls' governess did a wonderful job of organizing this display."

"Yes. She did indeed." That was all William said, but he looked at Samantha.

And she blushed.

Lady Stephens halted, and beside her, General Stephens halted, too. They looked from Samantha to William and back again. They were seeing too much in his gaze, in her lowered eyes and too-still figure, and others began to notice, too. William didn't want people nattering about him and his governess. Except that, if they did, everything would be so simple. If he destroyed her reputation with so simple a ruse, he would have to wed her, and for some reason, that sounded like a grand scheme.

Had she spun a web of magic about him, that he should think such folly?

"Well!" Duncan clapped his hands together loudly, making people jump, distracting everyone's attention. "Let's go in and eat. I, for one, can't wait, and I need a dinner partner." He swaggered toward Teresa.

Turning her back, Teresa walked ahead of him out of the door.

The guests gasped and gave their consideration to the scorned Duncan, who in typical roguish style said, "I'm irresistible to the ladies."

With much laughter, everyone walked toward the dining hall where the informal meal was laid out, one that would carry the guests through tonight's ball until midnight, when supper would be served.

Duncan sidled up to William. "Stop staring at Miss Prendregast."

Lieutenant Du Clos offered Samantha his arm, and she accepted it. She listened to the lieutenant, but her gaze brushed William's, and he felt the sensation from the cut of his hair to the tips of his toes. She affected him, every moment. He wanted to stalk her like a stallion after a mare. He wanted to mount her from behind, hold her hips and plunge into her. He wanted to lay her on her back and part her legs, and kiss her between them until she screamed with bliss. He wanted her to take him in her mouth . . .

As quickly as he could, he walked out of the music room. It was all very well to fantasize about being a stallion. It was quite another to look like one.

"That was close, and it involved my own humiliation." Duncan spoke in the soft voice he'd perfected on the long nights of hunting. "I hope you're grateful—"

William noted with approval that Lady Featherstonebaugh hobbled along on Lord Hartun's arm, listening closely.

"—But I see you're not," Duncan concluded. "It's a fascinating thing. You watch Miss Prendregast. Lady Marchant watches you."

"And you watch Lady Marchant." William nodded as the guests called out compliments on his children's singing. "What have you done that Teresa should snub you like that?"

In a deadpan tone, Duncan said, "She fancies me, and she doesn't want to fancy me."

"Really?" Without suffering a single pang of jealousy, William considered the situation. "And you fancy her?"

"Like mad. And, well, hell, you don't want her."

"I didn't say that."

"You don't have to. It's obvious to me, at least."

William accepted a glass of wine from a passing footman. "She's rich. You haven't a farthing."

Duncan watched Teresa's regal back as she led the guests to the buffet table. "I could make her happy." Stopping suddenly, he pulled William aside, out of the crowd and into the empty smoking room. "Wait. You mean . . . you don't care? Not one bit?" In a meticulous tone, he said, "I'm talking about seducing the woman who fulfilled every requirement on your wife list."

"She's not the only woman who does." William fixed Duncan with a stern glance. "And you should, just once, consider having honorable intentions."

Duncan examined William, and what he saw must have made him happy, for he relaxed and grinned. "I might, where Teresa's concerned, but I'll have to tread carefully. And you're a fine one to talk. You're doing a good job ruining Miss Prendregast's reputation, and with nothing more than a glance."

It was a day for admissions. "There's been more than a glance. I kissed her."

"Once?"

"Once."

"Hell, that isn't worth going to confession for. Are you tempted to do more?" Duncan laughed. "Of course you are. You've made that clear."

"I shouldn't." Not until . . . but he must concentrate on the success of their mission before he made his move.

"Why not? I told you the first time I saw her she was the one for you." Duncan nudged him with his elbow. "Come on! You've done what's right your whole life. Have a little fun."

"Take her as my mistress, do you mean?" William shook his head. "It wouldn't be fair to her. She's an innocent."

"Oh." Duncan's sideburns drooped, and he sighed. "Back to sleeping with your cock in your hand."

"Anyway, it's not possible." William was relieved. "I placed her in one of the cottages, far away from me."

Duncan stopped in the act of taking a sip. "You moved her—"

"Out of the house."

"—And into a cottage, where you and she can have a bacchanal all night long without worrying about your children?"

William's jaw dropped.

Duncan slapped him on the shoulder. "Good work, mate. You'll never sleep in your own bed again."

William followed Duncan and watched as his friend sauntered into the dining hall.

Is that what William had done? Is that why he'd

been so willing to let Samantha escape from under his roof? Had he, in the depths of his mind, been plotting to get her out so he could spend the nights in her arms?

He didn't know himself. He didn't know himself at all.

He stood listening to the clink of silverware, the voices . . . Samantha's voice. He loved her voice. Rather deep for a woman, husky and soft, as if she'd been making love all night long and had worn herself out with moaning. Her voice alone made a man want to see if he could make her moan. And William could. He knew he could.

She was alone in that cottage with only Clarinda for a chaperone, and most of the time, Clarinda had her duties in the house, so . . .

Duncan came out of the dining hall as if he were shot from a cannon. Out of the corner of his mouth, he spoke to William. "In your study. Now." He kept walking.

Now? No, not until William's condition had subsided, for Duncan would know what caused it and no matter how important the information he'd discovered—and from the looks of things, he had discovered something magnificent indeed—he would still take the time to mock William. Perhaps he had reason. By God, William was thirty-four years old, the father of six, a rampart of propriety and honor. To spend his time behaving like a randy schoolboy was embarrassing and . . . well . . . rather gratifying. He grinned. Better not tell Duncan *that*.

He strolled along, taking care to smile and nod

as he passed a single guest, hurrying to catch the meal, and when he reached his study, he was back to normal. Or what used to be normal, before the advent of Miss Prendregast. Stepping inside, he shut the door behind him. "What is it?"

Duncan stepped out of the shadows, and his usually cheerful face was gaunt and worried. "That damned fool Featherstonebaugh. Teresa heard him talking to Lady Featherstonebaugh."

At once, William concentrated. "Where?"

"In the music room, just now." Duncan pulled a long face. "It's not as if he's devious."

William nodded. "Why did Teresa come to you?"

"Because she thought the conversation odd, and you weren't in the dining hall to tell." Duncan's eyes flashed with irritation. "Listen! Featherstonebaugh said Lady Featherstonebaugh should give the map to Pashenka or there would be more trouble."

"Map?" William's mouth turned grim.

"Teresa didn't hear everything, but it sounds as if Lady Featherstonebaugh stole a map on the way up here and she's holding it as a surety so Pashenka won't"—Duncan shrugged and shoved his hands in his pockets—"kill her."

"So Pashenka did give her those bruises."

"I think we can safely assume that."

"I'd feel sorry for her . . . if she hadn't caused so many deaths." *His wife. Mary.* William's hands clenched convulsively. To think of her dying like that . . . "What map could it be?"

"They stayed at Captain Farwell's home on the way up here." Duncan stroked the whiskers that feathered down his cheeks. "Send a messenger to him and find out, but really, it doesn't matter. Lady Featherstonebaugh's a damned sharp woman. You know the map is important."

William's mind raced. "Where is it?"

"Featherstonebaugh didn't know." Duncan paced to the desk. "The old fool would betray her if he could."

"Probably." William had some of the most powerful, intelligent men in the nation at his party under his command, but none of them were in field operations. None of them were worth a damn in a situation like this. "Tonight, when the ball starts, you'll search their bedchamber, but she'd be as big a fool as her husband if she kept that map anywhere but on her person."

"That's what I thought." Duncan fiddled with the pens on William's desk. "We could arrest her and take it from her."

"But we want to send her back to him with all the false information she's gleaned at the party."

Duncan picked up one of the pens and examined it, then lifted a quizzical brow at William. "I don't suppose we can make an old woman strip down?"

"You're the great seducer." William grinned. "You do it."

Duncan stroked his chin and pretended to think about it. "I just remembered. I'm not such a great seducer, after all."

"We need to do an exchange."

Duncan nodded. "Give her a fake map for the real one."

"If we knew where it was, and if someone could pull off that trick, we'd do it." William considered and discarded strategy after strategy. "But who, and how?"

❧ *Chapter Twenty* ❧

Teresa viewed her pièce de resistance. To the wonderment of all, the peach-colored silks hung from the ceilings and draped down the walls, transforming the ballroom into a plush pastel harem. The crystal chandeliers sparkled above with a thousand beeswax candles. The orchestra played with precise brilliance. Champagne flowed freely, and the ladies were swamped with invitations to dance—of course, with the difference in numbers, how could it be otherwise? The gentlemen gathered in knots, talking in serious tones, and only occasionally did they visit the card room or go outside for a smoke—always a good sign that they were enjoying themselves. Even William was keeping his attention on the business at hand, rather than staring like a lovestruck adolescent at Samantha. In fact, he looked very serious, and Mr. Duncan Monroe was missing.

Good. If all went well, he would stay missing.

As Teresa gazed across the glittering assemblage, she couldn't remember doing anything dreadfully wrong in her childhood. She'd been reasonably obedient, willing to learn, smart enough to stay out of trouble, a comfort to her parents, but . . . obviously she was paying for some celestial sin, because nothing, absolutely nothing had gone right about this party. About this whole trip.

First, there was William with his ridiculous infatuation with the governess. Gossip spread like wildfire, but Teresa had not learned to handle social crises for nothing. Throughout the houseparty, she had frequently stopped and visited with Samantha, and always spoke of her in glowing terms to the biggest gossips at the party. She had even made sure Samantha's ballgown of royal blue satin broche was perfect, adding lace on the skirt and miniature white roses to the neckline. She had stifled the worst of the rumors, but if William continued to watch Samantha as he did, Teresa would be helpless to stem the tide.

And the longer she was with William, the more she wondered if she cared enough to have him. She liked him well enough. But . . .

Well. That led to the second problem, Mr. Duncan Monroe, formerly of the Third King's Own Light Dragoons and still a royal pain in the fanny. He watched *her*, Teresa. Watched her so hungrily she occasionally found herself fanning her hot cheeks and marveling at the power of that man's warm gaze. What he had not cared about before now interested him, and he couldn't have made it more clear. And she . . . she didn't want anything to do with it.

Well. She did. But pride stopped her. Pride, and . . . a woman made plans. A woman had a right to change those plans, but Teresa didn't change her plans under pressure, and Mr. Monroe was putting her under pressure. Not with words, but with that heart-stopping intense gaze. Flipping open her fan, she once against fanned her hot cheeks.

And now, further proof Teresa must have sinned at some point in her past—Lady Featherstonebaugh was limping toward her. Lady Featherstonebaugh, who started talking before she reached Teresa. "What an extraordinary young woman Colonel Gregory has hired as his governess."

Teresa viewed the older woman critically. Her straw-colored silk gown with its narrow sleeves and low lace collar would have been appropriate for an ingénue, never for any woman over forty, and certainly not for a lady forced to lean on her cane to walk across the marble floor. Her gilded feather fan and the gilded feather in her hair were nice touches, but somehow the shimmer made Lady Featherstonebaugh look tired. In fact, she had bags under her eyes as if she weren't sleeping well. Guilt, Teresa decided affably. Guilt about that mysterious map. She'd been furious with Lord Featherstonebaugh for mentioning the map, and Duncan had been in a dither when Teresa had told him about the conversation she'd overheard. Apparently, the map was of some importance, although why Teresa didn't know, or care.

"Miss Prendregast can play, she can sing, she can care for children, she has every man at the gathering panting over her . . . she can seduce her employer . . ." The orchestra played, the dancers swirled across the floor, and Lady Featherstonebaugh smiled beatifically. "Rather mortifying, heh, Lady Marchant?"

Teresa did *not* like Lady Featherstonebaugh. She had never liked Lady Featherstonebaugh, and Lady Featherstonebaugh energetically returned the favor as she did with every woman of her acquaintance. Teresa thought the woman vapid and cruel, and growing bitter in her old age. Here was the proof. The first conversation they'd passed, and Lady Featherstonebaugh was already sticking needles in Teresa's hide. Needles that drew blood. "Don't worry about Colonel Gregory. I don't. Miss Prendregast is a sensible female, as well as lovely, and she knows better than to set her sights on a man as wealthy and landed as he."

"Someone had better tell him, then. He's been making cow eyes at her for two days." Lady Featherstonebaugh flipped her hand, dismissing the subject now that she'd painstakingly planted the seed of apprehension. "But that's not why I came over. I wanted someone to confide in. Another woman . . . and there are blasted few in this gathering." Leaning closer, she lowered her voice. "I've remembered where I heard Miss Prendregast's name."

Teresa's ears perked up, although she took care not to let on. "Have you indeed?"

"Miss Prendregast is that infamous cutpurse who haunted London about six years ago. She used to hang about the theater and take the gentlemen's wallets, and all the gentlemen would brag about how she flashed them a smile as she escaped." Closing her fan, Lady Featherstonebaugh pressed the handle to her puckered lips. "I suppose Colonel Gregory should be told about that, eh?"

Stricken dumb, Teresa stared at Lady Featherstonebaugh, pristine in her chic garments that failed to promote the illusion of youth, with spots of rouge highlighting her cheeks . . . or was that the faintest of bruises?

Then the import of Lady Featherstonebaugh's revelation registered. *Damnation.* Teresa remembered the tale now. Adorna had taken the girl-thief under her wing and taught her how to walk, to talk, to read, to teach. As a governess, the girl had a reputation for being a fearless defender of her charges, and she'd taken down that idiot Wordlaw. Teresa had applauded her for that. Now . . . what should she do with this knowledge? She couldn't decide immediately, but she would enjoy spiking Lady Featherstonebaugh's guns. Taking a glass of champagne from a passing footman, she sipped it with a fair imitation of boredom. "I know who you're talking about, but dear, you've the name wrong. It's Miss Penny Gast"—she enunciated clearly—"who's the pickpocket. It's an easy mistake to make." She sipped again. "Especially for the elderly with their hearing troubles."

Lady Featherstonebaugh heard *that* well enough. She turned a delightful shade of purple. Her headdress trembled as she shook with rage, and for one moment, Teresa wondered if she should move out of range of that cane. Instead in a low, intense voice, Lady Featherstonebaugh asked, "Are you sure?"

"My dear lady, I like attention as well as the next woman, and Miss Prendregast is getting most of it." Teresa blinked in her patented, *aren't I innocent* look. "Don't you think I would take care of the matter if it were so easy?"

Lady Featherstonebaugh nodded and swallowed. "Yes. I suppose you would." Groping at her side, she found her black-spangled reticule and squeezed it until something inside crumpled. "I need to sit down."

"Would you like assistance?" Teresa meant it. Since her arrival, Lady Featherstonebaugh had been hobbling badly, as if all the gout in the world had caught up with her. Not that it didn't serve her right. Teresa had never met such a malicious old woman, but that didn't make watching her pain any easier.

"I can make it over to my alcove." Lady Featherstonebaugh grinned at Teresa with such implicit evil, Teresa stepped back. "I hear very well over there."

As she left, Teresa rubbed the goose bumps on her arms. If she could, Lady Featherstonebaugh would hurt her. Hurt them all. Teresa looked for Samantha and found her speaking to Lord Hartun. Certainly Lady Featherstonebaugh would hurt Samantha if she could—and she could.

Excuses could be made for Lady Featherstonebaugh. The woman's husband pranced across the floor with one of the young matrons, his hands meandering over her back. The filthy old lecher would drive any woman to folly and cruelty, but Teresa doubted he'd had much influence on his wife. Lady Featherstonebaugh was too strong-willed.

Teresa's gaze wandered to William. He stood speaking in a low voice to that worthless mongrel, Duncan Monroe, who had finally decided to put in an appearance. Duncan . . . William's best friend. Duncan—always taunting, always watching . . . always desirable. Damn his eyes.

She jerked her gaze back to William. William and Duncan had been having a lot of those low-voiced conferences. Duncan had certainly flown out of the dining hall when she told him about that map, and neither he nor William had made an appearance at the supper. And only the night before, when the other guests had gone to bed, she had sneaked downstairs to get a drink of whisky—ladies were never offered whisky, their constitutions were too delicate—and she'd heard their two voices in William's study. Although she'd pressed a glass against the door, she'd been unable to pick out more than a few words. *Featherstonebaugh*, and *Pashenka*, although when she'd left London Count Pashenka had put forth the rumor he was ill, when in fact everyone knew he'd left for some assignation.

Had he come here to the Lake District? Had William and Duncan accidentally picked him up on one of their night rides? It seemed a stupid mistake to make, especially for two relatively intelligent men, but they'd made the same mistake with her . . .

She stared down at the bubbles in her glass, and her eyes narrowed.

Featherstonebaugh. Pashenka. William and Duncan's thief-catching activities.

Her head jerked up. She scrutinized the ballroom.

Too many generals. Too many ambassadors. Too many dark-clad men who had neither the antecedents nor the money to be present at a party like this, but who exuded power and secrecy. Men from the Home Office. She had recognized them, although she hadn't realized the import of their attendance.

She saw William again, and Duncan. They hadn't stopped her coach because they thought her a bandit. They'd feared she was a spy, fleeing London on the heels of her leader, Count Pashenka. Oh, yes. Teresa had lived in India, known firsthand the rivalry between England and Russia for the riches of the East. Knew full well that spies operated in every city and on every mountaintop in India. She hadn't realized they were here in England, too.

Well. Now she knew better.

Spies. She had landed in a nest of spies.

* * *

Samantha thanked Mr. Langdon for the dance—his second and last tonight—and excused herself. The doors onto the veranda were open, the breeze billowed the peach silks, but as midnight neared, it was growing warm in the ballroom, and Samantha was growing weary. Weary of the dancing, the constant chatting, the endless flattery, and the fact that Colonel Gregory had not once sought that waltz from her. Instead, he'd been distracted, speaking seriously to Mr. Monroe, and then to Lord Hartun.

Not that Samantha cared, really. She might fancy herself in love with Colonel Gregory, but she valued love as it should be valued, as puffs of smoke up a chimney to hover and dissipate in the wind. Perhaps if she kissed other men, she would fancy herself in love with them instead.

Yes. That was a sound plan. She'd kiss and compare, and under the influence of other men's passion, this ache in the region of her heart would dissipate and she would once again be herself, Miss Samantha Prendregast, independent, willful, and sure.

She smiled, nodded, curtsied, nodded, smiled, and escaped to the elegant and empty ladies' retiring room. Mirrors lined the walls, stools sat before every table, with pitchers of water, handkerchiefs, and powder there for anyone's use. With a sigh of relief, she poured water into a basin, dipped in a handkerchief, wrung it out and blotted her face. It was cool. Blessedly cool. She closed her eyes in bliss.

At once the picture of Colonel Gregory sprang to

mind. No other man wore clothes as he did. His dark blue jacket hugged his shoulders, his brocade waistcoat embraced his waist, a pair of black trousers clung to his thighs like . . . well, like she would if she lacked good sense. But she had plenty of good sense, and just because she liked to look at him didn't mean she was slipping down the slippery slope toward dissipation.

And his face . . . a dozen men here were more handsome, but his features were noble, rugged, manly. A woman knew from the way he held himself, by his expression, that he would take care of her. And when he looked at Samantha . . . she slithered onto a stool. When he looked at Samantha, her knees went weak and prudence failed her.

She heard footsteps, light and sharp. Gorblimey. Someone was coming.

She arranged her features to an expression of ease. An expression she was hard-pressed to keep when Lady Marchant walked in in a billow of cherry-red silk and rose perfume, champagne glass in hand.

"I was looking for you," Lady Marchant said.

What had Samantha done now?

Lady Marchant seated herself on a stool opposite, and placed her glass on the table with a decided clink. She took Samantha's hands—a move that made Samantha decidedly nervous. "You're all alone in the world," she said. "There's no one to give you advice, so I'm going to."

"All right." *Why?*

"Du Clos is charming, but poor. You've made a conquest of Mr. Langdon. He's a widower with eight thousand a year. Of course, you'd have to look at that face every morning across the breakfast table, so that's something to consider. Lord Hartun . . . I would be careful. He's eminently eligible, but it's a noble old title and I doubt his family would accept you even if he lost his head so far as to propose."

Bewilderment fought with cynicism as Samantha tried to understand Lady Marchant's motives. Selfish, surely, but the lady looked so . . . ablaze with sincerity. Determined. And almost . . . uncomfortable with her role as mentor. Samantha swallowed twice before she could speak. "My lady, I don't . . . I'm not here to find a husband."

"Then you're a pretty fool." Lady Marchant's mouth was firmly set, her eyes decided. "You have them eating out of your hand. They don't care that you're a governess. With a little labor on your part, you could be a wife. You'd never have to work for a living again."

Samantha tossed the handkerchief into the basin, where it landed with a splash. "I like to work."

"Nonsense. I like you. I don't why. I shouldn't, but I do." Glancing toward the door, she lowered her voice. "Lady Featherstonebaugh has recognized you. From London. From the streets."

At once, Samantha comprehended. Recognized. Caught. A thief. Forever. Perhaps Lady Featherstonebaugh was telling William now, and the next time he looked at her, his eyes would flash with contempt. This was what she'd been afraid of. As she inhaled, the air hurt her lungs. "Ruddy 'ell." The words slipped out. She wanted to snatch them back, then she realized—what did it matter? Lady Marchant *knew*. "I suppose I'll have to leave. At once."

Lady Marchant grabbed her arm and shook it. "No. I covered for you. I told her she was wrong. You're safe. I'm telling you, if you catch a husband fast enough, he won't find out until it's too late."

Samantha didn't understand why Lady Marchant was saying these things. "That's . . . horrible. Then I'll be stuck with a husband who's ashamed of me."

"Better that than no husband at all." Teresa waved her hands impatiently. "You have a notoriety that already has a certain kind of luster about it. With a rich husband on your arm, you'll be feted, not avoided."

"And if my husband is angered at being so tricked?" Samantha well remembered how much a blow from a fist could hurt.

"It doesn't matter. You're pretty and exotic enough to keep him entertained for a year or so. He'll want an heir and a spare and then he'll be off with his mistress anyway. That's the way the game is played." Teresa toasted Samantha with her champagne, then tossed back the rest of it. "Is it any different in your lower classes?"

Samantha released an unwilling, cynical gust of laughter. "No. Marriage is the same everywhere. That's why I remain unmarried."

"Good luck to you with that." Lady Marchant's lips curled with distaste. "I'm a lady—a lady with a fortune, and I need a husband to be invited to all the right places and to be seen with all the right people."

Lady Marchant had been blunt. Lady Marchant had done her a favor. Samantha spied a chance to do both in return. "You've accomplished that. Wouldn't you rather be rolling, naked, under the sheets with the man you love?"

Lady Marchant took a sharp, shocked breath. "What do you mean?"

"You know very well what I mean. I like you, too. I don't why. I shouldn't, but I do." She was telling the truth, Samantha realized, and that both startled and amused her. "You're the kind of lady who's done everything right her whole life. Married the right man, entertained the right people, worn the right clothes, all for . . . what? Not yourself, that's for certain."

"I like my clothes and my . . . the people I entertain."

Samantha considered her, trying to understand, and at last she did. "You can't even call them your friends."

Pale and defensive, Lady Marchant said, "Friendship's not everything."

A pang of loneliness struck Samantha, a longing to talk to Adorna and the other girls at the Distinguished Academy of Governesses. "Yet I miss my friends." For a moment that befuddled, confused woman looked like a friend, too, and Samantha broke one of her own rules. She gave advice. "Mr. Monroe wants you so badly. He'd show you a fancy time."

"It wouldn't last," Lady Marchant said immediately.

"What does, my lady?" Samantha heard the cynicism in her own voice. "What does?"

Lady Marchant's mouth worked. Then she firmed her quivering chin. "By the time this party is over, I intend on acquiring a husband." Bending her gaze meaningfully on Samantha, she said, "The biggest prize of all."

Colonel Gregory. Of course. "If you do that, you'll both be cheated." When Lady Marchant would have protested, Samantha held up a restraining hand. "I've never doubted you would bring him in. I think it's a shame, when you have a man waiting in the wings who urgently wants you. Nevertheless, I wish you happy hunting."

Apparently Samantha's wishes weren't enough for Lady Marchant. "You can't have him. Do you know the story of his wife's death?"

"No, my lady." Samantha didn't want to hear, but she listened with morbid fascination.

Lady Marchant spoke rapidly, as if she wanted to get the tale out and done. "We were all stationed in Kashmir, a lovely place in the mountains. Cool, spectacularly beautiful. We each lived in our own compound, and I don't know exactly how to explain the loneliness of living in a country where everything was foreign . . . and the natives hated us. Someone would send out an invitation, and we went. We traveled miles to see old friends, to catch up on gossip from home, to hear English spoken without an accent." She stared at Samantha, but she was seeing a place and a time long gone. "There was always some sort of unrest, fed by the Russians, and when there was, William always volunteered to lead the battalion. Right before the biggest party of the year, our soldiers were called out to quash an uprising. So once again he marched away."

Samantha swallowed. Foolish to worry about a man who had obviously survived the danger . . . but she did.

"Mary was angry, and that was unusual, for Mary was the gentlest of souls. She adored William. She always let him get away with whatever he wanted. She wanted to return to England, but he didn't, so they stayed. She wanted the children to go to English schools, but he didn't, so they stayed. She missed her family . . . I told her so much indulgence wasn't good for a husband, but she didn't listen to me." Lady Marchant flipped her hand to indicate the dismissal. "Anyway, she never asked William for anything, but she wanted to go to that party to see her friends. He told her no, to stay home. I don't know why she disobeyed him that night—I suppose they'd quarreled—but she set off on her own. She never arrived." Her voice broke.

Samantha handed over her own handkerchief and wished she had another one. This was worse than she'd imagined, to hear about William's wife, to imagine how she'd suffered and died.

Lady Marchant dabbed tears from her eyes. "They found her body the next morning. Thieves had run the carriage off the road. Mary was killed instantly, thank God, but the thieves killed the coachman and the servants and stripped everyone of jewels and clothes."

Lady Marchant was reliving the horror, and she dragged Samantha into it with her. "Poor woman," Samantha said. And more important, "Poor children." Did they know their mother had been stripped and tossed into the ditch like offal?

"William was never a tolerant man, but after that, he was a man possessed. He became a martinet. He hunted down the robbers and had them hung. He hunted down every Russian and rebel and thief in Kashmir." Lady Marchant shuddered. "He brought the children back to England and established himself as the colonel of his own private regiment of girls. I have no doubt he told himself it was for their safety. He blamed himself for Mary's death."

"I would say he had reason," Samantha answered softly. Poor William, with that sense of responsibility that he both suffered from and cherished. How he must have mourned and raged at the death of his beloved wife. How he must have sought revenge . . .

"Absolutely, he did. He had taken Mary for granted. He didn't realize what he had in her until she was gone. God." Crushing the handkerchief in her hand, Lady Marchant breathed heavily.

Stricken by an epiphany, Samantha said, "You're angry at him for neglecting her."

"He won't treat me like that, I assure you." Lady

Marchant's eyes sparkled with a combination of tears and rage. "But Samantha, I swear to you. You'd better leave William to me. He would forgive you anything, but never being a thief."

❧ *Chapter Twenty-one* ❧

The music floated out of the ballroom, the moonlight silvered the lawn and the lake, and, to William's indignation, Samantha stood on the veranda speaking to a leering Lieutenant Du Clos.

What is she thinking? Only yesterday, she had assured William she would not be caught alone with the lieutenant, a decision William had applauded. Now she leaned against the railing, her body a graceful, desirable curve, and watched Du Clos so worshipfully the little twerp looked dizzy with his good luck. He leaned toward her . . . his lips almost touched hers . . .

William slammed the door against the wall. "Lieutenant!"

Lieutenant Du Clos jumped and swung around, fists up.

"Your presence is required inside!"

The lieutenant had the audacity to snap. "By whom, sir?"

By whom, indeed. "By your hostess. She needs partners for the dancing."

Lieutenant Du Clos hesitated, knowing it was nonsense, clearly wanting to challenge William, but not quite having the nerve. Clicking his heels together, he bowed to Samantha. "May I escort you inside, Miss Prendregast?"

Samantha watched them both with an expression of condescending amusement. "I'm fine where I am, Lieutenant Du Clos."

Lieutenant Du Clos bowed again and marched stiffly toward the ballroom. Stopping alongside William, he said, "Are you coming, Colonel Gregory?"

William stared until Lieutenant Du Clos's gaze dropped away. Then he said, "Don't be impertinent." Without watching the lieutenant's departure, he strode to Samantha and looked grimly down at her.

She tilted her already stubborn chin at a yet more obstinate angle. "I have resolved to kiss more men."

"What?" He hadn't followed her out here for *this.*

"Ever since you kissed me, I have been"—she seemed to search for the right word—"distracted. When I see you, I blush."

Leaning his hip against the railing, he crossed his arms. "It's charming."

She forged on. "I find I'm not eating well, and I have a tendency to go off into a daydream, frequently when others are in the act of speaking to me."

"Really?" She made him want to purr. To purr, and to roar, and to purr again.

She shook her head in reproof. "It's simply not acceptable, and upon reflection, I've decided the solution is to gain a little more experience."

"I agree."

She hesitated, then very quietly said, "Good."

"But," he pointed out, "experience need not be gained with other men. Especially not men like Du Clos."

"Everyone has warned me he's a lady's man, so he must be adept at kissing."

"He's adept at ruining young women. *I'll* help you learn more about kissing."

"But that wouldn't stop me from blushing when I see you."

"Perhaps I'll start blushing too." She was so clever, and so stupid. So beautiful and so . . . beautiful. Her skin glowed from the light of the candles inside. Her full mouth trembled—she was truly hurt. Worried. Unhappy. She didn't know what to do with the emotions cascading through her.

He did, but he shouldn't. Shouldn't wrap his arms around her. Shouldn't kiss her as he had done the other night. But somehow, *shouldn't* became *did*, as he slid his arm around her silk-clad waist, and drew her close.

She pressed her palms against his chest. She turned her head away.

"Samantha," he whispered, and bending his head, he found her lips.

Sweet. She was so sweet. So surprised, so giving, so willing, so inexperienced . . . he broke off the kiss, as if that would make him better, more honorable, when he was being the world's worst cad. Debauching his children's governess, and imagining ever greater debauchery.

He almost chuckled. He had been a career soldier. He would have told anyone he did not own an imagination, but it seemed he did. As he held her form against his, letting the warmth of her soak into him, feeling the soft mounds of her breasts, seeing the sculpted shoulders, his imagination showed him, in vivid color, the tangle of two bodies on a bed. He would hold her hips, and gently press himself into her, leading her on a tender path to passion. Making her a woman—his woman.

"Colonel, please." Samantha sounded stifled. "Someone will see."

Her hands were at her side now, as if she couldn't stand to touch him. Her chin was up, and she looked . . . angry.

Angry?

"And if someone sees, it won't matter to you. You're a respected member of society. I'm not. I'm a governess, and before that I was"—she caught her breath—"even less respectable. Please. I know I can't stay here now, but don't make it impossible for me to obtain a post at all."

He let her go as if she burned his hands. "You're right. I apologize."

She brushed at her skirt, and watched her hands as she did it. "So you agree I must leave?"

No. No, he didn't agree to that at all. But if she stayed . . . he couldn't fool himself. If she stayed, she'd be in his bed, if he had to carry her there.

"Perhaps it would be better to ask if the children will be getting a new mother, in which case a governess is . . . well, she would want to choose the governess." Samantha stepped away from him. "I assume Lady Marchant will be the lucky woman."

He still didn't answer. Now was not the time. First, he had to take care of the Featherstonebaugh matter. Not that he could do anything tonight . . .

But no. He had to be sensible. In measured tones, he said, "Lady Marchant fills every requirement on my list, and she has proved to be a hostess of incomparable skill. She is my logical mate."

"Well." Samantha smiled tightly. "Then I wish you all the happiness in the world." She turned jerkily and strode down the veranda, down the stairs, and out of sight on the grounds.

He fumbled for a cigar and lit it. His list of bridal requirements might as well be dust. On paper, Teresa *was* his logical mate. She fulfilled her duties admirably. She looked beautiful. William liked her. And he thought about wedding her with the same pleasure he experienced when he thought of going to a barber-surgeon.

Of course, in all truthfulness, Teresa seemed to think the same of him. She spent less and less time at his side, preferring to gossip with her friends, or supervise the servants—or avoid Duncan with such assiduousness that William wanted to laugh. His friends were infatuated with each other. God help them.

Very well. When Lord and Lady Featherstonebaugh were captured and Pashenka was on his way to Russia loaded with false information, he would propose to Samantha. Then he would marry her. That was the only possible resolution to this battle.

In the doorway behind him, he heard the rustle of silk.

Stepping onto the veranda, Teresa said, "I have had, in my day, a number of touching declarations, but that is the one I want framed. Perhaps I'll cross-stitch it. *She is my logical mate.* That gives me such a warm feeling inside."

Teresa was pleased to see he was at least smart enough to say nothing except, "Teresa . . ."

A most unusual impulse had come over her. It was noble. It was foolish. It would result in the loss of a great prize, both financial and social, and she didn't like the impulse at all. But she was tired of being clever and doing what everyone thought she should do. She was tired of all the proper men bobbing about her, wanting a piece of her fortune. She was tired of scheming and planning to save herself from a fortune hunter by marrying a fortune, when fortune hunters were always so much more charming than suitable gentlemen.

She lifted her hand. "Oh, don't! Don't 'Teresa' me. I don't know if you're going to propose marriage to me, or not propose marriage to me, but let me lift you off the hook. I don't want you. I won't take you. I already married one man who didn't love me. He liked me. He enjoyed me. But he didn't love me. He loved his military instead." Taking William's cigar, she took a puff of it. "You are so damned madly in love with that governess of yours—"

William drew in a sharp breath.

She didn't know whether it was because she swore, or smoked, or because she told him the facts. She didn't care. "You can scarcely keep your mind on your business—which, by the way, I have figured out." She took another puff. "Because I'm not as stupid as I pretend to be. In fact, I'm smarter than almost anyone here—and I'm tired of hiding that, too."

"My business?" he questioned cautiously.

She whispered, "The spying. Don't worry. I won't tell anyone." Raising her voice again, she said, "But I will tell you—go and get Miss Prendregast. You're an honorable man with honorable ideas of what's right and what's wrong and who should marry whom. You're so damned honorable you'd ask me to marry you because you thought it was the right thing to do, and you wouldn't take Miss Prendregast as your mistress because that was the wrong thing to do, and I'd wake up every morning knowing you didn't love me. Every time we rolled around in the sheets, I'd know you were pretending I was her. And I'm too good for that kind of treatment." She gestured widely with the cigar. "She's in her guest house, sulking or crying or, knowing her, trying to decide if she should go after you. I'd suggest you get over there and help her make up her mind."

He stared at her. At the cigar. At her sardonic expression.

He smiled. He picked up her hand and kissed the back. He bowed, vaulted over the railing, and disappeared into the night.

She snorted and took another puff of the cigar. What an idiot she was. An idiot, and she didn't care a whit.

"Well." A man's deep voice spoke from the deepest shadows near the house. "That was *the* most interesting scene I've ever had the pleasure to witness."

Swinging around, she watched with a sinking heart as a tall, dark shape moved toward her. Ruddy 'ell. It was *him*.

Duncan towered over her. "And here I've heard you brag you always get your man."

The light from the windows softly lit his face, and she could see the dimples in both his cheeks. The blackguard. "How long have you been listening?"

"I followed you out here, of course. I have rather a vested interest in the results of that little talk."

"Really? What interest could you have in whether I marry William?"

"Then you couldn't marry me."

She sucked on the cigar so hard she brought on a fit of coughing.

Duncan, in another one of his spasms of ungentlemanly behavior, smacked her on the back. "Give me that." He removed the cigar from her fingers and tossed it into the bushes. Taking her shoulders, he leaned over and kissed her.

She shoved at him and, as hard as she could, slapped him across the cheek. She hated him. God, how she hated him!

As she wound up for another shot, he grabbed her wrist. "That, my darling, was a mistake." Wrapping his arm around her waist, he pulled her hard against him and bent her backward.

And kissed her—a full-blown, open-mouthed, passionate raid.

She tried to scold, but his tongue was there, moving in and out in a brazen imitation of intercourse. He let go of her hand and cradled her neck. Off-balance, she grabbed for his shoulders. The railing dug into her thighs, and she wanted to be incensed. About the position, about the indignity, about his presumption.

But she couldn't. Not when a thrill swept across her skin unlike any thrill she'd ever experienced before. This was no gentlemanly buss. This was everything any woman had ever dreamed of, and it was happening to her. Eyes closed, she savored the encounter. She wanted to rub herself against him, over and over, getting pleasure from the mere contact with him. But he held her too firmly. He controlled her every movement, keeping her between him and the railing. When he came up for air, her sanity briefly surfaced. But he dipped his head again, sliding his open mouth along her jawline, taking her earlobe between his teeth and biting lightly. She jumped. She gasped. "That hurt!"

He chuckled, a soft puff of breath in her hair. "My darling, you don't even know what you like." He bit her again.

"God. Duncan." She clutched his hair in tight handfuls, wanting to wound him, too.

He didn't seem to care. He kissed her below her ear, kissed the pulse on her throat, lingered over one particular place which seemed to fascinate him, right where her neck met her shoulder.

She heard herself moaning, blatantly exposing her feelings like some madwoman.

Duncan didn't taunt her, though. He tasted her as if he couldn't get enough.

She stared up at the stars wheeling past and wanted . . . wanted his hands on her breasts, wanted his head between her legs. Blast him, she wanted the rogue in every way possible.

He kissed her lips again, entering her mouth as if sure of his welcome—and he was. Eyes closed again, she teased at his tongue, kissing him as she had never kissed a man before. And she hadn't. Not like this. Not with her whole body. Not with her whole mind consumed with desire for the man who held her in his arms.

When he lifted his head at last, she ran her fingers through his hair. In a husky voice she scarcely recognized, she said, "I'll meet you in my bedchamber."

"Yes," he whispered. "Later."

She blinked at him, trying to get her bearings. "Wha . . . what do you mean, later?"

"Dear girl, you have sent William on his way to meet his love. William is the host. That leaves you as the only one left to direct the ball, because you are the hostess."

She couldn't believe it. She could scarcely breathe. He wasn't on fire as she was. He wasn't out of control. "You did this to me. You did this on purpose."

"What? Kissed you? Damn right. You've needed kissing for years."

Humiliation clawed at her. "You brought me out here, and you forced me until I . . . you forced me."

"My darling, I'm not restraining you at all."

He wasn't. At some point in that last kiss, he'd stood her upright, and she still clung to his shoulders like some weak girl in need of a man. She snatched her hands back to her side and balled them into fists. She wanted to shriek. She wanted to kick him. She wanted to claw his eyes out.

"When the ball is over," he said, "I'll come to you in your bedchamber."

She could see the dimples in his cheeks again, and knew he was laughing at her. He hadn't been as involved as she had been. He had deliberately made her desperate for him, then proved he held the upper hand. "You will not be welcome."

"Maybe not initially, but we both know I can change your mind."

She lifted her hand to slap him again, open-handed and with the full strength of her arm behind her.

He didn't touch her, but his voice was suddenly cold and hard. "Don't hit me again."

She hesitated, lowered her hand—then it occurred to her. She had to go back in, and she'd been kissing Duncan Monroe in every lascivious way she knew. And he'd been kissing her. The bastard had already marked her. Of course. He wanted to humiliate her in front of everyone. Because she'd been so scornful of him, he'd taken his revenge, and a fine revenge it was. "Did you mess up my hair?"

"Not at all. I was careful not to." He carried her

shaking hands up to her head. "See? I didn't even slip out a hairpin."

"Did you unbutton anything?" She groped for her back.

"You are completely fastened. Your gown is as impeccable as it was when you arrived." He stepped back and viewed her. "Well, perhaps a little more wrinkled, but surely the dancing can account for that."

"Yes. Yes, I'm sure you're right." Taking a long breath, she straightened her shoulders. "You're sure you didn't do anything that would make me conspicuous?"

"My darling, you have an incredibly suspicious mind."

"And you can weave horseshit into gold."

He laughed. The bastard threw back his head and laughed in full-bodied amusement. She started to walk away, but he caught her arm. In between snorts, he said, "Your hair, your gown are perfect, and if you have a passionate, revealing glow about you, I can hardly be blamed for that."

"I'm going in."

"I'll be in your bedchamber tonight."

"Don't bother."

She sailed into the ballroom, her chin tilted upward perhaps a little too much, but she needed the confidence such a posture gave her. The guests smiled at her, toasted her with their wine, and she smiled back, grandly aware of her duty tonight. She *was* aware. That slip out on the veranda could scarcely be considered anything more than a moment's madness. She circulated, making her way to the stage. She stepped up with the musicians and ordered them to play a little trill. When she knew she had everyone's attention, she announced, "Colonel Gregory is indisposed, but he has asked that we enjoy ourselves, and in tribute to him, I think we should." A titter ran through the ballroom, and she smiled and nodded. "It's time for our midnight supper now. It will be served in the great hall."

Everyone smiled at her until she descended the stage, smiled with such amusement a cold trickle ran down her back, and her gaze swung to Duncan. Duncan, who stood silhouetted against the night, leaning against the open French door and like the lout he was, smoking a filthy cigar.

She jerked her gaze from his and strolled toward the great hall, leading the guests. But she casually glanced in one of the mirrors as she passed—and there it was. On her pale smooth skin, where her neck met her shoulder. A small, purple mark. A love bite. She stopped. She stared. She couldn't—didn't—restrain her gasp of horror. And in the mirror, she could see Duncan. Moving toward her. Across the ballroom. The focus of all eyes.

And in the light, clearly visible on his cheek, was the mark from her fingers.

He bowed, a great, sweeping gesture of obeisance, and mouthed a single word. "Tonight."

❧ *Chapter Twenty-two* ❧

William strode up on the porch of the guest house. In a rage of frustration, he discarded his jacket on the wooden floor, ripped off his waistcoat and flung it over the rail. Striding to the door, he lifted his hand to knock—and stopped.

This course he considered was not honorable. The young woman did not deserve to be debauched by her employer, regardless of the freedom with which she handed out her kisses.

He lowered his hand.

To him, though. Only to him. And he ought to be ashamed for kissing her, and more ashamed that he felt such pride in her response.

Her awkward, inexperienced response.

Certainly she gave no indication of being a woman of the world. Rather, she made clear her scorn for the society ladies who fluttered about their men, flattering them to their faces while discounting them in private.

He strode to the railing and clutched it so tightly the blood left his fingers. But he wanted Samantha. Everything in his body, in his mind, demanded he take her, possess her. He dreamed about her—about her blonde hair flung across his pillow, about the satin skin of her shoulder and how it would feel to his lips, about mounting her and having her, again and again. It was ruthless, the way he felt about her, as if she were an enemy to be conquered. He wanted to teach Samantha her place, and that place was in his bed.

He pounded the railing with his fist. Damn it. Damn it!

He was a civilized man, a soldier who had seen too much in his travels and who prided himself on his enlightenment. He should look on Samantha and remember her gentleness with his children, her kindness to his servants, her propriety with his guests.

Instead he remembered how openly she laughed at him, how cleverly she defied him, how she strode like a panther and smelled like a woman. Every emotion he experienced for her was primitive, coarse, and unregulated. He was a man out of control.

Behind him, the door banged open and he turned to observe Samantha, exiting in a flurry. She slammed the door so hard it bounced back open, and she growled as she turned to shut it properly.

That was all it took. The sight of her, the sound

of her. His lips felt stiff, but his voice low and dark. "Samantha."

She froze, then little by little faced him.

It was dark on the porch. The curtains muted the light from inside the cottage, the roof deflected the moonlight, but he could see the tense outline of her figure against the white wall. She wore the same garments she had worn at the ball, her arms and chest pale and bare. She stared at him, and her bosom heaved as she took a long breath. "You. How dare you come to me, here, tonight?"

Then she rushed him. Right at him.

He braced himself for an attack.

She grabbed his lapels, yanked him toward her, and kissed him.

He could almost hear the last fragments of his restraint crack.

She pressed her lips against his, slanting her mouth as he had taught her, and bit his lower lip. Gently, yet with an aggression that lifted the hairs on the back of his neck.

He sure as hell hadn't taught her *that*.

But he wasn't going to let her take charge. Not when lust pulsed through him: blinding, blood-red lust. Sitting on the railing, he spread his legs to brace himself. He wrapped his hands around the back of her head and held her in place. He drove his tongue into her mouth. He tasted her momentary surprise, a fleeting resistance, then the surge of her response.

She held nothing back. She tried to devour him,

skirmishing, answering his every feint. Her palms slid up over his shoulders, a deliberate caress that left a path of fire on his skin.

He nipped at her lips, then soothed the bite with small licks of his tongue.

She stepped between his legs and pressed herself against him. Chest to chest. Groin to groin.

Her breasts pushed against him, and he wanted . . . everything. Now. Now. He stood.

She whimpered as he broke the kiss.

Embracing her, his arms around her waist, he hurried her backward and pushed her against the cottage, trapped between him and the wall.

She gripped his arms and writhed against him. Not to escape, but like a cat enticing him to pet her.

He obliged, moving his hips against her, trying to scratch the itch she had created with her languorous eyes and pert mouth, her smooth skin and that body that moved with such sinuous sensuality. Sliding his hands up from her waist, he discovered . . . dear God, she wore no corset. No corset. No chemise. Her skin resided beneath a single layer of thin silk, and he would touch every inch. Soon. But not soon enough.

He found her breasts, and cupped them. Full. Sensitive, if that gasp she gave was anything to go by. "Were you coming to me?" He didn't recognize his own voice, it was so deep.

She leaned against the wall, her head thrown back and her neck exposed, the portrait of a woman in the throes of passion. "What?" She sounded as breathy as he sounded guttural. "What did you say?"

"Were you coming to find me?"

She didn't answer, she only rolled her head back and forth.

"Samantha." It killed him to step away, but he had to know. "Answer me."

She caught him, pulled him back against her. "Yes. You. I want you."

He rewarded her by circling her nipples with his thumbs.

She rewarded him with hardening nipples, and a heartbreaking moan.

The clear, smooth expanse of her neck beckoned, and he leaned down to kiss it, to taste the sweet cream of her skin. She intoxicated him. "From the first moment I saw you . . . on that road . . . I knew you would be trouble."

She laughed, a warm, husky chuckle of amusement. "You frightened me half to death."

"I would never have known." He fumbled with the buttons on the back of her dress. He'd lost his dexterity—or he was simply so desperate he couldn't . . . there! Three buttons in a row. Enough for him to slip the sleeves off her shoulders. "You stood up to me."

Grasping his shoulders, she arched her back to allow him greater access. "I thought you were stealing my reticule. Promise me."

The buttons opened easier now, and the bodice dropped to her waist.

"Promise me you won't get yourself . . . killed."

"No. No, I won't get myself killed."

He would have said more, but her breasts spilled into his hands, soft skin peaked with nipples as velvety and tight as ripe berries. He savored the weight of them. Wrapping his arm around her back, he arched her backward and caught the soft, precious mound in his mouth.

She gave a cry, strangled and uncertain. Then, as he suckled, a moan escaped her. She trembled in his embrace. She cradled his head. Stroked his hair back from his forehead. "William. Please, William."

The weeks of watching her, the nights of desiring her, drove him to a frenzy. He circled her nipple with his tongue, used his lips in wanton arousal, and struggled to control the mad woman he had created. He wanted to laugh with her, to dance with her . . . he wanted to plunge inside her until she acknowledged him as her master. He wanted to love her until she was as wild as he knew she could be.

And she . . . the little witch, she wanted to wrest control from him and drive him as insane as he had driven her.

With a swipe of her hand, she untied his cravat and cast it aside. She fumbled at his collar and discarded it. She spread his shirt wide, and slid her hand inside, on his bare skin.

Her hand . . . on him.

He could scarcely breathe. He bit down, gently, threatening her and pleasuring her at the same time.

She gave a choked cry, and slid one leg up around his hip.

If nothing stood between them . . . if his trousers had miraculously disappeared and her skirts were hiked up to her waist . . . he would be inside her. Thrusting his cock past the entrance to her body, into her depths. Stroking her to the depths of her womb. Making her respond to him as he demanded. If nothing stood between them . . .

Purposefully, her hands wandered down and latched onto his trousers. Her fingers stroked over him, touching his hip, his belly . . . my God. She found his cock and fondled the length of it. His heart stopped at her daring. At the gratification of her touch. It didn't matter that his trousers blunted the sensation, or that his undergarments stood between him and ecstasy, or that she didn't yet know how best to pleasure a man. She was his. His woman. His mate. And he responded to her from the marrow of his bones and the depths of his being.

He pressed her against the wall and caught a handful of her skirts. He lifted them, caught another handful, lifted them. With his knee, he separated her legs. There was no finesse about his gesture. He moved to conquer . . . and the choked cry she gave was not an objection, but simple surprise. He ran his hand up her thigh and discovered . . . he shouldn't have been surprised, but she was bare beneath her petticoats, her legs smooth and long and daring.

He laughed aloud, his triumph expressed in merriment. She had hoped to disconcert him. Instead, she'd sanctioned his brashest move. He slid his leg up until she rode his thigh. She gasped and tried to lift herself onto her toes, away from him.

He followed, giving her no surcease, pressing his knee against the wall, lifting her so her most sensitive parts rubbed against him.

"William," she whispered, and her voice quavered. "Don't."

He chuckled again, and reached between her legs. He found the thatch of curling hair, delved deeper and touched her. The barest, most sensitive skin. The vulnerable nub that could bring her— would bring her—the most exquisite pleasure. Using his fingers, he opened her so nothing remained between her and satisfaction.

"William." Her hands clawed at his shoulders. "Please."

"Don't?" he murmured. "Or please do?" And he raised his thigh. He held her bare hips and moved her, back and forth, allowing the weight of her body and the contact with his leg to work on her.

She couldn't get away. She tried, God knows. She squashed herself against the wall. She pushed at his chest. She tried everything, but at last she surrendered.

And as he'd always known, when Samantha surrendered, she surrendered everything. She held nothing back. She leaned her head against the wall. She bunched his shirt in her hands. She breathed harshly, haltingly. And as he held her, arm around her waist, she shook with the onset of climax. And when climax struck—she cried out until he had to cover her mouth with his own to stifle her. No one wandering in the garden could mistake that sound for anything but a woman in the throes of rapture.

He wanted to protect her from censure, and at

the same time—he wanted to puff out his chest and tell the world. He had brought Samantha to the peak. Forced Samantha to the peak. Controlled a woman whose heart and mind challenged everything he was.

Supporting Samantha in his arms, he slid his leg down. He held her, and kissed her forehead, and prided himself on his handling of her. He might be half-mad with desire, but he'd driven her over the edge.

Then he felt the tug of her fingers at his trousers. And his drawers. Somehow, she'd managed to unbutton him, and now . . . he caught his breath. He could scarcely breathe. Somehow, she'd managed to burrow beneath his clothing . . . she held his bare cock in her hands.

No woman had ever done that before. Held him, stroked him, fondled him in curiosity and provocation. She slipped her fingers along the length, tracing each vein on his straining manhood. She circled the head, and he thought for one incredulous moment he would climax in her hand. But he grasped at control . . . barely. "You don't know what you're doing."

"No, but I like it." She sounded deep, husky, like a woman sated on love.

He still held her bare hips. He'd show her satiation. Thrusting his hand between her legs, he opened her folds and with his fingers, found the entrance to her body.

She jerked and trembled—and grasped him more firmly than before.

He slid one finger into her.

A groan tore from her, and she tried to wrap her leg around him again.

"That's it," he decided. "That's all." He wanted between her legs. He wanted her now. He propelled her against the wall and pressed her against him, naked and bare, male and female. With two fingers, he opened her.

"That hurts," she said.

For an answer, he lifted her chin with his other hand and kissed her. Ravished her mouth with his. Gave her no reprieve.

She didn't back away. Not Samantha.

He had known she wouldn't.

Instead she kissed him back, bold and wild, and pressed herself closer again. Her whole body closer to his, and the way he stood, knees bent, ready to drive into her . . .

They paused.

He was just inside her. Just the head. Stretching her.

It was the beginning of possession. It was what they'd been fighting against since the first moment they'd met.

And this was inevitable.

Both of them stopped breathing, stopping kissing. They stared at each other in the dim light, not seeing each other with any clarity. Not needing to. She moved her hips, a slow demand that forced him a little deeper. And she sucked in a pained breath.

He put his mouth next to her ear. "You knew it would hurt you."

"Yes. I knew you would hurt me."

That wasn't what he'd said, but she pressed downward again, and he couldn't find the words to question her. The sensation was everything he'd ever dreamed. She was silk and sand, warm and tight. He wanted to get inside her and stay there. He wanted to finish quickly and start again. She wrapped him in a heat that thawed the frozen corners of his soul and made him whole for the first time in too many years. In his life.

A burst of laughter came from the manor.

They couldn't do this here.

He lifted his head and glanced around. "We've got to move."

"I don't want to." She drenched him with her arousal.

He retained some level of sanity, if this could be called sanity. "We'll be caught. Into the cottage." He picked her up, his hands under her bottom.

She wrapped her legs around him.

And he slipped all the way inside.

Her maidenhead broke. She gave a shout—of rage, of pain, he didn't know—and smacked him hard on the shoulders. "Ruddy 'ell!" She swore like a soldier as her muscles flexed around him.

In the sudden, overwhelming gust of desire, he forgot the need for privacy. The need for discretion. The need for anything but satisfaction. He let the wall support her back and slowly pulled out of her . . . almost all the way. And back in. And out.

Her breath sounded harsh in the night air. "William. Dear God. William."

She didn't sound like she was in pain anymore, and he couldn't have done anything if she was. His thighs, his calves ached from the strain of holding her up, but he couldn't stop. He had to take her, and take her, and take her, until she knew she was his.

She held his shoulders for balance, for support . . . this bliss was too exquisite to bear, and at the same time, he wanted her to hold him forever.

He moved more quickly, his breath harsh, his lungs laboring, his hips thrusting without tenderness. He couldn't get close enough. He couldn't reach that one place . . . that place inside her . . . the place that promised ownership, control. Of Samantha. Forever. He had to reach it. He had to reach it *now*. "Now," he demanded. "Now!"

Her legs convulsed around his waist. She moaned deeply. And inside, her muscles clasped him, milked him, as he plunged over and over, filling her with his seed.

Slowly, he collapsed onto his knees, holding her, sliding down the wall, groaning with satiation . . . and the need to take her once again.

Chapter Twenty-three

Samantha woke to the sound of the kindling igniting in the fireplace, and the solid thunk of logs being tossed onto the coals. The heat blazed up toward her face. Snuggling her cheeks against the sofa cushion, she smiled and waited. She wasn't disappointed. William placed the blankets over her shoulder and slid in behind her, pulling her against his warmth. "Um," she moaned, "you're like a stove."

His voice spoke right in her ear, profound and mellow. "Hot?"

"So hot." Opening her eyes, she slid around to face him. Firelight put streaks of gold in his dark hair, and gave his austere features a warm glow. He watched her with a smile, as if the sight of her gave him pleasure. Certainly the night had brought pleasure. After their stormy indiscretion on the porch, he'd carried her inside. They'd gotten no further than the sofa before desire swept them again. The cushions had ended up on the floor. Their clothes had ended up on the floor. *They* had ended up on the floor. There they'd stayed.

Now he brought the blankets and pillows from her bed, making a nest like a mighty eagle enticing his mate.

She skimmed her hand over his stubbled chin. "What time is it?"

Without a glance toward the window, he said, "Two hours until dawn."

"I'm wide awake." She looked down at his chest, then up into his eyes. "What would you like to do to pass the time?"

"Flirt." His fingers threaded their way into the fall of her hair. His blue eyes were almost black in the firelight, and stark in their intensity. "You're so beautiful. Slender, with the sleekness and strength of a thoroughbred."

She grinned. Because she could tease him. Because he made her happy. "Are you saying I look like a horse?"

"What do you think?"

The smile disappeared, vanquished by the power of his question. "I think that you really see me as beautiful. And I think . . . I'll bow to your superior perception."

"You confirm that you're wise as well as beautiful." With his palm on the small of her back, he brought her bare hips against his. He was aroused again, pressing himself against her. Yet he made no move to mount her, although she moved enticingly. "You're too new for me to take you again."

"But don't you want . . . ?" She moved her hands down his chest.

"Yes." He rose onto his elbow and propped his head on his hand. "But despite my disgraceful behavior tonight, I do know how to treat a woman."

She rose onto her elbow, also. "What disgraceful behavior?"

"I took you standing up on the porch."

"What's disgraceful about that? I have rather fond memories of—"

"As do I." He placed his palm over her lips. "But to initiate a virgin in such manner, so forcefully, without consideration to your comfort or your innocence!"

She shoved his hand away. "Comfort? We were supposed to consider comfort? The thought never crossed my mind."

"A man should cherish a woman her first time. Such roughness is for experienced lovers, not . . . not you." He frowned in his stern, military disapproval. "Not so soon."

"Are you feeling guilty?"

"I can't believe I so lost control."

"You did, didn't you?" Delighted, she stroked his shoulder. "Colonel Gregory lost his head over a woman."

"Not over any woman." He stroked her shoulder with as much pleasure. "Over you. Only you."

She liked him so much.

"Talk to me." Taking a lock of her hair, he

brought it forward, draped it over her breast, and over and over, he brushed her nipple. "Since we can't make love, tell me about your family. About your childhood."

That woke her from her sensuous dream. He asked questions for a reason. He wanted to know the truth about the woman who had made him abandon his vaulted principles.

He wasn't involved as she was.

He watched her so keenly, it was as if he could read her soul. "You look at me with those big brown eyes so accusing, when I'm trying to do the right thing."

"You want to know about the woman you've slept with," she said flatly.

"Lovers talk. They tell each other about their lives. Their memories."

She bristled with hostility. "Their families."

"I've made my choice. I want *you*. Not your family."

She knew it. She'd given him hints of her past. Tidbits of her reality. She could tell him about her mother and father, about her background, and he wouldn't change his mind. As long as she didn't push him too far . . . as long as she told him everything except what she'd done to so many people for so many years.

"You were raised on the streets of London, I think," he said.

"You guessed. Is it the accent?" She dropped into Cockney. "The way Oi use me fingers t' eat? Did ye see me wipe me nose on me sleeve?"

His eyebrows rose, but he showed an insight that frightened her. "You're angry."

No, she wasn't. She was scared. For the first time in her life, she desperately wanted something she could never have. What had Lady Marchant said? *If you catch a husband fast enough, he won't find out about you until it's too late.* William admitted he couldn't resist her. If she snatched him up . . . but he *would* find out. She had to remember that. She loved him, and she could never have him.

He rubbed the lines between her brows. "Someone must have hurt you very much."

A multitude of someones, and he was next in line. She dropped back into the crisp, upper-class accent she'd been taught. "I hurt them back, sir. If you truly believe that white is white and black is black and there are no shades of gray, then you should know I'm covered top to toe with coal dust."

He smiled at her with such passion, such admiration. "You are the most honest woman I've ever met."

Sitting up, she exclaimed, "No!" He was twisting this around. She was trying to warn him, and he admired her for it. But only because he didn't comprehend the depths of her iniquity.

"I know, I know." He gathered her to him again. "You're about to thrash me for being biased. But I'll say it right this time. You are the most honest *person* I know."

She ought to tell him. She ought to. But the air was cold, he was warm, and she was allowed one full day of happiness. She would take her day of happiness.

He pulled her back into his arms, and she went without resistance, collapsing onto his chest, letting him warm her with his heat. Stroking her hands across his shoulders, she tried to absorb everything about him. The way he looked, the way he felt, that fall of hair over his brow, his strong fingers . . .

With his thumb, he pressed the pad of her chin. "Tell me one good thing about your parents."

"They were married."

His eyes grew somber. "A little stark."

It was the middle of the night, the time for confidences. He was her lover, a man she wanted desperately to trust. Why not tell him everything? The worst that could happen was that he would turn away from her . . .

"Darling, you look as if you're in pain." He cradled her head against his chest. "Don't . . . I'm sorry I asked."

In a rush, she said, "My mother was a member of the minor gentry, a parson's daughter who worked in a great house as the governess."

She could hear the gust of breath into his lungs, rode the swift inhale beneath her cheek. "So you're treading in your mother's shoes," he said.

"I hope not." Was she? What would happen . . . after today? "My father met my mother in the park on her half-day off. She had a small inheritance from her grandmother, so he romanced her and against her father's wishes, she wed him. And she . . . descended into hell. She lost her position, of course. Her family wouldn't speak to her. And my father revealed himself to be a black-hearted blighter. He spent her money, then put her to work, not such work as she was used to, but sewing until her eyes ached. Begging . . . she hated the begging. Standing on the street corner, her hand outstretched, being spat upon by her former mistress, ridiculed by the lads, offered money for her services." Samantha buried her face in William's chest. "Da used to thrash the gents for that."

"Thank God!" He sounded appalled, yet pleased that her father had shown some small sign of chivalry.

She crushed his hope. "He didn't want her, but no one else should, either." Why had she started to confess? Now she was lost, wandering in the recollection of those nights which seemed to have no day and hunger always clawed at her stomach. "My mother gave birth to me under the worst circumstances while he was out romancing yet another lady. He liked fooling them, you see. Taking them down to his level. And sometimes they had money, and then we had money, too, enough to buy food and coal."

William stroked her hair. "You were cold and hungry?"

"Aye, sir, and me mum gave almost everything t' me." Remembered guilt clawed at her as she slipped in and out of her Cockney accent. "I knew it wasn't right, but I sat before the fire and ate her food."

"How old were you?" His hand slid along her spine, up and down, offering comfort, but beneath her, his muscles tensed.

"She died when I was seven."

"Seven? You were seven when she passed on? You made your mother happy by surviving." His hug was both tender and exasperated. "Dear girl, you are not a parent. I tell you the truth—once you've given life to a child, you'll do anything to keep her alive, even starve and freeze."

Samantha almost laughed at him, but that wouldn't have been kind. "You're naïve, sir. My father felt no such parental urge, nor did my mother's most holy parents. Mum told them they had a granddaughter. She begged them to take me. She, who hated to beg." Her fingers dug into William's shoulder. "They refused her, told her she deserved her fate as I deserved mine."

"You might pity them for their shriveled souls."

"Or hate them for turning their faces away." She did hate them. "When Mama died, Da sent them word. He didn't want me, and I suppose he thought he might reap some profit out of my sale." She shook her head. Why was she still talking? She'd never told anyone any of this. It was humiliating to be so poor and unwanted, especially by those who should have cared the most. Why couldn't she just shut up?

"How did you survive? A child of seven, with no one to care for her?"

"I sang on the street corners. I begged. I swept the crossings. I did what you see children doing every day in London."

He didn't say anything.

He must despise her now. She'd blabbed all her secrets—well, almost all her secrets—and he realized at last the kind of female he had embraced. She cringed as she thought of facing him . . . but she couldn't put it off forever, and at last she lifted her head and looked him in the face.

He observed her with . . . well, it looked like with affection. Admiration, almost. "You are a remarkable woman," he said, and cupping her face, he kissed her.

With a sob, she relaxed against him. She kissed him back, deep kisses she had shared only with him. She gave herself to him completely, and hope sprouted and grew in a spirit she would have sworn was barren. That was so dangerous, to think that because he accepted all the horror of her early life, he would accept her completely. But she couldn't help it. Perhaps . . . perhaps she had found a home at last.

Leaning her forehead against his, she looked into his eyes. "I've told you my secrets. Now tell me yours."

She didn't know what she expected, but nothing could prepare her for the truth.

"My secrets? I only have one. I catch spies."

She blinked at him. "What?"

"See how much I trust you?" His blue eyes twinkled at her. He smiled as if he were proud. "I swear to you it's the truth. I catch spies—"

How foolish she had been! "At night on the road. Of course." She clutched at him. "That's dangerous."

"More than catching bandits?" he teased.

She answered him seriously. "Yes, I think so. Bandits are usually people who have no other way to live."

He sobered. "You are too kind to people who deserve no kindness."

He didn't have a clue, and she was focused on him. His safety. "Spies are coldly ruthless. They don't want to rob you."

"Indeed they do. Spies rob us of life, of honor, of land, of military men who would serve their country to the best of their ability, of children . . . of wives."

The situation grew ever more precarious. Samantha felt as if she were in the middle of a frozen lake, with thin ice in every direction and no idea where to turn. "I thought your wife died in a . . . robbery."

"The thieves confessed before they were hung. They were paid by the Russians to wait until Mary left our compound, and to specifically set upon her. In my zeal to rid the countryside of Russian influence, I had proved to be a problem which they took steps to eliminate."

"Gorblimey."

"So I left India with my children, resolved to follow the line of traitors back to its source. And so I have. I've enticed one of the most important couples ever to betray England here to this party."

Layers upon layers. The party was more than a mating ritual between him and Lady Marchant. It was a trap for—"Who?"

"You are so honest, so outspoken, I fear if I confide in you, you'll not be able to hide your disdain."

She remembered the times she'd been caught with her hand in a pocket, the way she'd smiled and wheedled and acted the innocent. The times she'd talked her way out of arrest by imitating an upper-crust accent and a wholesome indignation. "I'm only outspoken with you, William. I can act with the best of Drury Lane."

"Lord and Lady Featherstonebaugh." He waited for her shocked reaction.

But she was thinking. Recalling the narrow old fool with his flirting and his prancing. Recalling the intent old woman watching the proceedings with narrow-eyed intensity. "Not him. Her."

William shook his head as if puzzled. "How did you know that?"

"I recognized the signs. She's hiding something."

"She is hiding something. She's stolen a map. Teresa overheard them talking, and we have more information now from . . . from the man she stole it from. It's vitally important that we recover it, but we would really like to make an exchange, to replace it with a map that would confuse the enemy." William's hands tightened on her shoulders. "If we could do that, we would save countless English lives."

Her breath caught, and caught again. Pain pressed like knives on her lungs. She spoke in a hoarse whisper. "You need a cutpurse."

"Yes. Do you know where we can find one?" He

chuckled, then halted. "I suppose you do know. Were you familiar with the thieves in London?"

"Yes."

Rubbing his chin, he focused over her head. "But no common thief could pretend to be genteel. I suppose we could put him into the party as a servant. But no, we couldn't get him here fast enough." He saw Samantha's signs of distress, and cuddled her close. "Don't worry, love. Somehow, we'll find a way. It's not your predicament. Don't worry your head about it."

He drifted off to sleep, leaving Samantha staring, wide-eyed, into the encroaching light.

William woke in the early hours to a wash of pale gray fog outside the window. Inside, the fire was blazing merrily, giving off a heat that roasted his backside and warmed the cottage. But Samantha wasn't in the bed. He lay with his eyes closed, breathing the scent of her on her pillow, feeling the relaxation that came with bliss, and waiting until she returned so he could tell her about the rest of their lives. How they would spend them together. They would talk about travel, perhaps, and children . . .

He heard the rustle of starched petticoats. His eyes popped open, and his gaze fell on Samantha, dressed in a pale green day gown of modest proportions, seated at the table. She was staring at him, her expression cool and expectant, not at all the loverlike delight he experienced on seeing her. But perhaps she was shy. Or perhaps she feared he would reject her as her father had rejected her mother.

Ah, yes. In that tale, she revealed all the uncertainty she must feel in his society. It was up to him to reassure her.

Smiling at her, he patted the cushions. "Come back, darling. Let me show the correct way a lover leaves the marriage bed." Her cool expression vanished, to be replaced by shock and, for a second, such stark pain he was taken aback.

"Marriage?" she said. "There was never any talk of marriage."

Her disbelief rendered him speechless long enough for him to look her over. Her hands were clenched in fists in her lap, her thumbs tucked under her fingers. She was breathing in short, shallow breaths. Some time in the middle of the night, she had fallen prey to doubts and fears—about him? About his intentions? But if that were the truth, surely his reference to marriage should have cured her misgivings. Gradually, without looking away from her, he freed himself from the blankets.

She observed without a flicker of desire or interest.

Collecting his clothing, he donned it, all the while trying to understand what had happened. Had he hurt her? He had, but he'd made it up. Had he frightened her? Nothing frightened Samantha. She'd been upset last night when he'd told her about the situation with Lady Featherstonebaugh— was she worried he would risk his life and leave her alone? But if that were the case, why had she set herself apart from him? "Tell me what's wrong."

She looked away, toward the window, and her lips trembled before she pressed them tightly together.

"Come up to the house with me," he commanded. He needed to coerce her into talking—and she shouldn't be alone. "I need to prepare for the day, dress in something other than last night's wrinkled garments, consult with Duncan."

At last she looked back at him, and the emptiness in her eyes showed him a soul barren and bereft. "I have something to tell you first."

❧ Chapter Twenty-four ❧

"Are you going to untie me, or leave me like this all day long?"

Teresa ceased her frantic dressing and looked over at Duncan, stretched out naked on her bed, bound to the headboard by her sash. "Yes, yes, I'll untie you." She strode forward with such purpose it was hard to believe that, a half an hour ago, she had been engaged in kissing his bum. She tugged at the knots she'd taken such pleasure in setting a few hours ago. "I need you to help me with my buttons."

"A pleasure, my lady." As his hands were freed, he caught her around the waist and held her in place. "But first I'd like to know what I said that distressed you so."

She looked down at him, her eyes damp with worry. "You said you needed a cutpurse. You said you and William required the assistance of a cut-purse."

"If I had known it would cause you such distress, I'd have kept my clabber shut. I thought that you seem to know everything about everybody, and that you might have someone to do the job."

Her expression haunted, she said, "I have to go warn Samantha."

His hands slid away, and slowly he sat up. "Warn Samantha? Miss Prendregast? About what?"

Teresa's movements were jerky as she walked across to the window and stared out at the foggy morning. "She isn't . . . she hasn't . . ." She turned to face Duncan. "Do you think William will confide in her?"

"I don't know." Reservations formed in Duncan's mind, but he didn't believe them. He couldn't imagine that that young governess . . . no. No, it was impossible. "I would have said never, but William is as daft in love as any man I've ever seen."

"But he won't tell, will he?" Teresa wrung her hands. "Because I fear Samantha would . . . but he won't tell her his dilemma. He thinks women are fragile creatures whose minds shouldn't be troubled by such thorny issues."

All of Duncan's suspicions coalesced, and he came out of bed in a rush. "Damn it. Are you telling me William is courting a thief?"

William marched Samantha across the lawn, clutching her arm.

The wench had the gall to try and wrestle free.

"You don't need to hold me. I told you so I could help you."

"You told me too late." He gripped her tighter. "I have already compromised myself and my honor."

She punched him in the ribs with her free hand, a sharp, painful, close-fisted jab she could only have learned in her perfidious past.

Grunting, he dropped her arm.

Before he could grab her again, she marched on ahead and in that mocking tone that scraped at his arrogance, she said, "I forgot you were the only one involved with the events of last evening."

In a few strides, he caught up with her. "The only one with honor to lose."

"I forgot that, too."

The fog wet the grass and illuminated the delicate filaments of a spider's web constructed between the branches of a rose arbor. Trees loomed out of the gray blankness, then disappeared behind them. If the fog persisted, it would ruin Teresa's plan for a gala farewell luncheon in the tents. But William rejoiced in the still dampness. It hid the house from them, and it also hid them from any prying eyes. None of the guests would be awake yet, of course, but their servants were, and he didn't need them reporting to their masters that Colonel Gregory had spent the night in the arms of his governess. Undoubtedly, a great many people realized he and Miss Prendregast had disappeared at the same time. He didn't wish to confirm any suspicions about his disgraceful behavior. His dignity, his standing in society, his very sense of worth was at stake.

"I am furious with myself." He didn't try to lighten the harshness in his tone.

"Aye, guv'nor, Oi know." She used that dreadful, low accent, but she didn't say anything else.

And he wanted her to. He wanted her to fight with him, to stoke the fire of his wrath, to prove how unworthy of his attentions she was. Because it was he who had been wronged. Not she. He hadn't wronged her. "If you'd told me the truth at once—"

"I would have been back on that train before the next day dawned. It was not an enviable fate a mere day after I arrived." She smiled faintly. "The train is looking better now."

That smile did what he wanted. It infuriated him. It justified his total and unequivocal rejection of her and her thieving ways. "Did you never think of your effect on my children? To associate with a cutpurse may have permanently scarred their unformed characters."

"If I have made a mark on their unformed characters—and I hope I have—it is not because of something I did in my adolescence."

"The taint of your crime still clings to you."

"In that case, you daren't see your children again, for the taint of last night's events must cling to you."

Whirling, he grasped her shoulders and jerked her to a stop. "Don't you dare insinuate I'm marked by you."

"I was pointing out how absurd you're being."

She sounded impatient, but her eyes were wise and sad.

"You stole from me. I'm missing a pen, a portrait—" Then it struck him—the significance of what he'd lost. "My God, what kind of person are you that would take the only things I have left of my wife?"

"Oh." She bit her lip as if troubled, and her gaze dropped away. "Oh."

This hurt worse than he'd imagined. Samantha had been stalking him, taking the remnants of his honest, lawfully wedded relationship and leaving him with her. With nothing. "Where are my things?"

"I don't know."

"Where?" He shook her as if he could rattle the truth from her.

"I honestly don't know." He would have shaken her again, but she knocked his hands away and said, "Sh."

He heard it, too. Two people, a man and a woman, arguing as they walked. The words were indistinct, but he recognized the voices. Duncan and Teresa. Sourly, he wondered if they had come to warn him about Samantha's shady past.

No. They didn't know about that. Perhaps they came to chide him for taking advantage of her innocence. But no, her virginity was nothing but a treasure to be sold to the highest bidder, and she'd hoped to trap him with it.

Teresa and Duncan broke out of the fog and abruptly stopped their conversation. Their . . . argument.

Elegant Teresa appeared somehow unfinished, although William couldn't decide how. Perhaps she'd forgotten to don all the parts of her gown. Certainly her shawl was only roughly knotted around her shoulders, and her hair, usually so sleek, was as tumbled as Mara's.

Hands outstretched, Teresa hurried forward.

William expected her to embrace him.

Instead she headed right for Samantha. Hurriedly, he let her go and stepped back.

Clasping Samantha's wrists, she tugged her toward the house. "Samantha! Darling! I came to find you. I need someone, another woman, to help me . . . decorate the inside tables." She spoke toward William, but her gaze seemed to avoid him. "You know, William, there are some things only another woman can do, and this is one of them."

Calmly, Samantha interrupted her. "He knows."

Teresa, the imperturbable, stomped her foot. "No. How?" Without waiting for an answer, she charged on. "You told him, didn't you? You had to do your duty, didn't you? You couldn't decide this was none of your business—"

"Sh!" Duncan said.

"But it is my business," Samantha said. "It's my country—"

William snorted.

Samantha ignored him. "—And innocent people are being killed."

"Sh!" Duncan said again.

The women looked at him, looked around, and nodded.

Duncan ruffled his hair—which already stuck

straight up—and very softly said, "I'm damned grateful, Miss Prendregast."

William turned on him. "What do you mean, you're grateful? We're not going to let her do this. She'd tip off Lady Featherstonebaugh for spite. I'm going to lock her in the attic and throw away the key."

"No, William, you're not." Duncan's voice was pitched to reach the other three, no further, but he spoke intensely, resolutely.

William's jaw dropped. At Duncan's words. At Duncan's tone. Drawing himself up to his full height, he looked down his nose at Duncan. "I beg your pardon."

"We're going to accept Miss Prendregast's help, and we're going to thank God that she's in the right place at the right time."

"How can you say that?" William asked.

"How can you not?" Duncan lowered his voice to an intense whisper. "We're desperate to get that map. Captain Farwell said it is of primary importance. We're damned lucky that Lord Hartun brought his secretary, and that he's an expert cartographer. The damage we can do to the Russians by replacing the real map with a false map can barely be imagined. And we have no way of performing either of these tasks without Miss Prendregast."

"You think dealing with this . . . this scarlet woman is the answer?" William pointed a shaking finger at Samantha, then tucked it behind him. As a commander, he was the best. He was cold. He was dispassionate. He knew better than to show such emotion, but right now, he couldn't seem to stop himself.

Samantha watched him serenely, her hands loose at her sides, as if the two of them had not spent the night pressed together. As if what he said meant nothing to her.

"She's not a scarlet woman—or she wasn't until last night," Teresa snapped. "And that outrage can be placed at your door, William. And mine, to my eternal shame." Taking Samantha's arm, she tucked it in hers and stared at him with ill favor. "You are not the man I imagined."

William wanted to shout at her. At Teresa, the women he had deemed suitable to wed.

But he couldn't bear to think of marrying her, and he didn't dare shout at her. Teresa, when she chose, had quite an imperious manner.

"Of course he is the man you imagined." Duncan took her hand, raised it to his lips and kissed it with loverlike fervor. "This morning, you knew he would react with outrage when he discovered Miss Prendregast's special gifts."

Samantha lowered her head.

But William saw her grin. She looked at Duncan and Teresa with an affection that encompassed them both. And he realized . . . it was early morning. Teresa was disheveled. Duncan was positively disreputable, unshaven, still dressed in last night's clothing and looking . . . looking a great deal as William himself must look.

They were lovers. Teresa had sent him to Samantha so she could take Duncan instead.

William ought to be incensed. Instead ... instead, he found he really couldn't be bothered by Teresa and Duncan. He could think of only one thing. One person. Samantha, who had so grievously betrayed him. In triumph, he produced the one reason he knew would sway his friends. "She has been stealing from me. She took Mary's portrait. My wife's portrait!"

Samantha's eyes flashed. Her fist rose.

For one moment, William thought she would punch him in the face.

Then her fingers loosened and dropped. Yet she didn't deny his accusation.

And something inside him mourned. But he denied that part of his voice, and instead turned triumphantly to the silent Duncan and Teresa. "Would you trust such a scoundrel with this mission?"

"You are truly a consummate fool," Teresa retorted.

Viewing their damp, disgusted expressions, William realized nothing he could say would change their minds about Samantha. So he did what he did best. He took charge. "I say we're not going to use Miss Prendregast."

Duncan stepped forward to face William. He snapped to attention, but he didn't capitulate as William expected. He said, "Then, Colonel Gregory, I relieve you of duty."

"What?" William roared.

"You're so enraged and illogical"—Duncan's gray eyes were formal, narrow slits—"you mentioned our mission and our target at a time when our most dread enemy could be ten feet away and listening, and you did so in a tone that reached far beyond our ears."

Duncan's guts took William's breath away—and his candor sent a chill up William's spine. Duncan spoke the truth. Anyone could be standing close enough to hear them speaking, and they wouldn't know he was there. Not Lady Featherstonebaugh. She was still limping badly. But Featherstonebaugh. Or Pashenka. Or any of the other myriad of spies being drawn to the Lake District by the presence of their master.

William and Duncan faced off.

Duncan didn't back down.

Before William could decide what to do, Samantha freed herself from Teresa and stepped between the two men. "I feel as if I'm a bone over which three dogs are at war. But I'm not a bone nor, regardless of my past sins, am I a traitor." She faced William. In a patient tone that tried his serenity, not that he had any left, she said, "You're arguing with Duncan when you have no choice in the matter. At this moment, at this party, there are no other cutpurses or pickpockets. This is a delicate operation. You need a professional. I'm your only recourse." She stared at him, right into his eyes as she had done last night. But nothing of last night's affection remained. This female was cool, focused, and logical.

Everything a woman should never be.

Turning to Duncan and Teresa, she said, "Now. Let us find a place where we can plot, and we'll get this thing done so I can leave at once—and never have to see Colonel Gregory's face again."

"Brava!" With mocking, measured tone, Teresa clapped her hands.

"Very good, Miss Prendregast." Duncan offered her his arm. "The gazebo, I think."

Teresa should have gone with William, but she ignored him and grasped Duncan's other arm. The three of them walked away, a triumvirate of determination and strength.

"Since William will be of no use to us as we plan, we'll have him patrol to ensure we're not overheard." Over his shoulder, Duncan asked, "Can you at least do that, William?"

William stalked after them, glad for the first time in his life to bring up the rear. In this situation, he couldn't take the lead. He couldn't bear to trust Samantha to do the right thing.

He couldn't bear to trust *himself* to do the right thing. He bubbled with emotion. He, the man who dismissed women as pleasant diversions, but not an integral part of a man's life. He, who imagined himself married to the military, to the quest for justice, but never truly passionate in the pursuit of love.

Samantha had unmanned him—and Duncan was right. William had lost his perspective. He'd been talking without caution, thinking with his cock. He couldn't weigh the risks of the mission judiciously. He dared not retain command.

The gazebo loomed before them, and without looking back, Duncan, Teresa, and Samantha entered.

Quietly, William walked around the octagonal building, checking beneath every rosebush. They were alone. Alone, and lost in the mist.

Closing his eyes, he rested one hand on the wall near the door. Yes. He was lost. He'd never in his life *not* known the proper thing to do, or the correct way to proceed. It was all *her* fault . . . and he detested men who blamed their problems on anyone but themselves.

What had he become?

He heard Samantha say, "It's in her reticule. The map's in her reticule."

Thrusting his head inside, William didn't bother to subdue his scorn. "How would you know that?"

"Shut up, William," Duncan said.

Samantha ignored them. Him. "That black spangled reticule. She wears it with everything, and more important, she fingers it all the time. I thought she was a laudanum addict, and that's where she kept her juice." She shrugged. "The map is in her reticule."

Duncan nodded. Teresa nodded. They both seemed to accept Samantha's assessment without reservation.

William ducked out and leaned against the gazebo, looking into the fog. Better that than staring at Duncan and Teresa. And Samantha.

Duncan asked, "Can you make that exchange?"

William strained to hear, but Samantha didn't answer.

Duncan spoke with more urgency. "Can you change the real map for a fake one?"

"Of course she can." William smiled disagreeably as he answered over his shoulder. "She's infamous."

"Shut up, William," Teresa said. "What's the problem, Sam?"

"Usually a pickpocket just cuts the strings or slips in and gets the cash." Samantha spread her hands wide. "I've never opened a reticule, taken something out, and replaced it with something else."

Teresa nodded. "I understand."

"On the other hand, Terry, it could be worse." Samantha grinned, one of those gamine grins that had formerly charmed William. "She could keep it in her bosom."

Duncan and Teresa laughed.

William glared. *Sam and Terry.* When had that happened?

Before William could yell at them, scald them with his contempt, Duncan stepped into the doorway. "William, make another circuit of the building. I want to know there's no one out there."

"There's not." But William, surly, set off at once, and looked as carefully as before, watching for footprints in the dew, for any proof that someone— like Pashenka—had decided to see how well his spies were doing. But so far, Pashenka had stayed hidden on the Featherstonebaugh estate. Of course. He stayed where he was safe.

William returned to the doorway as Duncan was saying, "Then that's the plan. Pray God, Miss Prendregast, that your hands are swift."

❧ *Chapter Twenty-five* ❧

It was almost finished, this horrible houseparty with its manor full of idiots. When the luncheon was over, Valda could leave the dining hall at Silvermere where Gregory and Lady Marchant, that slut hostess of his, had ordered luncheon served. Valda would go out into the swirling fog, step into her carriage, and go home to Maitland at last. She hadn't slept in two nights. She'd been kept awake by the pain from her bruised body.

And the worry about Pashenka. How to handle him. How to escape this situation alive and free.

Not long ago nothing could have kept her awake. Pashenka wouldn't have caught her unawares and kicked her. She would have considered eluding him a challenge, nothing more. Now a dreadful refrain played in her mind ... trapped. Old, and trapped.

But she wasn't. She wouldn't allow herself to be.

And there were advantages to being awake all night. She'd heard Rupert get up and start rummaging around in her belongings, looking for the map, and she'd lain there and smiled into her pillow beneath which rested her black-beaded reticule—and the precious map.

She would give Pashenka the map. Yes, she would. Right after she told him she had more information hidden away in her brain. That would keep her alive until she could get away.

Now she fingered the reticule that hung on her arm, and watched the guests milling around the table, smiling, gossiping, filling their plates with strawberries, breads, thin-sliced beef, and cold asparagus. She ought to be eating, but she wasn't hungry. She simply wanted to leave. She didn't even care about her clothing, and she wore a fabulous outfit of . . . she had to glance down. Oh, yes. Of bronze satin with silver trim. She wore the finest clothing here.

Rupert looked good, too. Thin, tall, more aristocratic than any of these military men or ambassadors. He spoke now with one of the young, country debutantes, smiling his most charming smile and following her as she edged away. Damn Rupert. If only he were reliable. Or faithful. Or less of a flaming coward. Then Valda would keep him. But there was no chance of that now. He had betrayed her on every level. At the proper moment, he would have to be eliminated.

Leaning on her cane, she tried to listen to the conversations. Why, she didn't know. She already had so much information to impart, she'd never recall it all. She'd been so groggy last night she'd even written some of it down. She, who had always remembered everything, had begun to lose the little details.

Furthermore, some people she saw had begun to look . . . odd. Every once in a while, from the corner of her eye, she would see a man who looked almost skeletal. A woman as pale as death. A child who spoke with a hollow voice. When she turned her head, they would be gone. It was as if the ghosts of those she had killed were haunting her.

Impossible. She needed to get some sleep.

"Lady Featherstonebaugh." Lady Marchant spoke right in her ear.

Valda jumped so hard Lady Marchant had to rescue her as she toppled over.

"Lady Featherstonebaugh, you must indulge in Colonel Gregory's luncheon." Lady Marchant forcibly steered Valda toward the table. "We want you to enjoy your last meal here."

Automatically, Valda moved into her benevolent old lady routine. "Dear, I'm not able to fight my way through the crowd. Perhaps you could fill a plate for me."

"My lady, your strength has always impressed me. Come this way." Lady Marchant applied yet more pressure to Valda's arms, guiding her deeper into the crowd. "You don't want to miss such a wonderful opportunity."

"Opportunity?" As Valda's sore ribs got jabbed with random elbows and the babble of the crowd filled her ears, her voice grew shrill. "It's no opportunity to eat this swill and drink such gritty wine. You chose badly, my lady, badly." Aware she had lost the good humor that had served as a camouflage for so many years, she tried to rein herself in, but couldn't. "You don't need to look at me that way." She saw one of those skeletal faces peering over Lady Marchant's shoulder. "So reproachfully. That's the risk you take, being an English soldier—"

"An English soldier?" Lady Marchant glanced behind her.

Valda blinked. Only Lady Stephens stood there, chatting with Lady Blair.

"What are you talking about?" Lady Marchant asked.

"Nothing. Nothing." A great shout rose from the guests.

Lady Marchant yanked her to a stop. "Look, they're brawling."

Jerked from her moment of madness, Valda stared through the opening in the crowd.

Colonel Gregory had Mr. Monroe by the throat.

The crowd was forming the traditional fighting circle around the two men. The faces were intent, staring at the two furious men.

And the men were furious. Colonel Gregory looked as if he would gladly kill Mr. Monroe. Mr. Monroe was flushed, his eyes venal.

Looking into Mr. Monroe's face, he shouted, "You liar! You haven't been riding out at night chasing spies."

With that one word, they captured Valda's attention. Spies? What did he mean, spies?

Mr. Monroe broke Colonel Gregory's hold.

"How dare you call me a liar? I have. I'm a hero. Better than you!"

"You're nothing. The spawn of a Scotsman." Colonel Gregory grabbed at him again, his lips drawn back like mad dog's. "You're a fortune hunter!"

To hell with fortune hunting. Valda wanted to hear about the spies. She leaned forward, her gaze intent.

"*I'm* a fortune hunter?" Mr. Monroe shoved Colonel Gregory's chest. "What about you? At least I love the woman!"

Beside Valda, Lady Marchant inhaled sharply.

Valda looked at the female beside her and realized—the men were fighting over *Lady Marchant*. Fascinating. And the men had mentioned spies. *Truly fascinating*. The pain of her ribs, her fear, even her awareness of her surroundings left Valda as she concentrated on the scene before her.

"I know what you've been doing," Colonel Gregory shouted. "You're after Lady Marchant—"

Now the entire crowd gasped. The circle tightened.

Eyes avid, Valda leaned forward.

Mr. Monroe swung at Colonel Gregory. Colonel Gregory went spinning away. Women screamed. Men shouted.

And Valda felt a tug on her precious reticule.

She grabbed at it. It still hung on her arm. She spun toward the person beside her—the person who tried who steal the map.

It was that thief. That tall governess with the white-blonde hair. That Miss Penny Gast. Swift as a snake, Valda grabbed that fiendish girl's wrist and twisted. "Give it back!"

"What?" Miss Gast pretended to be bewildered.

With her other hand, Valda reached into the pocket hidden in her skirt. Wrapping her fingers around the cool butt of her new pistol, she clumsily drew it. Pointing it at Miss Gast, she said, "Give it back!"

"Ruddy 'ell!" Miss Gast tried to step back as she stared at the pistol. The crowd hemmed her in, holding her in place.

Lady Marchant shoved at Valda. "Lady Feather-stonebaugh, what are you doing?"

People around them were noticing the pistol. The women screamed louder. The fight between Colonel Gregory and Mr. Monroe died.

"Give it back!" Valda demanded again.

Miss Gast held up her hands, showed her empty palms. "I don't have anything. See?"

"What's going on?" Colonel Gregory shouldered his way toward them.

Valda stuck the pistol in Miss Gast's stomach.

Colonel Gregory froze. "Don't move. Samantha, don't move."

"She stole my . . . my paper," Valda said. "Everyone knows she's a pickpocket."

That bitch Lady Marchant interfered. "No, she's not. I told you she wasn't. You've got her name wrong."

"For God's sake, Valda, are you mad?" Rupert stared over the top of the crowd.

"I don't have anything. See?" Miss Gast spoke in

this soothing tone which irritated Valda almost to madness.

Valda wanted to shoot them all, but she had only one bullet. One bullet to use on this bitch who had stolen the map. "No one steals from me."

Moving slowly, Miss Gast showed her empty hands. "Why don't you check on your paper? You'll see I don't have it."

Valda hesitated.

Miss Gast seemed sincere.

Lady Marchant sounded irritated.

Colonel Gregory looked . . . pale.

With her free hand, Valda squeezed the soft sides of her reticule. Inside she heard the crackle of paper. She began to feel ill. Cautiously, she withdrew the pistol from Miss Gast's stomach. No one in the crowd moved as she pulled open the strings that held the reticule closed and peered inside.

There it was. The map, folded into a stiff square, the distinctive red ink clearly marking its importance.

The pistol drooped in her hand. "I . . . I'm sorry, Miss Gast. I thought you had . . . I thought you were someone else."

"My name is Miss Prendregast." The young woman's voice was firm, but her hands trembled so hard she hid them in the folds of her skirts. "Miss Samantha Prendregast."

Slipping forward out of the throng, Mr. Monroe appeared beside Valda and removed the pistol from her grip.

The crowd gave a collective sigh of relief.

Lady Marchant put her hand to her forehead

and performed a most unladylike swoon, one that involved toppling over onto the marble floor so hard she bumped her cheek.

Mr. Monroe went onto his knees beside her, calling, "Smelling salts. We need smelling salts!"

Colonel Gregory grabbed Miss Gast and wrapped her in his arms.

For one moment, she looked as if she, too, might collapse. Then she lifted her head and fiercely said, "You don't like me, I don't like you, and I won't be punished for your wife's death. I won't be the scapegoat for your shame. So release me—now!"

The expression on Colonel Gregory's face was beyond price. Valda would gladly have stayed to hear the rest of the scene, but Rupert grabbed her and tried to hustle her toward the door. She resisted. But people were still looking at her. The ambassador and the head of the Home Office were eyeing her with peculiar intensity. Leaning down, she plucked her pistol off of the floor beside Mr. Monroe, tucked it into her pocket, and, head held high, sailed out the door with Rupert.

The last words she heard, spoken by a furious Colonel Gregory, were, "Miss Prendregast, pack your bags. You'll be returned to London first thing in the morning."

❧ *Chapter Twenty-six* ❧

William stalked into his bedchamber and pointed to his valet. "Out! Get out!"

"Aye, sir, don't have to tell me twice." Cleavers stormed out of the room and slammed the door behind him.

William stared after him. What the hell was wrong with him? What was wrong with everyone? Even his guests, who should have known better, had acted as if they couldn't wait to get away from him. They behaved as if he had drowned a kitten, when all he'd done was what any sensible man would do when he found a thief in his nest. He'd routed that thief. Never mind that she was beautiful and everyone loved her. Never mind that she'd brought peace and music to his household. Never mind that he'd taken her maidenhead with all the finesse of a rampaging sailor and she'd given it to him with all the grace of a . . . a woman. The woman for him.

But she was a thief, and once a thief, always a thief. She'd done him, them, England a favor, and risked her life doing so. If that had been all she'd done, he would have compromised his principles and married her.

But she'd also stolen from him. Just little things, some not important, some very much so. She hadn't returned them. Against all evidence, she hadn't admitted to taking them, had said she didn't know where they were, and he could tell by her expression she did. She was a liar as well as a thief.

He tore off his cravat and his collar. Discarded his tailcoat and his waistcoat. Looked out the window into night, trying to see the lights from her cottage.

He ought to imprison her here. Put her in the jail in Hawksmouth with instructions that she never be released.

But he couldn't. He was as soft as treacle pudding when it came to Samantha, and why?

Because he couldn't forget how she looked with the moonlight on her bare shoulders, and the pain of her upbringing, and, dear God, when he remembered how she loved his children . . .

Sitting in the chair, he began the difficult process of pulling off his tight boots.

So he would send her back to London. Foist her back on Lady Bucknell with a letter warning her of Samantha's larcenous bent. Then Samantha would be without honest employment. She'd be forced to return to the streets, to cut purses for a living, until they caught her and hung her by her slender neck.

Horror brought him to his feet. He stomped his foot back in his boot.

No. He wasn't doing the right thing. It wasn't right that he inflict Samantha on the London populace. Nor should he stand by while she went to hell with all the defiance of her fiery nature.

After all, she was not the only one at fault. He had seduced her.

He should have known better.

He was out the door and running down the stairs before he could reconsider. The footman jumped to attention and opened the door; then William was outside and racing to the cottage where Samantha was incarcerated. He slammed his fist on the door.

Clarinda came in a hurry, and even in the dim light on the porch, he could see her dismay. "Colonel! Miss Prendregast didn't wish want t' see anyone."

Taking Clarinda's arm, he pulled her through the entrance while he stepped inside. "Don't come back." He shut the door in her face and faced a room alive with the light of a fire in the central fireplace and a branch of candles set by the packed trunk.

"Clarinda?" Samantha called from the bedchamber. "Who was it this time? Please don't tell me it was one of the children. I couldn't bear turning one of them"—she stepped into the doorway and her voice trailed off—"away." She stood, silhouetted against the candlelight from the other room, arms upraised to brush her hair, hand holding an ivory brush. As she had the first time he kissed her, she wore her modest white nightgown, and her blue robe hung open.

Beautiful. She was beautiful. His heart ached at the sight of her, and he wanted only one thing. To have her for his own.

Seeing him, she stood immobile for a long moment. Slowly, she drew the bristles through her platinum blonde hair, smoothing the length over her bosom.

Then swiftly, quietly, she stepped back into the bedchamber and shut the door.

It was rejection, clean and final. His ire rose at her gall. When he heard the key turn in the lock, his rage took form.

Striding to the door, he kicked at the lock. The door was sturdy, but the lock was not. A trivial lock, one created for privacy, not safety.

He kicked at it again.

The lock creaked.

He flung himself at the door and smashed through, stumbling into her bedchamber.

And she said in a cool voice, "The window's open. At thief school, they teach us to take the easiest route."

She knew she shouldn't taunt him. He stood, hands hanging loose at his sides, shoulders hunched, head down, watching her like a bull about to charge. Heat radiated from him; he wanted to somehow pay her back for besmirching his reputation.

She didn't care that violence set his fingers trembling. She wanted to hit, too. She wanted to throw caution to the wind. She wanted to shriek and shout and slap, because once again, William had taught her a lesson she should have learned so many times before.

It didn't matter that she'd changed her life. That she worked to be better. That she stole . . . nothing.

She had once been a pickpocket, and she was forever tainted.

And he . . . the man she loved. The man she'd given herself to. He should have believed in her, and he was the first to condemn her. To condemn her, and to use her for his own ends.

Her hand tightened on the brush handle until the ivory marked her hand.

He took a long breath, one exhausting in its length. "I've decided to marry you."

She took a breath to match his—then released it in a burst of raucous laughter. "Marry? Me? Have you lost your mind?"

His fists clenched. Red rose from his neck to his forehead. He wasn't a man anymore; he was a beast, grunting and primal, trying to cover himself with a veneer of civilization. As if that would save him from his real self. "You were an innocent in the physical sense, at least, and I took that from you."

"Ah. So *you're* a thief too." She smiled brightly. "Well, like follows like."

He growled. There wasn't another word for it. He definitely growled. "I am not a thief. But you are, and I can't in all honor allow you to go out and wreak crime on the world."

"So you're making a sacrifice by taking me to

your bed." The words were acid on her tongue. "You really are noble."

"You have a good heart. You need a man's guidance."

His? He must be jesting! With one hand she smoothed the nightgown over her breast, her belly, her thighs, showing him her form, taunting him with herself. "Are you sure of your motive? Are you sure you're not marrying me because you . . . want me?"

"No. I'm not sure." His guttural voice vibrated with desire. "I do want you."

She smiled with wicked delight.

"I'll watch you. I'll keep you honest. I'll keep you pregnant with my babies." He stood straighter as he spoke. "You probably already are pregnant."

Her smile faded. "I spoke with Terry, and it's doubtful. She says it's the wrong time of the month."

"I'll keep you here, and we'll see. In the meantime, I'll keep you so busy you won't have time to indulge in your predilection for larceny."

Fury blazed up as hot as hell's fires. "Blighter. Bloody damned blighter!" She threw the brush at his head. "How dare you? How dare—"

He ducked. He charged. He caught her around the waist and carried her backward onto the bed.

She landed on the mattress, on her back, with him on top of her, and the rage of the past day blew like a blocked teakettle. She struck out at him blindly, hitting his head, his chest, his shoulders. She landed a few good, hard blows before he caught first one fist, then the other, and trapped them over her head.

They sank into the feathers, his weight bearing her down when she wanted to jump up and . . . no, not flee. Nothing so intelligent. She wanted to kick him. "Get off of me, you flaming . . . righteous . . . stupid . . . bully."

He didn't get off her. He bit her throat, a light scoring of teeth across her skin.

She screamed and thrashed beneath him. He was a beast, and she hated him with all her heart.

He restrained her as she fought, holding her wrists, keeping his body atop hers, until the first flurry of struggle was over and her strength failed.

Then he licked the spot he had bit.

She panted. From the struggle. From his weight. "I wouldn't marry you if Queen Victoria herself offered you on a silver platter."

He lifted himself above her.

She got a look at him. His blue eyes, fringed with dark lashes, blazed with emotion. Fury . . . no, passion.

He wasn't biting her as a punishment. He was marking her. He was making her feel what he wanted her to feel, and that was . . . "Anger. You want me to be angry. You don't care how furious you make me."

"Why would I? I like it." His chest heaved against hers. "It's something, my darling, that we have in common."

Her captured hands curled. Her nails bit into her palms. "We share *nothing* in common, remember, guv'nor? Oi'm a street urchin, a thief, a cutpurse, an' ye're a ruddy colonel in 'Er Majesty's army. A commander who never in 'is life ever did anything dis'onorable."

He laughed, deep, low, menacing. "I remember one thing we have in common." He transferred both of her wrists to one of his hands.

She knew what he was going to do. No matter how she detested their empathy, she could read his intentions, and she writhed away from him.

Pulling his knife from his pocket, he flipped the shining blade open.

Her throat dried.

"Don't move," he whispered. Tucking the blade into her neckline, he sliced her nightgown open.

The material tugged, but the blade was sharp and worked only too well. His hand slid past her chest, over her breast.

His black hair curled over his forehead. The candles cast a golden glow over his complexion. His jaw was carved marble, but his lips . . . as his hand brushed past her breast, his lips curved upward in the kind of buccaneer smile she never expected—never wanted—to see from him.

What an idiot she was for loving him. And how this love heated and burned.

He sat up, straddled her hips, and sliced the material down past her knees.

"What are you doing?" she shouted. "Are you mad?"

"I want the nightgown off. I want the robe off. I want you bare and defenseless. It's the only way to deal with you, Samantha. If it were up to me, I'd imprison you in a tower and keep you there."

He sounded so intense, so sincere, she noted the stirrings of fear deep in her belly. But she mocked him. "I would *steal* away."

He closed his eyes. When he opened them, he was smiling again. He made a show of clicking the knife shut and putting it in his pocket. With his free hand, he unbuttoned his trousers, loosened his drawers.

She watched, eyes wide, as he freed himself.

As slowly as a man dancing a minuet, he slid his knee between her legs.

She struggled to keep her thighs together.

He separated them. Bending close to her ear, he murmured, "Do you understand ruthlessness?"

He wouldn't . . . would he? She knew that he wouldn't . . . but she also knew he wouldn't cut off her nightgown, or keep her captive by his weight, or imprison her wrists.

She didn't really know him. She didn't know him at all.

"I'll never forgive you for this," she answered.

"For what?" He layered a kiss on her lips. "For making you like it?" He kissed her brow, her eyelids, her blazing cheeks. With his tongue, he circled the petals of her ear, and sucked on the lobe.

And she realized what he meant. He might hold her wrists. They might be sprawled sideways across the bed. Resentment and hurt might be eating at both of them. But between them burned a fire nothing could quench.

There was a reason why she'd come to him a virgin. There was a reason why he'd been celibate since his wife died. They'd been waiting for each other. Waiting for the conflagration that consumed them. Nothing could halt its advance. No matter what hurt stood between them or the insults they flung at each other's heads, they wanted each other. Nothing could change that.

The scent of him enveloped her, earthy and male. His shirt, loose, white and soft, brushed the tips of her breasts, over and over. His thigh nudged between her legs, a pale imitation of intercourse. Making her want the real thing. His mouth on her skin, his hands holding her down, his knee . . .

"No!" She turned her head away, kicked at his legs.

In the soft voice of pure menace, he asked, "What's the matter? Do you like that too much? Does it make your skin flush, your loins burn?" He trailed his lips over her chin and down her throat. "If I put my fingers in you, will they slide in because you're damp and slick from wanting me?"

Everything he said was true, and hearing him say so made it worse. It was almost as if he could talk her to an unwilling climax.

"I ought to cut your robe off completely," he mused.

"No!"

"No, you're right. I like holding you like this. Helpless, waiting and wondering what I'll do next." He gazed down at her bosom, and his smile produced a most peculiar tightening in her belly. "You have such pretty breasts. I never got to see them properly last time. It was dark and I was desperate. But they're everything I imagined. Pale, with rose-colored nipples that tighten when you're excited. As you are now."

"I'm cold."

He knew she was lying, but he pulled an expression of concern over his features. "Then I shall warm you." Dipping his head, he took a nipple into his mouth and rolled it across his tongue.

Irresistibly, her eyes closed. Her back arched. Her legs clamped around his knee.

Opening his mouth wide, he took as much in as he could, then suckled with a strong motion.

They'd spent only one night together. How did he know how to rouse her so precisely? How did he know to sweep his cheek across the lower slope of her breast, then slide up her body and nibble at her lower lip? Her mouth was open as she gasped, and he took pitiless advantage to enter her with his tongue.

She strained upward, trying to increase the contact between them.

He kissed her until she thought that, even if she got away now, she would recognize the taste of him forever. Then he whispered, "Samantha."

She lifted her lids to see him looking down at her. His mouth was damp from hers, his gaze as merciless as a peregrine's hovering over its prey.

"Don't get up. Don't move. Remain just as you are, or you'll not get out of this bed until the vicar comes to wed us. Do you understand?"

Never taking her gaze from him, she nodded.

Even so, he didn't believe her, for he let go of her wrists, then hovered there as if waiting to make another grab for her.

Pride required she make another attempt at escape. But pride was stupid, and she was not. She was practical. She was no-nonsense. She was a cutpurse from the East End of London.

She didn't have a chance. He was bigger and probably faster.

More important, she wanted this. Not as he wanted it, as a forceful fortification of the bond between the two of them, but because she wanted a sweet farewell. And because—*tell the truth, Samantha*—because she couldn't not. She loved him too much to deny him, or to deny herself.

He ripped his shirt off. He looked to see if she was still lying there. He shoved his trousers down. He looked again. Grasping the last remaining connected inches of her nightgown, he tore it all the way through the hem.

And she remembered—he was furious. She was new to this. He could hurt her . . .

But Colonel William Gregory would never hurt *her*. Not physically.

And he had already broken her heart. What more could he do?

He placed one tender hand on the inside of each ankle and rubbed his palms up to her knees, up the insides of her thighs. Slipping his hands under her legs, lifting them onto his shoulders.

"What are you doing?" She tried to fight her way free.

He tightened his grip and laughed. "Just what it looks like."

He nuzzled between her legs, blowing air into the curling blonde thatch of hair.

She realized he could see her. There. Between her legs. The candles at her bedside flickered, giving light where they should not. And he was planning to . . . kiss her? Where she ached and wanted?

She couldn't bear it. She couldn't. Trying to escape, she twisted sideways.

He laughed again, opened her and thrust his tongue inside her.

This time when she twisted, it wasn't to escape, but in excitement. It was like . . . the deepest kiss, the greatest intimacy. When he was down there, he knew she was aroused. All her secrets were exposed; she could hide nothing from him. And the way he entered her, his tongue stabbing at her like a velvet lash.

She grasped the sheets, twisting them in her fists. She rocked her head back and forth. Within her, a fist of passion tightened almost past bearing. She was dampening his tongue, she knew it, but she couldn't stop. He drove her toward climax, ruthless in his decision to conquer her, to take her and make her realize they were mates.

And she did realize that. Just as she realized their story would end in tragedy.

But it would not end, not tonight.

His lips captured her clitoris, and he milked it in a motion that brought her to the edge. Close. So close. But not quite. Not yet—

He thrust his finger inside her. And it *was* now. Every muscle within her contracted. A scream burst from her throat. Her hips rose, rocking in the ancient motion of intercourse, in orgasm, in acceptance.

And in one smooth motion, he slid up her body and entered her.

She was damp and slick, so desperate for penetration she accepted his length without difficulty.

He was hot and hard, so insistent that he rode her orgasm all the way in.

Then, grinding his hips against hers, he started her all over again.

She didn't stop. She had no control. She climaxed again and again, digging her nails into his buttocks, trying to hold him still for a moment of respite. "Please," she whispered. "Please, William." But she didn't know what she begged him for.

Perhaps she begged for his love.

He moved slowly, then quickly. Deeply, then barely entering. He taunted her with his motions, holding one of her thighs up on his arm, using the other hand to caress her as he pleased—on her breasts, her stomach, between her legs right above where he entered her.

She whimpered and moaned, growing more exhausted with each culmination, yet the motion never stopped, and her response grew greater. It was as if he were weakening her defenses and strengthening their bonds at the same time.

His strokes speeded up. He allowed her leg to rest on the bed, put all his weight atop of her, pressed her into the mattress. "Samantha. Look at me."

She scarcely understood him.

He wrapped his hands around her face. "Look at me."

She made the effort to lift her eyelids—and

stared right into the soul of his passion. This man, so strong, so cultured in appearance, was a primitive to his bones. He had made his claim; he would accept no denial. "You're mine," he said. "Mine."

❧ Chapter Twenty-seven ❧

Samantha woke with the first light. The fire had gone out, she wore not a stitch, but she was warm, snuggled up against William's back. He'd removed his boots and his trousers completely, and now she held a naked man in her arms. A gloriously naked man, his bottom tucked into her belly, his back against her chest, their legs tangled together.

He had made his point last night. Now she would make hers. With as much expertise as she'd learned in the last two days, she would show him her love, and show him what he would miss for all the long years they'd be apart. It was little enough revenge, for the pain as she knew she would suffer.

The arm beneath her rested across his shoulders. The other was tucked around his waist, and her hand . . . she smiled. Her hand was most conveniently placed.

Softly she stroked the fur that grew on his chest, marveling at the sculpted muscles beneath. His ribs rippled beneath his skin, and she ran her fingertips over them, first one side and then the other, and smiled as he took a long breath.

Was he awake yet? She didn't think so. With the flat of her hand, she stroked down his ridged belly and into the thatch of hair at his groin. There she found what she ultimately sought.

He might still be asleep, but parts of him were stirring. She grinned into his shoulder. She didn't know anything. She didn't know about pleasing a man, but she knew how to please William. Everything she did pleased him . . . sexually.

Only in other ways did he find her lacking.

Her smile turned bitter. To her, it was the other ways that mattered. Eventually to him, too. So she would leave him and live a life barren of richness or sensuality or love.

But she would have her pride.

She snorted softly. Pride was a cold bedfellow, but to spend the rest of her life knowing her husband watched and suspected her of a moral corruption that might involve affairs, treachery . . . murder? Once William's imagination went to work, she would never be without surveillance.

So she had this morning to taste him, caress him, and build her memories forever.

She cupped his genitals. His balls were hot and hairy, wrinkled and heavy for their size.

But his member . . . smooth, hairless, magical, it stirred beneath her touch. It fascinated her, this male organ that hardened so swiftly. She wrapped her hand around it, palm and fingers, measuring its width. Then she stroked its length, enjoying the texture, the ridges, and at the top, with her thumb, she circled the sensuous cap. A drop of moisture beaded there, and she drew it out in a little circle.

"Dear God. Samantha." William's voice was drugged, sleepy.

She lifted herself on her elbow, and kissed his shoulder—and bit it.

He jumped, and rolled over to face her, the blanket wrapped around his waist.

To her surprise, his eyes were alert. Had he been awake all the time? Or was this the way the spy catcher and soldier woke up?

It didn't matter. She wouldn't be here long enough to learn the answer. "I owed you that," she said.

His gaze flicked to the mark of his teeth on her neck, and he reached out to encircle her.

"No." She pushed his hands away. "It's my turn."

Still he tried to embrace her.

"My turn," she said firmly.

His lashes drooped. "You'll make me sorry."

"Oh, yes. That is my plan." She caressed his chest and watched his face, taking delight in that magnificent structure, in the pure blue of his eyes, in the lips which had provided so much delight. She would remember everything about him, but she would cherish the memory of his face as he looked right now, strong with anticipation and faintly wary.

His legs shifted beneath the covers. "I'm sorry

already, if that makes any difference."

She smiled at his treachery. "Not a whit."

The sun was rising over the mountains, bathing him in light, showing him in all his beauty. She'd never imagined such a magnificent man could exist; heavily muscled, with valleys and peaks of definition that came only from hard riding and constant activity. She wanted to ask what he did to keep so fit. Fencing? Boxing?

But it didn't matter. If she knew, it would be one more fact she had forever to brood about.

Flipping her hair over one shoulder, she bunched it like a whisk and brushed at his throat. She saw his Adam's apple move up and down as he swallowed.

His hands closed on her shoulders, and he massaged them in deep, warm circles.

"You don't have to do anything," she murmured against his skin.

"If I don't, I'll take you now."

"We can't have that." She brushed his hair back from his face, delighting in the curl that clung to her fingers like a living thing. He was so beautiful . . . but that was the wrong word. Not beautiful, but craggy. The bones of his face gave him an intimidating strength. His nose—she chuckled—his nose could only be called big, but no one dared say that for fear he would take umbrage. Or perhaps laugh, depending on his mood, because he wasn't vain and cared so little for others' opinions. His beard was a dark shadow across his jaw that scraped her fingertips as she passed over it. His ears she admired for their neat set against his head, and because they enticed her to nibble at the lobe. And when she did that, his hands spasmed on her shoulders. Encouraged, she licked the folds.

He groaned.

Leaning her forehead against his, she looked into his gaze. "I've found something you like."

"Anything you do to me."

His lips moved with such etched precision, she couldn't take her gaze away. His lips . . . full, smooth, created solely to give pleasure to her. Bit by bit, she lowered her mouth to his and took his full lower lip between her teeth. She nibbled softly. His tongue came out to lick at her upper lip. And they were kissing, kissing like people starved of passion, of desire . . . of love. How she loved him! She feasted on his open mouth, tilting her head back and forth, dipping again and again into the sweet well, sucking at his tongue with tantalizing greed.

He remained still beneath her kiss, beneath the hands that rubbed his chest and stroked down his arms. His only response was to the kiss itself. He followed her lead, a male leashed by his own permission.

His neck was strong and thick, his shoulders so muscled his collarbones were almost invisible. Parting the hair on his chest, she lowered her mouth to his nipple and sipped delicately.

"My God." He arched back on the pillow. "Samantha."

"Hm?" She loved this. To have a strong, invincible man at her mercy. To drag her nails down his ribs and feel his stomach collapse as he sucked in his breath. To know that beneath the blanket waited her reward. Nothing could interrupt these last moments between them . . . hastily, she wiped a tear off his chest.

Showing a sensitivity she wouldn't have expected, he asked, "Samantha?" He tried to lift her chin.

She slipped away, down his body, trying to distract him with the simple expedient of kissing him at the place on his diaphragm where his ribs met his breastbone.

"Samantha?" His voice sounded fainter, but still he tried to look at her face.

She slid her hand over his hip and down his thigh. His thigh . . . she tried to wrap her hand around one and squeeze, but it was too broad. Too hard. "I could write an epic poem about your thighs."

"That would amuse polite society rather too much, and I wouldn't like that."

"I wouldn't either." She pressed her cheek to his belly. "I can't think of a word to rhyme with marble column."

He chuckled.

She heard the sound beneath her ear, and rewarded him with a kiss on his navel, probing with her tongue, reveling in the scent of his skin.

His hand slid beneath her and cupped her breast.

Taking that hand, she placed it on his chest and patted it. "I told you. I'm doing this." *I'm memoriz-*

*ing your body. I'm storing up pleasure. I'm making good
and sure you will never forget me. Or I you.*

"If you expect me to keep my hands to myself,
you'll have to tie me to the bed."

She lifted her eyebrows. "It's a thought." Rather
a good one, since she knew he would argue when
she left . . . and for him, she was weak. Far too
weak.

Taking his hands, she wrapped them around the
posts on the headboard. "Pretend I've tied you.
That should help."

"I doubt it," he rumbled, but he held the bedposts.

She slid her hand under the covers, lifting them
as she went, peering beneath as if whatever was
there could only be a surprise. As it was, in a way.
Rising from the froth of pubic hair was . . . "What
do you call it?"

"What?" He sounded almost shocked.

"I can't keep calling it '*it*.' What do men call their
part?"

"What men say is seldom for a lady's ears."

She delighted in his repressive tone. "Then you
can tell *me*."

Unclasping his fingers, he reached out to touch
her cheek. "Samantha . . ."

Exasperated, she took his wrist and carried his
hand once more to the headboard. "Tell me what
you call it."

"You're a lady if I say you are."

I can never be a lady. I don't belong in your world.
She took a quivering breath. It was better this way.

He would see. So would she. Someday . . .

"Samantha, listen to me . . ."

"What is this?" She feathered her finger along his tumescence.

"When I marry you, you'll be a lady."

She stroked him. "What do you call it?"

"You're a lady because—"

She touched her lips to the tip of his penis, and ran her tongue around in a circle. "Tell me what you call it or I won't kiss it anymore."

The muscles in his arms and his legs bulged. His knuckles turned white. At last, he was distracted. Thank God, he was distracted. "Dear heavens, Samantha." He sounded hoarse with shock . . . and delight.

She took her mouth away.

He spoke as rapidly as possible. "Prick, cock, the old horn."

She lavished a kiss on him—and stopped.

"Roaring jack, old Adam, roosterswain."

She sucked lightly on the tip, just once and no more.

"Privy member, bushwacker . . ."

His voice trailed off, and she looked up.

"If you don't put yourself on top of me soon, I'll finish in your mouth and you'll have to wait an hour for your satisfaction."

"Oh, we could invent something for you to do," she drawled. But she had a coach to catch. *A life to seek.* So she slithered up his body, taking her time, trailing kisses and rubbing herself against him like an affectionate cat. Then she faltered.

"What's wrong?" he asked gutturally.

"I'm not sure how to proceed."

"I'd show you, but I'm not to take my hands down."

She narrowed her eyes at him. He dared taunt her? Now, in his position? "I'll figure it out."

She'd been beside him, stretched out or on her knees. All she had to do was skate her leg over the top of him and take him. He'd shown no hesitation. A smile flirted with her lips. Why should she?

Well, possibly because he wasn't opening himself to her. He wasn't making himself vulnerable. She was. Yet even last night, when he'd been reduced by anger and frustration to a beast, he had never hurt her. He never would. She knew that just as surely as she knew she would always love him.

Without further hesitation, she mounted him. The mattress sank beneath her knees. The white sheets were rumpled. William was sturdy beneath her, big-boned and well-muscled, so strong she reveled in the dominance she held. His hands still clutched the bedposts, his abdomen rippled as he breathed, and he was hers, all hers—for now.

Placing herself over his hips, she pressed onto him, opening herself along his length, teasing him with the knowledge that he was close, so close, to entering her. But she held power, and she murmured, "Not yet, not yet." Because it felt good to rub herself against him, to see him strain and writhe. She scraped her fingernails lightly through the hair on his chest. She circled his nipples, she caressed his abdomen. Leaning over him, she kissed his lips, and whispered against them, "You're so gorgeous, stretched out like a gift I've opened but in which I've yet to take pleasure."

Below her, he rolled his hips. "Take your pleasure."

The movement lifted her, placing all of his parts firmly against hers, and bringing her a rush of such desire she flushed and grew damper yet.

If he did that again, she would be lost. Desperate to draw this out, this last time, she said, "Don't move. I'm the one in control."

He laughed, a husky, mocking laughter. "Control? You're not in control. I'm not in control. We're at the mercy of our passions, swept together and clinging madly to one another." He laughed again. He looked into her eyes, challenging her, as he made a show of loosening his grip from the bedposts. Slowly, he reached for her, touched her thighs, slid his hands up to her hips . . .

Her spine sagged, her body softened in the sweet rush of passion. He was right. It was passion that swept them along, changing them forever.

He urged her to rise on her knees, adjusted her and himself, and found the damp, warm center of her. Together, they paused, savoring the anticipation.

Waiting was ecstasy.

The gradual push of his body into hers was more, greater, grander than any moment had ever been in her whole life. She took him in slow increments, with hesitations in between so gratifying they brought tears to her eyes. With each forward movement, his breath rasped in his throat, and she gave a moan of helpless need. The joining, for all that they'd done it twice before, was still new, a miracle of pleasure. He reached the deepest point; he touched her so deeply inside, with so much heat, it was as if he branded her. She moved away quickly, almost tearing herself apart from him, but he caught her hips and entered once more.

The two of them groaned out loud, caught together in the trap of rapture. She moved faster, the mattress bouncing beneath her knees. She loved this; the scents, the sounds, the warmth, the closeness.

Moving with a strong rhythm, she leaned down to put her face close to his. "I'm yours."

"Yes!" His eyes blazed with triumph.

She pulled him into her. "And you are mine."

"No."

"Oh, yes." *I love you. I love you.*

"Don't ever leave me."

I do love you.

He threw his head back, straining in agonized pleasure. He clasped her tightly against him. His hips surged and he filled her with warmth and wetness. With seed. With him.

✣❦ *Chapter Twenty-eight* ❦✣

As William slumbered, Samantha slipped from the bed. Last night, Clarinda had laid out her traveling garments; Samantha gathered them and tiptoed into the main room. Her trunk was there, packed and ready to be loaded, as well as her gloves, her hat, and her coat. As she donned her clothes, she looked around the room, seeking anything she might have forgotten, but there was nothing. She had left no mark on this place where she'd found heaven and descended into hell. She supposed that was good, except . . . from her reticule, she took her knife and knelt beside the table where William had showed her so much love. Underneath on the unvarnished surface, she scratched her initials, and William's, and encircled them with a heart.

Stupid, really. No one would ever see it. But she would know it was there, forever, and she wanted there to be something of forever in her love.

Or rather . . . her passion. William was right. That explained why a man like him would want to wed a woman he despised. Why a woman like her would seduce a man witless and harsh.

Glancing out the window, she saw a line of figures: six girls, twelve to two, dressed in dark blue ankle-length gowns, their hair tightly braided and their black boots shined. Emmeline had only one glove. Vivian's hat hung down her back. They all looked slightly sleepy, and they stood staring at the little cottage, doggedly waiting for . . . well, she didn't imagine she would get away without talking to them, did she?

With a heavy heart, she walked into the cool air and over to the solemn little line. "Girls." She held out her arms.

They stared at her with accusing eyes.

"The housekeeper says you're leaving," Agnes said. "You aren't, are you?"

Then Emmeline broke, and ran to her, and the others followed, hugging her, holding her, sniffling into her skirt.

"Miss Prendregast, Miss Prendregast, don't leave us," Henrietta begged.

"Yeth, Mith Prendregast, we'll be good," Emmeline said.

In a mature voice so unlike the petulant child of the last week, Agnes said, "Miss Prendregast, you've been our best governess, and you've been my best friend. Please, please, can't you find a way to stay?"

She broke Samantha's heart. They all broke Samantha's heart, and she hadn't thought it could break any more. She took the little ones' hands. "Let's go for a walk."

"That means *no*," Kyla whispered.

The subdued little group trudged through the dew-dampened grass, leaving a trail of footprints.

Samantha knew she had to say something. Something wise. She had to say the right thing. And she feared there was only one right thing, and she had only one chance to say it. "Do you know why I'm leaving? Did Mrs. Shelbourn tell you that?"

The children shook their heads in doleful unison.

"Because, when I was very young, I was a thief."

The children gasped.

"Oh, yes. I was the worst kind of sinner. I robbed people of their money and their belongings. I cut their purses." She stopped walking and looked at each one of them. Poor, wide-eyed, shocked little dears. They didn't know what to say. They didn't know what to do. "I was good at what I did, and I was famous. I even had a nickname—the Theater Pickpocket. The wealthy used to brag they'd had their pockets picked by me. Even people who hadn't, bragged. But one day I cut the wrong purse, and the owner of that purse took me in hand. Lady Bucknell made me see the error of my ways, and I reformed." Samantha swallowed. This was the hard part. The part that hurt. "But once you've got a reputation, it is yours for all time.

When people hear that I was once a thief, they think I must still be a thief. When something goes missing and I'm anywhere near, they blame me."

"Did you take my mama's miniature?" Vivian accused her with expression and words.

Samantha swayed, hurt yet again when she didn't think she could hurt anymore.

"No, she didn't!" Mara smacked Vivian.

Samantha walked backward until the back of the bench touched her skirt, then she sank down. "You see? Already Vivian is suspicious." She looked down at her gloves, then up at the children. "No, Vivian, I didn't, but your papa thinks I did."

"I thought you helped him catch the bad lady last night," Mara said. "Doesn't that make him like you more?"

"I did help, but that made his opinion of me worse, really. I used my pickpocket skills to help him, and proved conclusively I had been a thief. I was condemned no matter what action I took."

"Who took Mama's miniature?" Agnes asked. "If we could discover that, you could stay."

Samantha had to tread carefully. "I can't say who took your mother's miniature, but even if we knew, I wouldn't stay. You see, your papa thinks the worst of me, and I will not remain and wait to be accused again."

"Miss Prendregast, I'm sorry." Vivian ran to her, sat next to her, and wrapped her arms around Samantha's shoulders. "I shouldn't have blamed you."

"It's all right." Samantha stroked her hair.

"Other people have made that mistake."

"We wanted you to be our mother," Agnes said.

Oh, dear. "I would love to be your mother, but you know, and I know, that a former thief, a governess, and a woman with no background and no family can't marry a man as important as your father."

"You can thso." Emmeline's eyes flashed.

"Also, I would do you children no good as you went out for your debuts."

Agnes bunched her fists at her waist. "I'd like to hear someone say anything bad about you."

"You will."

"Father's in love with you," Henrietta said.

Samantha caught her breath. Is that why he insisted she stay? Because he thought he was in love with her? Or was it because he'd taken her maidenhead and he believed in some murky, shamefaced little corner of his soul that he had to make things right? "Maybe he thinks he is. He'll get over it soon." From the depths of her bitter soul, she dragged the words, "Men always do."

"It's not fair," Kyla wailed.

Samantha discovered an incongruous smile playing on her lips. "Life never is, dear. The thing to remember is—when you're doing something that you know is wrong, to stop it and make things right."

"We're only children." Mara's chin raised belligerently. "How do we know if something's wrong?"

"If you feel sick to your stomach all the time, waiting for someone to find out, then you're doing wrong. If you find yourself hiding, afraid the light will reveal you, then you're doing wrong. If you cause hurt, then you're doing wrong." Standing, Samantha went to Mara and touched her chin. "Mara, listen to your heart, and everything will come right." Enough of that. That was perilously close to a lecture. "Now. I have to go. I'll never forget any of you." Gorblimey, that was true. So true. "I'll keep you in my heart always." She hugged each one of them, trying to find something special to say and failing miserably. Maybe she wasn't cut out for this governess stuff. Maybe it was better that she leave.

She left them standing there, a forlorn little group that held her fragile heart in their hands.

As she walked back into the cottage, she saw that her trunk was no longer in the main room.

A bad sign.

She found William standing in the bedchamber, fully dressed, looking absolutely delectable and staring at the rip in the sheets he'd made with his boots the night before.

"That will cause gossip in the servants' hall," she said.

He looked up at her so calmly, she knew he'd heard her enter. He scrutinized her, and while his expression was pleasant his blue eyes scorched her with their heat. "Why are you wearing your hat and gloves? You surely didn't plan to go visiting so early on this fine morning. We have our wedding to plan."

He made her want to cry.

He made her want to rage.

She would only allow the rage. "As I'd planned, I'm leaving. I'm going back to the Distinguished Academy of Governesses, and once there, I'm going to suggest to Lady Bucknell that I'm an unsuitable governess. I would be better as a companion to an elderly woman, or as a director of a school, or any position that requires me to stay away from men."

He strode toward her so quickly she backed up, an instinctive retreat that ended, not in the other room as she'd hoped, but in an ignominious smack against the door's casement.

"I'm afraid I'd have to write Lady Bucknell and tell her you can't be trusted in any position which allows you access to other people's money or possessions."

The pain caused by his accusation took her breath away. What an idiot she was, expecting that a night of breathtaking sex would make him see her true character.

It hadn't, obviously, for he not only still believed her a thief, he believed that she would stay with him. "Yes, and between you and the last man who took a hatred to me, I suspect I'll be unable to obtain a position in England." She shrugged with a fair imitation of insouciance. "I shall have to go abroad."

"You can't do that." He sounded direct, calm, as certain as a god making a pronouncement. "What would be the purpose? You can stay here and be my wife, with more possessions than ever you can as a governess—or a thief."

He couldn't tell her what to do. He'd lost that right. "But there'll be no illicit thrill, will there? The excitement of picking a pocket. The thrill of sneaking about and having an affair. That exhilaration will be gone."

Placing his foot on the wooden chair, he leaned his elbow on his knee. "You can steal anything you like of mine if you'll stay."

She looked at him, dressed like a buccaneer, with the confidence of a lord. "If I married you, it would all be mine, anyway. I can't steal from myself."

He watched her so closely. Too closely, weighing all her reactions, reading everything but the truth. "At least give me back the miniature of my wife."

She closed her eyes against a sudden rush of tears.

No. No tears. The rage was better. "Your wife's possessions are a small enough token of your appreciation for the job I did with Lady Featherstonebaugh."

As if she'd taken a lash to him, he caught his breath. Then he took her wrist, a slow, gentle capture. "Was it your father who taught you to steal?"

"Yes, but don't let that influence you. I was good at it, and I liked it. I liked the excitement of it. Sometimes I even miss it." She bit her lip. That was true, but also tantamount to claiming she hadn't stolen his wife's miniature. And she would not waste her time with claims of innocence that he would disbelieve.

"You didn't eat if you were unsuccessful."

"That's true of a thousand thieves, William. Don't start feeling compassion now. You'll end up confused."

He stood over the top of her, let her feel the heat

of him, looked at her with those amazing eyes. "The children need you."

"The children will do just fine." That much was true.

"I need you." He caressed her cheeks with his fingertips, and said the words that, yesterday, she would have killed to hear. "I love you."

Did he believe it? Yes. Of course he did. There was no other reason for his amazing offer of marriage. He thought he loved her—but he didn't trust her.

This time she couldn't keep back the tears. "Is this what love is? A commodity that falters at the first sign of difficulty? Emotion without trust? An empty mind and a busy cock?" He tried to speak, but she put her hand over his mouth. "Don't answer. That *is* what love is. I've seen it time and again, and I reject it. I don't want your kind of love." She pushed his hand away. "I deserve better."

He looked at his fingers as if her touch had burned him. "I can't stand this. This hurts too much."

"Good. Your paltry little emotions don't come close to mine."

Looking down at her, he smiled, a smile stiff with pain. "As long as you're suffering as I am."

William sat at his desk, shoulders slumped, his head in his hands, and wondered how everything had gone so wrong so quickly. He'd fallen in love, passionately, madly in love. He'd abandoned his morals to take Samantha, standing on the porch while the music played and the candles glowed, while he should have been at the ball as host. A woman not of his own class, of unknown origins, and he'd been so swept by passion . . . well. This proved that his morals were the correct morals. He should have never given in. He should have demanded to know who her family was. He should have investigated her background so this would have never happened.

Except . . . he wanted her again. Right now. Here. On the desk. On the floor. On the sofa. He'd been so mad with passion he had been willing to abandon everything he believed and expose his children to Samantha's thieving ways so he could have her.

And she had rejected him.

He groaned. He writhed with mortification. That lying little thief had slashed him with her scorn and walked out his life.

He would heal, of course. He would get over her, of course.

But right now, he felt as if he was bleeding in his gut. In his heart. And he couldn't stop the one thing that ripped at his peace more than anything.

Doubt.

What if she hadn't stolen those things? What if pride had made her claim she had, and all the while he had another thief in the house, one who knew of her past and for some nefarious reason wished to separate them? But there had been no change in staff.

This misgiving was only the desperate groping of a man in pain. Samantha had done it. She *had*.

He didn't bother to lift his head when he heard

the door open. He didn't care who it was. He just wanted them to go away. "What do you want?" he asked.

"I've got the report from the coast," Duncan said.

"Did it go well?" William didn't care.

"It depends on what you mean by well." Duncan stood in the doorway, unwilling to come close. No one wanted to be with William now. "The ship weighed anchor in the bay. The boat came in to transport the passengers out. Pashenka did as we anticipated. He snatched Lady Featherstonebaugh's reticule, ran into the water, clambered in the boat and ordered them to push off. Featherstonebaugh brayed like a donkey and chased after him, into the water and almost into the boat."

William lifted his head. "What do you mean, almost?"

Duncan seemed to alternate between horrified and amused. "Lady Featherstonebaugh lifted her pistol and shot him."

"My God! Is he dead?"

"Quite dead. Amazing shooting for a woman with a popgun like that." Duncan blinked. "We rushed in then, shot all around the boat while Pashenka ordered them to row for their lives. We took Lady Featherstonebaugh into custody, but William . . . she seems quite mad. She was talking to people who weren't there."

"Perhaps the judge will have pity on her, and confine her to Bedlam."

"If you call that pity. I'd rather hang."

"So it's over at last." Odd, to think William had nothing to do now, no mission to accomplish. He had avenged Mary's death, and he had thought to feel jubilation. Instead, he felt only pain.

Duncan watched William almost . . . sympathetically. "Are you all right?"

"I'll survive."

"I know that. But will you ever admit that you made a mistake?" Duncan sighed. "Don't answer that. I'm off, then. Taking Teresa home by way of the vicar's. I'll get her wed yet."

William tried to be glad for his friends. Was glad for his friends. But so envious, too. Standing, he moved around the desk and walked toward Duncan, hand out. "Good luck to you."

Duncan strode forward and shook hands.

The two men looked at each other, and William remembered all the months and all the patrols, all the deception and all the exhilaration. Each laughed, William with hoarse amusement, and gave each other a brisk hug. "Congratulations," William said. "Teresa's a wonderful woman."

"I don't deserve her. But don't tell her that." With a wave, Duncan went out the door.

William heard him say, "Good morning, L'il Bit. Going in to see your papa?"

"N . . . no," a small voice stammered.

Mara.

William knew it was selfish, but he was glad she wouldn't come in to see him. He didn't want to try and explain to his accusing children why Samantha had left. He didn't have an answer, except that he'd failed in the most important mission of his life. Making his way back to his desk, he sank back down in the chair and put his head in his hands again.

But he wasn't to get off so easily.

"Father?"

He looked up quickly.

Pale and frightened, Mara stood staring at him.

He modulated his tone to be kind and fatherly. "Mara, is this something that could wait? I'm really busy here."

She glanced back at the door as if the thought of escape enticed her. Then she shook her head and dragged the toes of her boots on the carpet as she slowly walked in.

He managed not to snap out an order to march briskly with her head up and her shoulders back. If he were to be fair—and if Samantha were here, she would insist he be fair—he wasn't currently a portrait of military demeanor himself.

Mara got to the other side of the desk and stared at him with large, wondering eyes. "What is it, Mara?"

In an incredulous little tone, she asked, "Father, have you been crying?"

"No. Not crying." Not with his eyes, but with his heart.

Looking down, she dug in her pocket and brought out a small gold frame. Her hand shook as she extended it across the desk.

He caught her skinny wrist.

It was his wife's miniature.

"Where did you find this?"

"I didn't find it." She took a quavering breath. "I took it."

His hand loosened. His mind blanked. He didn't

know what to think. What to say. He gazed at the painting of Mary held in that small, shaking hand.

His own daughter. His own blood. Once a thief, always a thief. Black is black and white is white and shades of gray never existed.

He could scarcely speak. "Did you take all of Mama's things?"

Mara nodded, her complexion so white it was almost green. Her mouth worked as if she was trying not to bawl. He saw her swallow.

What had he done?

He stood.

Mara skittered backward, a little girl who had worked up all her courage just to face her father and tell the truth.

Moving slowly, careful not to frighten her more, he sat again. He shoved back his chair. He patted his knee. "Come and tell your papa all about it."

❧ *Chapter Twenty-nine* ❧

The coach careened down the mountain and with each curve, Samantha smacked the side of the coach, and all of the backward-facing passengers smashed into her. Then, as the coach straightened out, they pulled themselves back into seats and waited grimly for the next bend, the next slide across the crowded seat. Eight people, four facing front, four facing back. Six men, two women, all suffering passengers, stuck in a stifling coach with the windows closed to keep out the dust, all anxious for their arrival in York.

Samantha stared out the window of the coach, trying hard to be glad to leave these rugged fells behind. She hated the country. She had always hated the country, with its fresh air, waving grasses, and carnivores waiting to devour an unsuspecting city girl. Yes, she couldn't wait to be back in London, with its constant noise, the smell of rotting refuse, the filthy fog that painted everything from the buildings to a woman's best gloves black. Adorna would not be happy to see her . . .

"Whoa!" she heard the coachman shout. "Whoa, there."

"Why're we stopping?" The burgher from Edinburgh lowered the window and craned his neck out. "Ach, 'tis a tree doon in the road."

The passengers groaned.

Samantha tried not to indulge in a leap of joy. The tree was an unnecessary delay, an inconvenience . . . and one that would give her a few more minutes here, in the Lake District. Minutes standing on the road, looking at Devil's Fell, at the waterfalls, at the drystone walls . . . and crying because she had to leave. For no matter what she told herself, the truth was she'd grown rather fond of the region. Or rather—of the people she'd met here.

"Stand and deliver!" The cry sounded from off the road.

Stand and deliver? Samantha frowned. And a tree down in the road. Coincidence, surely. That was *not* William's deep voice, made menacing with practice. He would not have come after her. Not after the bitter words they'd exchanged. She had made her thoughts quite clear.

The housewife on the other side of the coach fell back against the seat, her hand clasped to her ample bosom. "Highwaymen." Her voice grew louder. "Highwaymen! They're going to rob us and rape us."

"You first," Samantha muttered. She really had to get a grip on her misery.

"There're a lot o' them." The Scotsman squinted with puzzlement. "Some are wretched short."

Short? What did he mean, short? But she was afraid she knew. "Like children?" she asked.

The robber outside shouted, "We're looking for a female, tall, thin, beautiful."

Lowering her head, Samantha slid down in her seat. It was William, and she would never forgive him as long as she lived.

And at the same time . . . she wanted to laugh.

"Blonde hair so fair it's like moonlight. Give her up to us, and we'll let the rest of you go."

Every gaze was fixed on her.

"She's not beautiful," the housewife declared, "but she fits the rest of the description."

One of the men kicked the door open.

Everyone in the coach lent a hand to lift Samantha out of her seat and shove her out. She stumbled and landed in a heap on the road.

"Now see here!" the coachman shouted at the six little highwaymen and one full-sized highwayman, all with scarves pulled up over their noses. "I can't have ye abductin' me passengers. I'll get a bad reputation, I will!"

The tallest of the children shouted, "You already got her fare. What do you care if she's abducted?"

Agnes. Agnes was participating in this outrage. In fact—Samantha staggered to her feet—all of the children sat, masked, on horses beside the road.

Well, the two littlest highwaymen were on ponies with leading reins.

The whole Gregory clan had come to get her. Although why they'd bothered . . . she flashed a glance at William.

He looked exactly as he had the night she'd arrived. Dressed all in black. Too tall, too broad, too masculine. Unreasonable, domineering . . . and those eyes. Those brilliant blue eyes that watched and mocked and lusted. At her.

She blushed, but lifted her chin at him.

"I can't allow ye t' take her," the coachman protested. "Miss Prendregast is me passenger an' I have a dooty t' perform."

Samantha saw Vivian nod to the littlest robber.

Right on cue, Kyla piped up, "She's my mama and I miss her."

The coachman cranked around to glare at Samantha. "Geeze, lady, ye're leavin' yer kids?"

"These are not my children," Samantha said crisply.

The passengers gasped in shock.

"Mama, how can you say that?" Agnes whined. "We miss you."

"Mama." "Mama." "Mama." Depending on their ages and prediliction toward drama, the children whimpered in various tones of despair or hilarity.

Arms crossed across his chest, William watched the touching scene.

Samantha ignored him and flayed the children with her gimlet, teacher's gaze. "I might have expected something like this from your father, but I insist on better behavior from you children."

Hanging their heads out of the window and the door, the passengers listened avidly.

The large lady made a pronouncement. "This isn't a robbery. This is . . ." Words left her, and her gaze narrowed on Samantha.

"But Miss Prendregast." Emmeline pulled her scarf down. "You stole something."

Samantha caught her breath in outrage, and slashed William with a look.

He impassively stared back.

Emmeline said, "You stole my heart."

"You stole my heart, too," Kyla said.

Samantha wanted to groan at this farce. Instead she found herself torn between sappy tears and exasperated laughter.

"You took all of our hearts." Agnes dismounted, walked to Samantha, and took her hands. "Please, Miss Prendregast, won't you stay with us?"

Samantha gazed at the girl. Gazed at all the girls.

Looked up at William. Stripping off his riding gloves, he touched his chest over his heart with his fingertips.

To her embarrassment, her own heart squeezed with passion. That eternal, desperate passion.

With a grunt of disgust, the coachman untied Samantha's trunk and dumped it onto the side of the road. The tree was moved. The coach rumbled off leaving a trail of dust that drifted away on the breeze.

The rest of the children dove out of their saddles. They jumped up and down. They hugged Samantha. "Weren't we good, Miss Prendregast?" "Did you want to cry?" "Aren't you happy you're staying?"

She hugged them back and laughed at their antics.

"All right, girls." William dismounted and clapped, once, loudly. "Give us a few minutes alone."

The children looked at each other and giggled. Then Agnes herded them toward their horses. The older girls helped the little girls into the saddles.

Samantha tried to watch them. Tried to ignore William. But he commanded her attention. Filled her vision. Stood too close and breathed too much of that abhorrent fresh air. He must be breathing too much of it, because she felt rather faint and breathless.

"We love you, Miss Prendregast," the children called as they rode off, towing their father's horse with them.

She waved feebly.

The sun shone, caressing her face with its warmth.

The breeze blew, fluttering the scarf at his throat. "So. Here we are. On the road again." He took her gloved hand, and with great deliberation, worked the glove off. Bowing, he pressed his lips to her palm. "Alone at last."

His warm breath sent goose bumps up her arm. Her traitorous nipples beaded at once. She tried to shift backward, but he followed, and what she gained by stepping away she then lost by his advance.

"Thank you for agreeing to listen to me."

He was making assumptions already. "I didn't agree to anything."

"You didn't run away. That's something. That's enough." He gestured toward a fallen log inside the shade of the woodlands. "Would you do me the honor of sitting with me while we talk?"

She had to talk to him, but she hesitated.

He knew why. "I'll check for snakes," he reassured her, and he didn't appear to be smirking at her fears.

So she walked through the grass beside the road into the rich brown humus laid down by ten thousand years of autumn leaves, and allowed him to roll the log back and forth to chase away any creatures that might be lurking. Peeling off his black riding coat, he folded it and placed it on the log. She seated herself, taking care to sit in a ladylike manner, as if that would wipe her wanton behavior from his mind.

Then, to her horror, he knelt on one knee before her.

"Please don't." She tugged at his arm. "Colonel Gregory, please, this isn't necessary."

He didn't budge. "Colonel Gregory? You called me William . . . this morning."

Color warmed her cheeks. "Yes, but before we had just . . ." But she was being foolish. "You're right, of course. Since we already *have*, it's ridiculous to pretend we didn't."

"Quite."

"But please, don't kneel."

"I'm a great believer in protocol. I believe that

one should curtsy to the queen. I believe one should salute one's officers. And I believe that a couple should court before they wed, that they should come to the marriage bed only after the ceremony, and a man should propose on his knees." He took her other hand, the gloved one, and removed that glove, also. Both gloves went into his waistcoat pocket, and he clasped her bare hands in his. "I've done everything wrong with you."

She remembered last night. And this morning. And blushed again. "Not everything."

"Thank you for that, at least." An enigmatic smile played around his mouth. He banished it, and in a serious tone, said, "I also believe a man should kneel to beg a lady's pardon when he has grievously wronged her—as I have wronged you. Mara took my wife's things."

A tightly wound part of her relaxed. After Samantha's lecture, Mara had confessed. Samantha had done one thing right. "I know."

His eyebrows shot up. "How did you know?"

"A thief always recognizes another thief." Samantha gave a little shrug. "She's the child in the middle. Unlike Agnes and Vivian, she's not growing into a woman. Not yet. But she's not an endearing little girl anymore, like Henrietta or Emmeline or Kyla, so she's lost."

He looked thunderstruck. "I hadn't even thought of that. How did I handle my children before you came along with your insights and your wisdoms?"

Samantha wanted to accuse him of flattery—but

it was true. He'd been heading for trouble, and she'd saved him a great deal of grief.

"She told me the memory of her mother was fading. When she was lonely at night, she tried to see Mary's face, but she couldn't remember her. Mara took Mary's things in an attempt to bring her mother back. For comfort."

Samantha choked, "Poor little girl."

"I'm having the miniature copied, one for each of the children." He kissed Samantha's knuckles on both hands. "And I'm hoping to get them a new mother who will tuck them into bed."

She looked away.

"If I can convince her to forgive me for accusing her on the basis of her past."

All the hurt, all the rancor, all the years of abuse and scorn, rose to the surface. She swallowed. She wanted to do it. She loved him so much she should be able to forgive him anything . . . but she couldn't.

There were some things, she discovered, that were unforgivable. She shook her head. "I can't."

He shifted uncomfortably, spoke more quickly. "I've been unbending in my ethics. Everyone knows the difference between right and wrong, and never could there be a good enough reason to cheat, to lie . . . to steal. But my daughter, my own flesh and blood, requires my compassion, and I will not reject her for her wrongs." He pulled a long face. "Although she and I are going to have serious discussions about morality."

"Yes. Good. But Mara is always going to be the one who tests the limits."

"I'll need you to help keep Mara on the straight."

She looked away again.

He took a breath. "Even before I knew about Mara, I knew I had to change. I had to change, or I couldn't keep you with me, and I hated that. It was hard, so I thought I could change a little bit and make you change a lot."

Amusement and animosity mixed in her until she couldn't tell the difference. She wanted to laugh. She wanted to choke from the pain.

"But you rejected me. I offered my belongings. You didn't care. So I admitted I loved you. You scorned my love."

She brushed at her eyes. "I didn't want to. No man has ever told me he loved me."

"So now I'm on my knees. I'm groveling." He crawled closer, so close he was pressed against her side. "I was wrong about you. I was stupid and pig-headed. I was righteous and self-serving. Please, please forgive me."

"All right!" She shouldn't have given in. "Of course." But she couldn't help it. "I forgive you." She wanted him. She loved him.

"Then . . . won't you look at me?" He spoke softly in her ear, so close his breath brushed against her neck.

She glanced at him, and down at their joined hands.

"Samantha, I can't change the past any more than you can." With his thumb, he massaged her palm. "All I can do is promise not to repeat my mistake."

She had to struggle not to snap at him. "Not even a little? Not even in the deepest recesses of your mind? The next time you misplace something, or when a disgruntled servant steals the silverware, you won't secretly wonder if it's me?"

He was silent for so long she longed to shift, to move away . . . to do as he asked, and look into his eyes. When she did, she saw a critical comprehension that made her squirm.

In measured tones, he said, "I guarantee I shall never suspect you of being anything except a beautiful, kind, intelligent woman, because I believe in you. But I can't force you to believe in me." With a painful grimace, he got to his feet. "No wonder you can't find it in yourself to love me. You doubt my truthfulness and my character."

"No, I don't! I don't doubt you at all. I . . . everyone else always . . ." She couldn't believe she was saying that. Such a feeble excuse to cover such a great fear. For if she gave herself to William for all time, she opened herself to hurt. It was a gamble, one so great she was willing to spend her life poor and in service rather than take a chance as William's wife.

Except for one thing. She rose, took his wrist in her hand and stared soberly into his face. "I do love you. I've loved you since the first time I looked up at you on horseback and thought you were a dangerous, handsome devil."

Now he tested her. "You love me enough to trust me with the keeping of your heart?"

"Do you promise to take good care of it?"

"Indeed I do."

"You would never lie to me." This time she didn't hesitate. "I love you, and I will marry you."

Without taking his warm gaze away from her, he called, "Children! Everything's settled. Miss Prendregast has agreed to be my wife."

They grinned at each other, imagining the children's joy.

"Girls!" he called a little louder.

She glanced around. She was a little surprised they weren't watching from the bushes. "Where are the children?"

"You don't suppose . . . they decided to guarantee the outcome they desired?" He nodded and stroked his chin. "Marvelous tactics. I must compliment them."

"How would they do that?" Her eyes widened. "By abandoning us in this wilderness?"

He chortled, then with one look at her panicked face, he attempted to sober. "It's not a wilderness," he said in a soothing tone. "They probably thought that if we were forced to spend the night together, we would have to reconcile. At the very least, we'll be irrevocably compromised and forced to wed."

She couldn't believe the children would do such a thing. "That's diabolical!"

"It is, rather." He chortled again.

She glowered. "You're proud of them."

"Not proud. Not really. Just . . . impressed with their logical thinking." He cleared his throat and changed the subject. "If we stay on the road, someone should come by in the next couple of days."

"In the next couple of days?" she shouted.

"If we follow the road, and no one drives by, it

would take us two days—four at the most—to reach Silvermere." Sliding his arm around her back, he pulled her close against him. "On the other hand, if you trust me, I know a shortcut through the forest."

His closeness made her dizzy. "How long . . . ?"

"I'll have you home tomorrow morning."

Breathing hard, she stared at him, then at the green patch of trees that stretched off the side of the road. "Are there wolves?"

"No wolves. No bears. It's safe."

"We'll starve."

"I can feed you. Trust me."

"Where will we sleep?"

With a grimace, he walked to a bag dropped on the side of the road. "I would guess our children left this for us." He opened it. "Yes. Blankets. Canvas. I'm a soldier. I've built a shelter with less." Returning to her side, he wrapped his arm around her shoulders. "Think about it. You and I under the stars . . ."

"Moths. Bats. Little creepy crawly things."

"Darling, when it's dark and you're frightened, I'll do my best to distract you." He looked down at her.

She knew he was going to kiss her. She knew it was going to be special. She leaned into him, clasped his lapels, turned her head to meet his lips. It was everything she hoped. A sweet mingling of breath, then a sensory feast of lips and tongues, a sharing of pleasure, a sanction of their vows.

"Did that distract you?" he asked.

With her eyes still closed, she nodded.

"Shall we go into the woods? Do you trust me?"

She nodded again.

"That's all I ask." He flung the strap of the bag over his shoulder and led her into the trees. "Tonight you can tell me why you thought I was such a dangerous, handsome devil."

If he were lucky, she'd be thoroughly compromised and they'd be married before she discovered a village was only two miles further down the road.

His children weren't the only tacticians in the family.

America Loves Lindsey!
The Timeless Romances of
The New York Times Bestselling Author